"I don't do casual."

Gabe's solemn expression added weight to his warning.

"And I don't do relationships...at least not well," Lindy amended with a subtle frown. "So what do we do?"

"Nothing."

"Nothing? I don't think that's going to work. We're both dealing with some hefty attraction, right? I mean, I know I'm not in a one-sided situation in this. So...maybe we should just kiss and get it out of our system and see what happens."

"I know where kissing leads," Gabe said, his eyebrow lifting in a sexy yet sardonic arch that Lindy found insanely attractive. "Don't you?"

"I have an idea," she murmured, biting her lip against the surge of arousal that followed his silky statement. "And that's bad?"

Dear Reader,

Lindy and Gabe...what can I say about them, other than *wow.* Simply put, I loved writing their love story because both needed to grow and change before they were ready for the commitment of a relationship. And they did so, beautifully.

Peeling back the layers of complex people is one of the perks of my job as a writer, and I had a ball exposing these characters' vulnerable spots for all the world to see. It's a deep, soulful journey that I hope you will enjoy as you spend some more time at Larimar with the Bells as they live and learn as a Family in Paradise.

You won't want to miss Lilah and Justin's story, *Something to Believe In,* coming in January 2013.

Hearing from readers is a special joy. Please feel free to drop me a line via email through my website at www.kimberlyvanmeter.com, or by snail mail at Kimberly Van Meter, P.O. Box 2210, Oakdale, CA 95361.

Kimberly Van Meter

Playing the Part

KIMBERLY VAN METER

HARLEQUIN®
entertain, enrich, inspire™

Recycling programs
for this product may
not exist in your area.

ISBN-13: 978-0-373-71802-3

PLAYING THE PART

www.Harlequin.com

Printed in U.S.A.

ABOUT THE AUTHOR

Kimberly Van Meter wrote her first book at sixteen and finally achieved publication in December 2006. She writes for the Harlequin Superromance and Harlequin Romantic Suspense lines. She and her husband of seventeen years have three children, three cats and always a houseful of friends, family and fun.

Books by Kimberly Van Meter

HARLEQUIN SUPERROMANCE

1391—THE TRUTH ABOUT FAMILY
1433—FATHER MATERIAL
1469—RETURN TO EMMETT'S MILL
1485—A KISS TO REMEMBER
1513—AN IMPERFECT MATCH
1577—KIDS ON THE DOORSTEP*
1600—A MAN WORTH LOVING*
1627—TRUSTING THE BODYGUARD*
1694—THE PAST BETWEEN US**
1700—A CHANCE IN THE NIGHT**
1706—SECRETS IN A SMALL TOWN**
1778—LIKE ONE OF THE FAMILY***

HARLEQUIN ROMANTIC SUSPENSE

1622—TO CATCH A KILLER
1638—GUARDING THE SOCIALITE
1666—SWORN TO PROTECT†
1669—COLD CASE REUNION†
1696—A DAUGHTER'S PERFECT SECRET

*Home in Emmett's Mill
**Mama Jo's Boys
***Family in Paradise
†Native Country

Other titles by this author available in ebook format.

To my firstborn son, Sebastian,
as he finishes one journey to start another.
I hope you find every success out there
in the world. I love you.

CHAPTER ONE

LINDY BELL STARED in growing horror, the plunger dangling from her fingertips ineffectual against the choking, gurgling and overflowing toilet that was burping water all over the tiled floor of Bungalow 2 at her grandparents' resort, Larimar. She jumped out of the way before disgusting toilet water washed over her flip-flops. Oh, yes, most definitely, without a doubt—this was hell. And she was going to kill her sister for dragging her here and then putting her on maintenance detail just because she knew the difference between a Phillips head screwdriver and a flat head.

Normally, Heath Cannon—her sister's boyfriend— was in charge of the maintenance but he'd fallen off the roof and banged himself up pretty bad so he wasn't going to be any help for a while. It wasn't that she minded pitching in—hell, she was here, wasn't she?— but right now, she wanted to murder someone.

She caught movement at the corner of her eye and turned just in time to see a small blond head duck and disappear as light laughter tinkled after her.

"You monster," she muttered, dropping the plunger to chase after the girl, not caring at the moment that she was supposed to be the adult because she was about to tie the little nuisance to the nearest tree. "What did you stick down there this time?" she shouted, rounding the corner and nearly skidding into a tall man who was

sheltering the aforementioned monster in his arms as if
Lindy were the villain and the kid was actually a victim.

"What's going on?" he demanded, rubbing the girl's
back with soothing and gentle motions, as if Lindy had
traumatized her. If anyone was suffering from an emotional upheaval it was Lindy. Being dragged to Cruz Bay
in the Virgin Islands on family business and forced on
janitor duty was punishment for crimes she hadn't even
committed yet. Unemployment sucked but unemployment in the entertainment industry was downright brutal. Her last gig had lasted only a few months and now
she was on the hunt again, or rather, her agent should
be hunting. In the meantime she had no choice but to
stick it out at the resort with her sisters. At the moment
she was looking at troubleshooting a clogged toilet—joy
of all joys—that seemed to have been filled with sand,
by the looks of it.

"May I ask why you're chasing my daughter with
murder in your eyes?" the man asked.

"Probably because I want to kill the little brat," Lindy
quipped, her kicked-up heart rate keeping time with her
temper. "She filled the toilet with sand."

"How do you know it was Carys?" he asked stiffly,
but Lindy suspected it was an act. Anyone with a kid
that wretched had to know they had the devil's spawn
on their hands. "Maybe the problem is simply the fault
of the plumbing."

"Yeah, sure. It can't have anything to do with the
beaches' worth of sand she poured down its throat. Or
the fact that this isn't the first time maintenance has
been called for problems with your toilet. Last week
we fished five ties—presumably yours—from the trap."
At his startled look, she smirked. "You ought to check

your underwear drawer. She might be throwing your boxers away next."

"She's lying, Daddy," the little heathen shouted before burying her face in his Hawaiian shirt. Nothing said *I'm on vacation* more than a rayon shirt with giant magnolias on it. Lindy looked away in disgust as the girl fervently assured her father. "I didn't put the sand in the toilet, Daddy. I swear it."

"This is the first I'm hearing about the previous incident," he answered, having at least the grace to look discomfited by the revelation. "Five ties?"

"Yeah. Five. Expensive looking, too. We threw them out because they were mangled." Ugh. That kid of his was a great testament as to why some animals ate their young.

"Perhaps it was an accident...."

"Whatever," Lindy said, exasperated and severely annoyed by the whole situation and the man's inability to admit that his precious daughter was a nightmare. Turning on her heel, she added over her shoulder, "Expect to see a plumbing bill on your invoice. Thanks for staying at Larimar. Please feel free *not* to come again."

Lindy stomped away from the two, her temper still percolating, and abruptly changed direction toward the beach. One of the perks of living on a tropical island was the ready access to paradise and right about now, she needed a good dose of calm before she dealt with any more resort issues.

As she walked the path to the private beach belonging to Larimar, she realized someone was calling after her.

She turned and groaned. Great. Little Miss Perfect's Deaf Dumb and Blind Father. What she wouldn't give for a guilt-free plane ticket back to Los Angeles. "What?" she asked when he'd caught up to her, thankfully sans the hellion. Maybe he'd dug a pit and pushed her into it. Ha. One could dream but she wasn't holding out hope. She couldn't help the irritation in her voice or her expression. Too bad his kid was such a pain in the ass. He wasn't half-bad-looking for a lawyer type, which wasn't *her* type, per se; she liked rugged guys whose trucks were usually crusted in mud from four-wheeling through rough terrain. This guy, with his clean cuticles—probably got manicures—and short-cropped dark hair—probably paid a fortune for that look at some high-priced salon—likely drove some overpriced European number—either a Saab or an Audi—and paid a valet to park it. But even with all those points against him, Lindy had to admit…he wasn't hard on the eyes.

GABE WESTON STALKED after the striking long-haired honey-brown brunette, choosing to focus on his ire rather than the fact that she was wearing a lemon-yellow bikini top that lovingly cupped her breasts and a sarong that hugged the womanly swell of near-perfect hips. She pushed her white, wide-rimmed sunglasses atop her head and fixed him with a look that was both appraising and annoyed, if there was such a thing.

"Do you know who I am?" he asked, mentally cringing that he'd actually said those words. He sounded like a pompous ass but her casual dismissal poked at his ego and frankly, after the situation with Carys, the filter he usually reserved for his mouth had fallen off, allowing him to spout crap he wouldn't under normal circumstances. But seeing as he was already making a *fine* impression, he might as well go all the way. "My name's Gabe Weston and I'm the one spending gobs of money at your resort right now during a down economy so I think a little respect or at the very least professional courtesy is warranted. An apology wouldn't be out of line, either."

"I agree. Your kid is a brat. I have a feeling there's probably a long list of people she ought to apologize to."

He didn't appreciate her quip—it hit too close to the truth. Carys was a handful and nearly everyone she came into contact with wanted little to do with her for long. Secretly, it horrified him that his daughter had become such a terror but he couldn't seem to find the answer as to how to return her to the little girl she'd been before his wife died.

"I want to speak to your manager," he said quietly.

"Good idea, and while you're at it make sure you let her know how your kid flushed a pound of sand down the toilet and how it'll likely take three plumbers to figure out how to unclog it without having to rip open the sewage line. It'll save me a trip." She smiled. "Somehow I think I'll be forgiven for my less-than-courteous delivery. And if not, oh well. My family owns this resort. So, do your worst but don't get your hopes up. Like as not, I'm here for the duration."

"That doesn't give you license to abuse your guests," he said.

"And it doesn't give our guests license to be destructive. Listen, we don't have a whole lot of rules here at Larimar but when your kid is doing her best impression of a rock star by trashing the place, someone has to say something and—lucky me!—I got the short straw. So, get control of the kid or we'll have to ask you to find another place to chill. We savvy?" She slid her sunglasses back in place, obviously finished, and continued down the sandy walk to the beach, both him and his daughter seemingly forgotten.

Gabe stared after the woman, half tempted to follow

but what did he have to say? Not much. His daughter was a hellion. And he didn't have a clue as to how to change that fact.

Biting off a string of silent curse words, he returned to the bungalow, hoping against hope that Carys hadn't destroyed something else in his short absence.

He found the bungalow eerily quiet, something he'd grown to mistrust, and went to Carys's bedroom door. "Are you in there, honey?"

"I didn't put sand in the toilet," she called out with a watery sniff. "That woman was lying."

He sighed. Yeah, he suspected someone was lying but it wasn't the brunette who had every right to be pissed off.

In a *Time* magazine article about the modern-day shark in the boardroom, Gabe, CEO of Weston Enterprises, was once described as being a man who ate his competition with all the violent, single-minded focus of a great white. In short, he bit and chomped and what he left behind wasn't enough to feed a goldfish.

And yet, as he struggled to rein in the desire to pound on the bedroom door of the rented bungalow, he was most certain an eleven-year-old girl was going to be the death of him.

Or more specifically—an eleven-year-old girl who bore half his DNA and was bound and determined to turn every single strand of his hair gray.

"Carys Deanne, I'm not playing around. We need to talk about this latest stunt," he said, feeling more than a bit foolish for speaking to a door but unwilling to invade his daughter's privacy. "This is very serious business, which will likely be very expensive to fix. You're lucky we have two bathrooms in the bungalow or else we'd be in a jam when either one of us needed to use the restroom."

"I said *she's lying!* I hope she drowns in the ocean for what she's saying about me," shrieked his daughter in a shrill voice, eliciting a frown from Gabe. "Why do you believe her—a stranger—over your own daughter?" There was a short pause, then a barely audible, "Mom would've believed me."

He winced even as he recognized the ploy to manipulate him. "Carys, leave your mother out of this," he said sternly. "The issue is about the property damage. You're going to apologize."

"Will not."

"You will."

"You can't make me. I'll spit in her face. Try me."

"That's not very nice, sweetheart," he chided her gently. "I know you don't mean what you're saying."

"I do mean it. And if you try to make me, I'll stay in my room until I die," Carys said with the theatrical flair that had always made him and his wife laugh when she was smaller. But since Charlotte's death a year ago, Gabe had found little to smile about when it came to his daughter's antics.

He'd brought them to Cruz Bay, St. John, with the hope that a change of scenery would help his daughter's increasingly bad attitude. But she'd just managed to terrorize and scare away the second nanny in as many weeks and he wasn't sure what to do any longer. He'd hoped to find a way to channel her destructive behavior into something productive but she'd sabotaged the art classes, sulked through the native dancing classes, and flat-out ditched the music lessons he'd managed to find on the small island.

He was plain out of ideas *and* patience. "Carys, you

will apologize even if I have to drag you from that room and plop you in front of the woman you're so adamant is the one lying. Your behavior is out of control. Time to get a grip, kiddo."

"You can't make me!"

"Yes, I can," he said, tight-lipped. He sent a quick look toward the heavens where he liked to think his wife was watching and chuckling over his bumbling attempts at being mom and dad and muttered, "I need a little help here.... At this rate, she's not going to live to see twelve!"

He stalked away from the door before his temper got the best of him and went to the kitchen to find a bottle of water. What was he going to do with her? His daughter's behavior was nearly beyond his ability to handle.

He knew she was grieving—losing Charlotte had been a blow to them both—but it didn't seem as if Carys was even close to healing. His daughter was mired in anger and plenty comfortable in her own little mud pit of sorrow. He cracked the top of the plastic bottle and swigged the water. The humidity was brutal that day. It was hurricane season in St. John, which meant temperamental weather. One minute it was sunny and hot, the next it was time to batten down the hatches and tie down the patio furniture.

His smartphone buzzed in his pocket and he fished it out. A work call. He paused a moment, torn between taking the call and having another conversation with Carys, but the decision became easier when he heard something hard and heavy thump against Carys's closed door. His little darling had just thrown something. He closed his eyes for a brief second and then walked away. "Hey, Gary," he answered, switching gears almost gratefully. "How's the Mercer and Jones acquisition coming?"

Standing at the helm of a multimillion-dollar company was easier by far than handling the fickle emotions of one eleven-year-old girl.

Heaven help him.

CHAPTER TWO

"Seriously?" Lindy gaped at her older sister, Lora, both incredulous and irritated all over again. "Did you not hear what I said about the toilet? The same toilet that the plumber fished five ties from?"

"Yeah, I heard you. She's a terror, I get it," Lora said, pinching the bridge of her nose and pulling her long, thick black hair into a quick ponytail to escape the smothering humidity of St. John. "But we can't afford to be scaring off patrons, especially during the off-season. If you'd take a minute to sit down with me and look at the numbers you'd see we need every penny. Larimar is in serious trouble, Lindy. It's time you set aside your natural inclination to say and do whatever you like and go apologize to Mr. Weston for calling his kid a brat."

"She is a brat," Lindy countered mulishly. "And I'm not apologizing."

"Lindy," Lora warned, looking as exasperated with Lindy as Lindy was with the whole damn situation. A few weeks ago she'd been cruising Mulholland Drive with freshly colored hair to lighten her natural mousy brown, living the Hollywood dream—or nightmare, depending on the day—and now she was back home in St. John, working with her sisters to save the family re-sort because she didn't have it in her to say *sayonara* to the whole situation. To make matters worse, after a few weeks in the Caribbean sun and salty water, her very expensive dye job was going to turn into an ugly mess. So much for making an investment into her future.

Okay, so she wasn't as cavalier about some things as she'd like to let on, she grumbled to herself. But Lora was on her last nerve and making it increasingly difficult to keep from boarding a plane back to California, right now. "C'mon, is it really so hard to just say the damn words?" Lora asked.

Lindy shot her sister a cool look. "I don't know. How hard is it for *you* to apologize?"

Lora had the grace to flush, effectively ceding the point but she didn't give up. "Yes, the kid is a monster, but do you realize Weston is paid up for the entire month? That's serious cash and we need *serious cash*. The next IRS payment is due around the corner and I can't liquefy any more assets without steep penalties. So, in order to keep the peace and keep Weston from taking his money and going elsewhere, I suggest you march your ass to his room and put those acting skills to work and pretend that you're contrite."

Lindy clenched her fists, fighting the urge to stomp her feet like the kid in Bungalow 2. "This is bullshit," she spit out just as her twin sister, Lilah, drifted into the room humming. She stopped short when she saw the standoff.

"What's going on?" Lilah asked, her sudden frown marring the clear, dewy skin of her twin's face as she played nervously with the long strands of her blond hair. Although many thought Lindy and Lilah were identical, in truth they were not. While Lindy's hair color came from a bottle, Lilah's was simply sunkissed naturally. Lindy had often wondered how Lora had been graced with such dark hair while Lindy and Lilah had landed on the lighter side. In their most heated spats, Lindy had often tried to convince Lora she'd been adopted. It might've worked if their faces weren't so similar. "Anything wrong?"

By the anxious tone to her voice, Lindy knew Lilah was fearful of the answer. Lilah hated confrontation and generally avoided it, but as of late she'd gotten a bit tougher it seemed, if only marginally so. "The little demon spawn in Bungalow 2 has been up to her usual antics."

"What'd she flush down the toilet this time?" Lilah asked.

"Sand. Lots and lots of sand," Lindy answered.

Lilah made a face. "What are we going to do? Should I have Celly call the plumber again?"

"Yes, please. And while you're doing that, our sister dear is going to apologize to the demon spawn's father for being so rude," Lora said.

Lindy narrowed her stare at Lora. "If you want an apology, why don't you go give one and say it's from me and call it a day? I'm afraid if I go near the kid I'll commit a felony."

Lilah shared a look with Lora—and the fact that her twin seemed ready to side with the big bad older sister gave Lindy momentary pause—then said, "Lindy, I know you don't want to but Lora's right, we can't afford to lose him as a patron. Larimar needs his money. I'm sorry. Just get it over with and then I'll make sure to handle the calls for Bungalow 2 from now on if you think that would help."

"Forget it," Lindy muttered with a scowl. "I'll do it. But I just want to go on record as to say that this sucks and you both suck, too."

"Duly noted," Lora said drily, then gestured. "Go before they start packing."

Lindy bit down on the impulse to tell Lora where to stick it and headed toward Bungalow 2. It wasn't Lora's fault that Larimar was sinking in financial quicksand. Lindy understood they were all doing what they could to save a beloved sinking ship but Lindy was not above feeling a bit emotionally manipulated into helping when she had her own life to live.

In Hollywood, it was crucial to be seen. How was anyone going to see her here? Before leaving L.A. she'd been hoping and praying that she'd landed the national commercial gig she'd auditioned for but she'd been sorely *vexed,* as the St. John locals would say, to discover the part had been awarded to the woman who'd no doubt said yes to the director's vulgar suggestion that had involved her mouth and his genitals. *Disgusting little pig of a man,* she thought, remembering with a shudder. Oh, who cared? Who wanted to be in a tampon commercial anyway?

Lindy trudged through the sand to Bungalow 2 and, drawing a deep breath, knocked on the door and tried channeling a calm and peaceful vibe when in fact, she was still sporting a distinctly uncooperative attitude.

The little bugger herself opened the door. *What luck,* Lindy thought drily. *Just get it over with,* she told herself.

"Is your dad here?" Lindy asked, forcing a smile that she didn't feel.

The girl, Carys, had the look of a child accustomed to getting her way at the expense of others. Lindy knew this look because half the kids in Hollywood wore it well. "What do you want with my dad?" she asked, lounging idly against the door frame. "Gonna tell him more lies about me?"

Lindy ignored that and bared her teeth in a wretched facsimile of a wider grin. "So, here or not?"

"Your hotel sucks," Carys announced, watching for Lindy's reaction. "We've definitely stayed in better, you know. In places with toilets that actually work," she added with a sly look. The brat was trying to bait her. If Lindy collected a paycheck she would've said she didn't get paid enough to deal with this crap.

"I take it he's not here," Lindy said, cocking her head to the side, openly assessing the kid. "Otherwise you'd be watching your mouth a little more closely. I get your act, kid. You play the sweet innocent girl for your dad but when his back is turned you show your true colors. You're spoiled, mean, selfish and cruel," Lindy said, taking pleasure in the way the girl's face had begun to redden. "Oh, and chances are no one really likes you, which is something you probably know but pretend not to care about because, let's face it, being a jerk is a lonely life. But let me fill you in on a secret, short stuff, this lonely childhood of yours is only going to get worse because unless you change your attitude, no one is ever going to want to be around you...not even your dad."

"Shut up," Carys said.

"Hey, kudos, kid, for the lip tremble," Lindy said, being quite brutal, probably more than what was required but Lindy was still pissed about the toilet. "Pretty convincing. If I wasn't already wise to your act, I might've bought it."

At that Carys's eyes actually welled and Lindy felt a pang of remorse for taking it to that level but the kid had it coming, for sure. Today Lindy was Karma's handmaiden.

"I'm telling my dad," she whispered, her voice cracking a bit. For a split second Lindy actually saw something in the girl's raw expression that smacked of genuine emotion. A moment of doubt crossed her mind as she thought to soften the harsh words but the moment passed as quickly as a tropical storm and suddenly Carys screamed before slamming the door in Lindy's face, "My daddy is going to sue you for every penny you own for being so mean to me!"

"Yeah, well good luck with that!" Lindy shouted back, forgetting her earlier doubt. Then she added, "Brat!" for good measure.

Well, that hadn't gone well. But surely Lora had to have known it wouldn't. Maybe her sister had set her up. Customer service wasn't her specialty or niche. And curse her own stubbornness. Maybe she ought to have let Lilah handle the situation with Bungalow 2, after all, because clearly Lindy simply wasn't cut out for this touchy-feely stuff. *Damn, damn, damn,* Lindy thought grumpily. She had a feeling this wasn't going to end well for anyone. At this rate, she might've single-handedly ruined Larimar's chances of pulling through this disaster in one day. *Good job, Lindy!*

"AND THEN…AND then…" Carys's voice hitched on a hysterical hiccup as Gabe cradled his daughter as she sobbed in his arms. "And then, she called me…she called me…a bad…n-name, Daddy!"

"What sort of bad name, sweetheart?" he asked, barely holding his temper in check. "Go ahead, you can tell me. I'll take care of this once and for all if you just tell me what happened."

Carys ground the tears from her eyes and then wailed, "She called me a…*b*-word!"

The b-*word.* Hmm…well, the range could land between a whole lot of different insults from mild to harsh.

He'd only been gone for an hour and a half, just long enough for Carys to calm down so they could discuss her behavior, but in the space of that time, that woman had apparently returned to the bungalow to call his daughter names. A small niggling doubt worried at his thoughts even as his temper reached a dangerous place. Carys was only eleven; the woman had no right to call his daughter names no matter what she'd allegedly done to the damn toilet. Still, that one percent of doubt countered with grim logic. Carys was…a handful. The *b*-word was the least of the insults recently hurled at his daughter. In fact, her last nanny…well, he was pretty sure the woman had called her something quite unpleasant in Swedish.

"Honey, why would she just show up and start calling you names?" he asked, unable to bury that small doubt under his instinct to defend his daughter. "Maybe it was a misunderstanding…."

"Daddy, you don't believe me?" Carys's head popped from his shoulder, her eyes hard and mean.

"It's not that I don't believe you, sweetheart," he said evenly. "But sometimes there are misunderstandings."

"I'm not stupid or deaf. She called me a *b*-word. How am I supposed to *misunderstand* that?"

Ah hell, he'd walked into that one. Carys was much too smart to pull off that kind of deflection. He sighed and shook his head. "Carys…be honest with me…. Why do you think a relative stranger would just start calling you names? That doesn't make a lot of sense. Did you, possibly, say something that might've been offensive?"

"Why are you taking her side?" Carys said, openly wounded and rapidly growing angry. "You're supposed to be on my side! Not hers. She's a nobody. I'm your daughter! Doesn't that mean anything to you?"

"Of course it does," he said sharply, not liking what

was happening between them but it seemed to happen more often these days. "I'm just saying—"

"Don't you love me, Daddy?" she cut in impatiently, wiping her nose with a quick swipe of the back of her hand.

"Carys," he warned, disappointed by her obvious attempt at manipulating him. "Stop it."

Her lower lip trembled and she pushed away from him, the action actually skewering him in the heart. "I hate you," she said quietly. "Mom would've believed me. She was the only one who truly loved me."

"Damn it, Carys," he said, growing angry himself, but mostly doubling over inside from the pain of what was happening between them. It was as if Charlotte's death had taken the light and laughter from his daughter and he'd been left with the dark and dour shell that could neither laugh nor smile and he was at a loss of what to do. "This has to stop. Just stop it already, all right?" His voice almost sounded desperate and if he could hear it, so could she. He moved to the window, a mass of equal parts frustration and despair, as he felt the need to escape. No, he told himself firmly. *Fix this. Somehow.* "Listen…" He turned to try again, to apologize for being short with her but before the words could leave his mouth, she was running out the door.

"Carys!"

CARYS RAN AS fast as her legs could take her, as fast as she'd ever run before. Her bare feet slapped on the dark asphalt road as she burst from the private grounds of the resort where her father had imprisoned her; running almost blindly as tears sprang from that empty, yet strangely painful place she held deep inside. She hated it here. She hated her father. She hated everything and everyone. No one understood what she was going through, how every day felt worse than the last.

Her father didn't care. All he cared about was his business and making money. She hated money. Hated that her father took business calls at all hours of the night, during dinner, when he'd promised to read to her, when he'd canceled their snorkel tour. Everything came before she did—everything!

He probably wouldn't even care if she dropped into the ocean and sank to the bottom and got eaten by a…a…stingray! A sob broke from her chest and she heaved as her side screamed in pain from the all-out sprint. She held her side as she limped, realizing with a cry her big toe was bleeding. Somehow she hadn't noticed that her big toenail had been partially ripped off. She sank to the side of the road and held her foot, crying. Nobody cared. Nobody!

"Momma…" she whispered. Just saying the word made her heart spasm with raw grief. Everyone had told her time would heal the hurt, but they'd lied! Every day was more painful than the one before and she didn't care anymore what anyone thought or said about her. She just wanted her mom again. And if that meant…well, then that's what she meant.

She wished she were dead, too.

CHAPTER THREE

LINDY STORMED PAST the reception desk where Celly, the local Crucian woman Pops had hired, arched her thin brow and clucked at Lindy's angry pace. "You got a bee in yah bonnet, supahstar?" Celly asked, using the nickname she'd given Lindy once she learned she was an aspiring actress. Funny thing was, Lindy wasn't quite sure if she was being facetious or complimentary.

"You could say that," Lindy muttered. "Where's Lora?"

Celly shrugged. "Not that woman's keepah, you know dat," she said, adding with a sniff, "she likely eatin' young children's souls for breakfast somewhere."

Lindy would've laughed because that was damn funny, but she was too keyed up to appreciate Celly's wry island humor. She had to talk with Lora before the she-devil in Bungalow 2 had her daddy bellowing to bring the resort down. Maybe if she gave her side of things… Oh hell, why even bother. She'd been harsh, but the kid had needed to hear a few harsh truths. She probably deserved to have her mouth washed out with soap, too. Luckily for Carys, Lindy hadn't had any on hand.

"Yah got murder in yah eyes, girl," Celly warned with a chuckle. "Must be good, whatcha got?"

"The spoiled monster in Bungalow 2… Lora told me to apologize for having the audacity to call the kid out for flushing two tons of sand down the toilet but I didn't quite manage the apology part."

"No?"

"Not quite. I probably made it worse," Lindy admitted with a private grimace. "But in my defense, I told Lora I wasn't in the mood to play nice with that little brat and so it's really sort of Lora's fault for making me do something I knew wasn't going to go well. She never listens."

"None of yah do," Celly said, chuckling. "Yah all de same. Stubborn, de lot of yah."

"Oh, really? And suddenly you're an expert on the Bells?" Lindy quipped wryly. "You've worked here for all of a year or so?"

"Dat mouth de same as de rest." Celly tapped her dark head. "Hard as sea coral and just as rigid."

Yeah, well, maybe. But she didn't have time to argue the finer points with Celly so she let it go. "If you see my sister can you please tell her I need to talk to her?"

"Yah," Celly said, though Lindy wasn't quite sure if Celly was just saying what Lindy wanted to hear or if she'd truly give Lora the message. Lora and Celly didn't get along. Under normal circumstances, anyone who bumped heads with Lora was an automatic friend to Lindy but Celly was different. She wasn't all that friendly and she rarely did what anyone told her to do unless it aligned with what Celly had already planned for herself. Lora had tried to talk Pops into letting Celly go but the man had stubbornly refused. Plain and simple, he liked the ornery woman. So she remained. The only one who didn't seem to rub her wrong was Lilah, but honestly, her twin had the disposition of a wet sea sponge—as in she gave absolutely no resistance to pressure; she simply caved. So of course Celly would have no problem with Lilah.

It was one of Lilah's most aggravating qualities to be honest but Lindy would never say that to Lilah because, well, everyone protected Lilah. It was their thing.

Lindy exited the lobby and ran smack into the very person she didn't want to face just yet—Gabe Weston.

She opened her mouth to defend herself but he blew past her, wearing an anxious expression. A feeling of dread settled in her stomach and she hurried after him against her better judgment. "What's wrong?" Lindy asked.

He barely acknowledged her, but answered tersely. "Carys is missing. She wasn't in her room and she wasn't down at the beach."

"I'm sure she's just hiding out," Lindy said, swallowing a really big lump of something that tasted like apprehension. Had she caused this kid to do something stupid like run away? The island was a safe place, *mostly,* but it certainly wasn't smart for a kid to go wandering around by herself. "I'll help you look."

"That's not necessary," he said, cutting her a short look.

"I know the island and two sets of eyes are better than one, right?" she said, trying to appeal to his logic, but she saw an arctic storm blowing behind his eyes. She supposed she couldn't blame him. "How long has she been gone?"

He made an agitated gesture that spoke of private guilt as he admitted, "I don't know, exactly. We were having a discussion and then she got really upset and ran out the door."

"Did she say what had upset her?" Lindy asked, though she could guess.

"Actually—" he stopped to pin Lindy with a sharp stare "—she said you called her the *b*-word."

Lindy gaped. "The what?"

"The *b*-word, which I can only assume is *bitch*. Is that true?"

"No," Lindy answered truthfully. "I hate to break it to you but your little angel lied to you. I called her a brat but I'd never call a little kid that other word, no matter how much they deserved it."

Gabe processed her answer and slowly came to his own conclusion. "I was afraid of that." He sighed and pushed his hand through his hair. "I've been having some…issues with Carys."

"I can only imagine," Lindy said wryly. "But we'll find her, don't worry. There are only so many places she can hide on this island."

"I thought she probably needed a little cooldown and went to the beach but after about thirty minutes I went to find her. She wasn't anywhere."

She could hear the guilt in his voice and felt bad for him. She wasn't a mom and didn't know what it entailed but she knew for certain, she wasn't interested in the job description from what she knew so far. "Okay, so she's either gone to Hawksnest Beach or she went to town. My vote is for town. I'm guessing she has cash or a credit card?"

He looked discomfited, as if Lindy's assumption only solidified her opinion that Carys was a spoiled rich kid, but he nodded nonetheless. "For emergencies," he clarified, as if that made a difference. In Los Angeles, a rich kid's emergency could mean there was a new pair of Jimmy Choo ballet slippers at Nordstrom. Lindy supposed rich kids were the same no matter the zip code.

"Well, that's good. If she has cash, she's probably

blowing off some steam in the shops. I mean, isn't shopping its own brand of therapy?"

"I wouldn't know. I don't particularly like to shop. That was my wife's department," he answered grimly.

Wife…likely a divorcé and he ended up picking the short straw with the kid this vacation. "So where's the missus right now?"

"She passed away a year ago."

Ouch. She bit her lip and the pink of shame heated her cheeks. "Oh. I'm sorry," she said and actually meant it. She knew how it felt to lose a mother. With a pinch of conscience she grudgingly saw Carys in a different light. Maybe the kid was hurting and lashing out because she missed her mom and buttoned-up dad wasn't cutting it in the emotional healing department. She skewed her gaze at Gabe and another apology hovered on her tongue. He started to veer toward the parking lot where his rented luxury car waited and she tugged at his magnolia-covered shirt, gesturing for him to follow. "C'mon, I'll drive. I know my way around and some of these roadways are tricky."

He seemed poised to argue but thought better of it and followed her to the Jeep. They hopped in and after Lindy fished around under the seat for the spare key, they were rumbling out of the parking lot.

"Do you always keep the spare in the vehicle?" he asked, clearly a bit incredulous. "I mean, anyone could just take off with your vehicle."

"They could but they don't. It's a private resort and everyone's pretty honest." She barked a laugh at a private memory. "We've only had one car thief in all the years we've owned Larimar," she shared without shame. "And it was me. I took the Jeep and skipped off island to St. Thomas, where a few friends were having a party, and I didn't come home until morning. In my defense, how was I supposed to know that the ferry didn't run past 11:00 p.m.? I was grounded for a week after that escapade but it was worth it."

He shook his head, not quite sure what to think of her. Lindy didn't take it personally. She was a bit of an odd bird, so she'd been told. "Oh, come on, you mean to tell me you never did anything crazy when you were a kid?" she asked, trying to take his mind off his daughter and ease the frown on his face.

He exhaled a short breath as if he was wise to her attempt but he answered with a short shrug. "I guess. But it feels a whole lot different when it's your kid doing the crazy stuff."

She bit her lip, her smile fading. Yeah, she supposed that was true. Now she wished she hadn't tried to make light of the situation. "We'll find her. It'll be okay," she said. "I grew up here and it's pretty safe. Almost boring. In fact, in St. Thomas they call St. John *St. Yawn* if that tells you anything."

"She's only eleven," he reminded her.

"Yes, but something tells me she's pretty damn resourceful, even for an eleven-year-old. Am I right?"

At that he nodded grudgingly, rubbing the skin above his brows. "Yeah. I guess you could say that. She can be a bit precocious."

"Yeah," Lindy agreed. "I recognize it. That's how I was, too. My grandmother had her hands full with me, but I turned out pretty well, so likely she will, too."

They drove into the plaza where the shops converged in a marketplace hub and Lindy grabbed the first parking space she could find, sliding into a tight spot that barely qualified as legal. Gabe looked uneasy at her parking job but she simply hopped out and waited for him to follow. She waved away his concern. "I know it looks illegal but it'll be fine. Besides, we'll be gone before anyone starts to raise a fuss. Trust me," she said, scanning the plaza. Several tourists were snapping pictures of an iguana lazing on a tree branch at eye level until he tired of the attention and lumbered farther up the tree. Lindy turned to Gabe. "Let's split up. We'll cover more ground if we do. You take the upstairs shops and I'll take the bottom level. We'll come back to this spot in thirty minutes. Okay?"

"Okay," he said and struck out, his pace brisk. She blew out a short breath and focused on where an eleven-year-old kid would likely want to hang out. The shops in this plaza were mostly geared toward tourists and she doubted the kid was looking to buy a coffee mug or T-shirt. Lindy closed her eyes and thought hard. If she were a kid with money at her disposal and she was so angry and hurt that she just ran away, where would she go?

Off island. The answer seemed simple enough. A rich kid with resources and enough savvy was going to try to find a way off the island, possibly to purchase a plane ticket in St. Thomas to fly back to wherever she came from. Knowing Carys, the kid probably knew her way around a terminal. The wealthy were usually well traveled; some kids in L.A. were bicoastal with divorced parents so a plane ride was as natural as hitching a cab in New York.

Lindy jogged to the marina and began scanning. She spied her old friend Billy Janks, unloading scuba gear from his charter. She waved and grinned when his dark brown face split into an easy smile.

"Yah a sight for sore eyes," he exclaimed when she stepped aboard and gave him a fierce hug. "Heath told me yah were here but I couldn't believe yah left all dat Hollywood glamour for little ol' St. John."

"I didn't leave permanently," Lindy said, smiling. "Just a little break until things get more settled with Larimar." She admired his beautiful boat. "Man, you've come a long way. I remember when you were just a snot-nosed island kid like the rest of us. Now you own your own charter company? That's damn sweet, Billy."

He grinned and nodded. "Saving up for yah to make me an honest mon, sweet."

Lindy laughed. "As if I'd keep you from all the ladies who want a piece of that dark island candy," she teased. "I'd never be able to live with myself if I kept you all to myself."

"True dat," he said, laughter in his voice. "So what da real reason yah here? Come for a ride?"

She shook her head. "No. Unfortunately not. But I'll take a rain check on that, though. Actually, I was wondering if you saw a little imp of a girl come through looking to pay someone to ferry her to St. Thomas. She has serious cash but she's only about eleven."

Billy sobered and nodded. "She came tru here about fifteen minutes ago. I told her to go home. She plenty mad when I say dat. I tole her to cool off with a cold drink at the boathouse."

"Thanks, Billy," Lindy said, relieved. At least Carys hadn't found a way off island yet. She waved at Billy and headed toward the boathouse. She stepped inside and spotted Carys immediately. She was trying to haggle with a captain Lindy didn't know.

"I have cash," she said, her small face gathering into a dark scowl. "What's the problem? I'll even pay you more than the trip is worth! I mean, you'd be stupid to pass up a deal like that!"

Lindy could tell the kid was about to get tossed into the water headfirst by the annoyed captain and for a split second, Lindy was tempted to let him. The kid deserved that and more, but in the end, not even Lindy could allow herself to let that happen.

"C'mon, kid, your dad is worried about you," she said, startling Carys until she saw it was Lindy, then her face screwed into a fierce glower. "I know, I know, you're mad. You can be mad in the car. Your dad is about to turn this whole island upside down to find you and you can't even comprehend how that will make my life hell and I think you've done enough of that for one day."

"My dad doesn't care," Carys shot back, but there was a slight tremble to her lip that gave her away. Beneath all that bravado and bad attitude, the kid was hurting. Lindy sighed and wondered why she had to be the one to see it first.

"You know he does so let's stop with the games and the lies." Lindy drew Carys away from the clump of island natives and took her to the bar.

"I'm not lying," she shot back heatedly.

"You told your dad that I called you a *b*-word. You and I both know I didn't do that."

Carys slid her gaze away. "I didn't say *which b*-word. It's not my fault he jumped to the wrong conclusion," she said with a shrug. "He didn't believe me anyway."

"That's not the point. You can't just make up stuff about people. Someone could get hurt."

"If he loved me, he'd believe whatever I said." Lindy's surprised laughter caused Carys to scowl. "What's so funny?"

"You, kid. Loving someone doesn't give you an all-access pass to being a manipulative brat," she said, pausing to order two Shirley Temples. "I don't know your dad but he seems like a decent guy. You and I both know you were the little twerp who ruined our plumbing so let's just get that out of the way right now. I see what's going on, though. You're trying to get your dad's attention because you're hurting but trust me, this way isn't productive and it just hurts you in the end."

"How do you know?" Carys said, her voice small but defiant. "You don't know anything about me or my dad."

"True. But I lost my mom when I was really young and I remember how it felt."

The defiance in Carys's body language lessened a bit as she asked, "Really? How'd your mom die?"

"Cancer," Lindy answered candidly, surprised when the admission still had the power to sting. She straightened and focused on Carys. "How about your mom?"

"Same. Dad said she didn't suffer too long, though. By the time the doctors found the cancer, it'd spread everywhere," Carys said, her small voice getting even smaller.

Lindy blinked back an unexpected show of tears. It'd been a long time since she remembered everything her mom had gone through. It'd been tough, but fast, too. Lindy had always wondered if her mom had simply given up because of her divorce. Her mom had never quite recovered from the shock of her husband splitting without warning.

"Dad doesn't like to talk about it, though," Carys whispered. "He says it's not going to bring her back so we shouldn't dwell on it."

"How do you feel about that?" Lindy asked.

"I hate it."

"Yeah, I would, too. My mom was a special woman. I'm sure yours was, too."

"She was." Carys sniffed and swallowed. "She was the best mom in the world."

"And I'm guessing she thought you were pretty awesome, too. I mean, something tells me you didn't act like this when she was around."

A hint of pink crept into Carys's cheeks and Lindy smiled in understanding. "Listen, how about this... I'll make a deal with you. If you promise to stop trying to kill our septic system with your antics—" Lindy took a deep breath, shocked about what she was going to offer to the kid "—I'll make a promise to listen to you anytime you want to talk about your mom. We can share stories about our moms if you want. Moms are special ladies. They deserve to get a little shout-out, even if they're not with us anymore. Is that a deal?"

"You'd listen to me talk about my mom? About anything I wanted to say?" Carys asked.

"Yes," Lindy answered, realizing she was making a big promise but deep down she knew the kid needed it. "Anything you want. Your dad is trying to do the best he can but you have to cut him some slack, you know? He's probably hurting, too."

At that, Carys's eyes watered and Lindy knew she'd hit a nerve. Carys didn't really want to hurt her dad but she was a little girl who was lashing out because that's all she knew how to do. "Okay," Carys said, nodding. "Want to shake on it?"

"Absolutely. A deal's not a real deal unless we shake on it. And maybe spit, too."

Carys hesitated and then spit in her hand before holding it out to Lindy. Oh damn, Lindy thought with a grimace. She'd been kidding about the spit part. But what the hell and after spitting in her own hand, she sealed their deal with a squishy shake.

"Great," Lindy said, quickly wiping her hand on the seat of her sarong. "Now can we get out of here and get your dad before he has a heart attack?"

Carys grinned. "Yeah, I guess so."

Lindy nodded and, as they walked out, knew she'd just made a reluctant friend in an eleven-year-old girl.

CHAPTER FOUR

GABE'S HEART WAS racing and his stomach had turned queasy. He'd pushed Carys too hard; he should've backed off. But he was at a loss as to what to do with her. He knew deep in his bones that Carys was guilty of all the things she'd been accused of and probably even a few things that hadn't been caught yet but he just couldn't understand why she was being such a terror. He'd tried about everything under the sun to help her heal—Disneyland, a new pony, the best birthday party money could buy—and it seemed her attitude only worsened.

And now this? If something happened to her he'd never forgive himself. He never should've listened to that woman when she talked him out of going straight to the police. They needed a search party right now. Changing direction, his thoughts almost manic, he startled when he heard Carys's voice behind him.

"Hi, Daddy," his daughter said, smiling as if she hadn't scared the living daylights out of him. She walked beside Lindy as if they were old friends, which made him do a double take. An hour ago Carys had been hollering for the woman's head. Now they were buds? Lindy's brow went up ever so slightly, as if encouraging Carys. His daughter drew a deep breath and—Lord help him, he was going to have a heart attack—apologized. "I was real upset but I shouldn't have run off like that. I'm sorry, Daddy."

With his daughter looking up at him with those gorgeous baby blues, appearing more sincere than she had in months, Gabe found himself floundering with the wind sucked from his sails. He'd been prepared to yell, cry, kiss and chastise but instead he simply nodded, unsure of what to do. "It's okay, sweetheart," he said, shooting an uncertain look Lindy's way. He was willing to bet she had something to do with this remarkable transformation.

If he wanted answers, he would find them with the woman he really wanted to avoid. When Charlotte had been alive, he'd been a faithful man and even after her death that hadn't changed. He knew he wouldn't be much of a partner to anyone new after Charlotte died and he'd wanted to make sure he was making good choices, particularly now that the parenting burden fell squarely on his shoulders. So that meant smothering the inevitable awakening of his libido, which chose to flare to life at inopportune moments. And up until that moment, he'd been successful. But there was something about this woman that made his decision to remain single and celibate very difficult.

"I'm hungry," Carys announced, grabbing her dad's hand. "Let's go to that hamburger place we went to the other day…Sailor's, I think?" She looked to Lindy for confirmation and Lindy nodded.

"Best burgers on the island, maybe even all the islands, but then I'm partial. I've been eating there since I was a kid."

"You grew up here." Gabe suddenly remembered, wondering if her unique, exotic environment had created the slightly wild persona he saw now, or if it'd been her nature to begin with. A shudder threatened to shake his spine as his thoughts touched on an off-limits area.

Of course, she had a body men dreamed about, but there was more to Lindy Bell than her body. He had to admit, he was curious. Which was exactly why he needed to steer clear. Curiosity led to seeking answers and sometimes the answers only spurred a deeper hunger for information. There was no way he was going to get mixed up with this wild woman. If he were truly ready to start dating, he'd start looking in more traditional pools, such as the country club, or the endless stream of fundraiser dinners that he was invited to because he owned his own Fortune 500 company. Realizing late that Lindy and Carys were already engaged in a conversation that didn't include him, he interjected himself with a firm smile. "Thank you, Ms. Bell. I think we can take it from here."

"I drove you here, remember?"

"We can take a taxi back to the resort."

Carys's expression fell, clearly displeased, but he needed to have a conversation with his daughter that didn't include strangers. Lindy seemed to understand his need for some privacy and smiled. "Well, sounds like you have everything under control here. Glad the rug rat is safe and sound." To Carys she said, "And remember what I said…" She held up her hand and pointed at the center of her palm, which appeared empty to his eyes but to Carys there seemed to be something of value there. "Catch you later, kiddos."

Once Lindy was out of earshot, he turned to Carys and asked, "What was that all about?"

"We made a deal," Carys answered without hesitation but failed to elaborate. "I'm starving, Daddy. Let's go. Can we walk to Sailor's from here?"

Distracted, he glanced around, not quite sure how to find Sailor's from the plaza. He hadn't been paying enough attention, and even though the island wasn't overly large, one could still get turned around. "We'll find a taxi, sweetheart. Now tell me more about this deal you made with a stranger?" he prompted, trying to keep his voice light and amused, but really he was uncomfortable with the idea that Carys had made some sort of deal with a woman she barely knew.

Carys turned and seemed to evaluate him, as if testing whether or not he could be trusted with the information and then when she simply shrugged, he realized he must've failed the test. Pressing his lips together, he made a mental note to talk with Lindy herself about what was going on, then switched gears and hailed a cab for them.

Once they had their burgers and were eating their weight in perfectly cooked beef—Lindy might be right, the burgers at Sailor's were pretty damn good—he tried to strike up a conversation with his daughter. Once they used to talk about everything under the sun; now they barely managed two words without it turning into a fight. "I was thinking we could take a drive to see the sights tomorrow. Maybe go parasailing or something?"

Carys shrugged without answering and continued eating her thick-cut fries. "Lindy is pretty cool," she announced, clearly demonstrating her attention was nowhere near the conversation Gabe had been having. He withheld an aggravated sigh and shrugged, not quite sure how to answer. What did he know about Lindy Bell aside from the superficial? She was hot-tempered, but beautiful in a way that made his teeth ache, and he had to focus really hard not to allow his imagination to run wild with all the pent-up desires he'd been trying his best to smother for over a year.

Carys continued, thankfully oblivious to Gabe's struggle. "I didn't like her at first but she's better than I thought. She's just got this way about her that's, I don't know, really cool. Like when I talk to her I feel like she's really listening."

"I listen," he countered, mildly offended. He felt as if he'd been bending over backward to get Carys to open up to him but she'd rebuffed his every attempt. "You know if you ever want to talk—"

"What if I want to talk about Mom?" she queried sharply and he shifted in discomfort.

He knew he needed to tread carefully but talking about Charlotte… It was so painful for them both so why would he want to encourage that? "Your mom would've wanted us to go on with our lives, not wallow in sadness. You know that, right?"

"When people die it's sad," Carys countered bluntly. "Lindy said it's good to talk about it. Somehow it makes you less sad."

He drew back, freshly irritated. "Talking isn't going to bring Mom back," he told Carys firmly. "Of course we miss her. But the best way to honor her spirit is to move on with our lives in a positive manner." At that Carys's eyes flashed and she shoved a fry in her mouth. He was losing her again. Damn it. "Carys, you know I loved Mom more than anything, right?"

"Yeah, I guess," she answered, shrugging.

"What do you mean, *you guess?*"

Carys glared. "If you loved her like you say you did I don't understand why you won't ever let me talk about her. You never even mention her name. It's like you're trying to erase that she ever existed."

"That's not true," he said, stung. "I just don't want to get stuck in an unhealthy pattern of emotional pain. And I don't want that for you, either."

"What are you talking about?" Carys asked, confused

and annoyed. "I don't even know what that means. Emotional pain? What else are you supposed to feel when someone you love dies? I guess I didn't get that memo on what's supposed to be healthy and whatever."

Somehow, once again, their conversation had eroded into an angry standoff and he was bewildered how they got there. He sighed and gestured at her cooling food. "Eat your burger."

"I'm not hungry anymore."

"Fine. Then we'll take it with us. You can eat it later."

"Whatever."

"Can we not do this?" he asked, hating that he was pleading with his daughter.

"Do what?"

"Fight."

"I want to talk to Lindy," she said, folding her arms across her small chest.

"What?"

"I want to talk to her."

"About what?" he asked, incredulous. Carys's mouth tightened, telling him he wasn't going to get an answer. He signaled for the check with a brusque motion. "This is getting ridiculous, Carys. I've tried to be understanding. I've tried to be accommodating but you've stonewalled me at every turn. What does Lindy Bell—a stranger, I might add—offer you that I haven't?"

"You wouldn't understand because you don't listen," she muttered, glancing away. "She understands because she lost her mom, too. And she says it's good to talk about it."

Gabe stared, hit by the knowledge that in one conversation Lindy had managed to reach his daughter when he had failed repeatedly. He also realized that Lindy had forged a tenuous bond with Carys through a similar experience. But Lindy wasn't the kind of person Gabe would like his daughter hanging out with on a regular basis. From what he could tell, it was likely Lindy didn't care about the things he felt were important and hoped to instill in his daughter. Maybe it was unfair to judge a book by its cover but he didn't have the luxury of getting past the surface when his daughter was involved. "I'm sorry, Carys. I don't think that's a good idea. We don't know Lindy very well and she might seem like a very nice person but I'd rather not invite strangers into our business."

Once again he was the bad guy, he thought with an unhappy sigh. But he had broad shoulders. He could take it. Carys would realize someday that he was only doing what was best for her.

He just hoped their relationship didn't sustain irreparable damage between now and then.

CHAPTER FIVE

Lindy returned from the marina and went in search of something to eat. She found her grandfather puttering around in the kitchen, fixing himself a sandwich. She slid onto the barstool and smiled with love in her heart for the old guy. He hadn't changed much physically. Maybe his hair had a bit more gray and he wasn't as robust as he once was but he still had that same indescribable quality about him that made him Pops. Even if he was slowly losing his grip on reality.

"Whatcha got there, Pops?" Lindy asked, bending to take a sniff of his plate and opening her mouth as if she were going to gobble it down right there in front of him.

"Hey now, get your own," he warned and pulled the plate from the snap of her jaws. "There's plenty. Celly just stocked the pantries."

Lindy cocked her head. "Celly?" she asked, curious. "She does the shopping now?"

"Well, your grams…she's hard to find these days for the little stuff, like grocery shopping and whatnot, so Celly offered to do the shopping. She's also a great cook. Have you tried her boiled bananas yet? Damn near as good as anything they sell at The Wild Donkey."

"The Wild Donkey," Lindy murmured, remembering the popular local hangout. "I can't believe they're still in business."

"Nothing much changes around here, just the people,"

Pops remarked, taking a hefty bite of what appeared to be a turkey and cranberry sandwich with lots of sprouts. "Mmm…that's good," he said with a grunt of approval. "Your grams talked Celly into all this healthy stuff and at first I was skeptical, but damn if she doesn't have me eating like a rabbit and liking it, besides. Wonders never cease, huh?"

Lindy smiled as she pulled the fixings for her own sandwich. "So…Pops…how is Grams feeling these days?" she asked, feeling out the framework of Pops's elaborate fantasy. "She okay?"

"Fit as a fiddle," Pops answered with a faint scowl as if he were annoyed that Lindy had even asked. "Why? She say something to you?"

Lindy's mouth curved in a faint smile as sadness brushed across her thoughts. She'd been fifteen when Grams had gotten sick. It'd been a horrible time. Sometimes she wished she could forget, too. Lindy blinked back the sudden moisture in her eyes and focused on her sandwich. "Nope," she answered brightly, slathering mayo on her bread. "Just making sure everyone's good and healthy. I've been gone awhile so you know, just want to make sure I haven't missed anything important."

"Everything's fine, sugar bird," he assured her with a smile, biting into his sandwich. "Everything's just fine."

"Good." She dumped a handful of turkey on her bread with a little more force than necessary. Pops looked up with a quizzical expression and she forced a laugh. "Oops. My bad."

Pops switched subjects without her needing to, saying, "Lindy…I'm worried about Lilah. I think she's going through something…and you two have always been so close. Maybe you could talk to her?"

"Sure, Pops," Lindy answered, sprinkling her sandwich with a liberal dose of salt and pepper. She liked it almost inedible to most tastes. The first time her friends had watched her doctor her Subway sandwich they'd nearly fallen over in shock. Of course, it could've also been for the fact that she was eating a full six-inch instead of cutting it in half to save for the following day. She sank her teeth into the sandwich and groaned in happiness. "What makes you think Lilah is bothered by something?" she asked around the bite in her mouth. "She seemed okay to me yesterday."

Actually, that wasn't entirely true, now that she thought about it. But then Lilah had always orbited her own planet and no one thought to question her flight pattern. Lindy loved her twin desperately, but she did worry about her at times. She'd tried to get her to move to Los Angeles, but even as the offer had fallen from her mouth she knew that was never going to happen. Lilah in Los Angeles would be like feeding a lamb to the lions. She'd stick out like a sore thumb in Lindy's circles; worse, some sleazy producer type might try to sleep with her. Lindy sighed and took another bite. "Yeah," she repeated, mostly to herself. "I'll talk to her, Pops."

"I knew I could count on you." He rose from the table and tossed his trash, then brushed a quick, smacking kiss on her cheek. She smiled at the contact and watched as he went on his merry way, likely to go find his wife.

How did someone lose their grip on reality like Pops? He seemed completely lucid, unless you considered the fact that he held conversations with a woman who'd been dead for almost ten years. It broke her heart, but what could she do? Pushing reality on him seemed to make it worse—Lora had learned that the hard way—but eventually his grip on everything was going to slip, right? She hated to think of that moment, so she didn't. Finishing her sandwich, she burped with total satisfaction just as Lora walked in and gave her a disgusted look. "What? In Europe that's considered a compliment to the chef."

"We're not in Europe," Lora reminded her. "Hey, I'm glad I found you. We're going to have a family meeting tonight to discuss the situation with Larimar. It's time to start implementing some strategies."

She groaned at the overly bright light in Lora's eyes. In her previous life—before she lost her job and Heath dragged her back to St. John to help fix this mess facing the resort—she'd been something of a marketing shark. And judging by the look on her face, she missed the action. Likely, if she saw a spreadsheet she'd shudder with ecstasy. But Lindy wasn't hardwired that way. She hated the words *marketing strategy, loss leader* and anything that would compel someone to open an Excel spreadsheet. But she hadn't returned home to hang out and spruce up her Caribbean tan. She was here to pitch in. *More's the pity.* She sighed grumpily. "What time?"

Pleased with the fact that Lindy hadn't tried to get out of it, Lora actually smiled as she grabbed a banana on the go. "How about seven? That way dinner is out of the way."

"Good. And drinks can follow," Lindy quipped, adding drily, "and they should. Lots of them if we're going to get through the evening without killing one another."

Lora's smile faded, but she didn't call Lindy out for her bad attitude. Thank God for small favors. Lindy wasn't in the mood to start a word war with her older sister.

"Did you apologize to Mr. Weston?"

Lindy chewed her bottom lip as she quickly processed an easy answer to her sister's pointed question. She could tell the truth, but then that would lead to all sorts of exclamations and recriminations over her bad attitude and the consequences of her sharp tongue—blah, blah, blah—and since it had all turned out fine in the end…

"Yep," Lindy answered with a short smile.

"Good." Lora smiled, seeming relieved. "I have to confess I was a little worried you might make things worse."

Lindy scowled. "If you thought that, why'd you insist I apologize?"

Lora's smile widened. "It was a leap of faith. I think."

Lindy bit back the sarcasm dancing on her tongue. She supposed she couldn't be too peeved; in a way her sister's fear had been accurate. But at least Lindy had managed to fix things, and that's what counted anyway.

"One less reason to worry. Thanks, Lindy," Lora said and breezed from the room.

Lindy rubbed her full stomach and headed to her room to grab her iPod. She was hoping to catch some rays before the day was finished, and the sun was quickly sinking into the horizon.

Of course, as luck would have it, that was not in the cards.

"Miss Bell?" A voice called out at her back and she grimaced, recognizing the firm timbre as belonging to Carys's father, Gabe Weston. She pivoted on her heel and pasted on a perfunctory smile for his benefit in an effort to be nice.

"What's up?" she asked.

"I wondered if I might talk to you for a minute…. It's about Carys."

A ripple of unease followed. "What's wrong? Everything okay? What's the kid done now?"

"Nothing," he answered with a faint scowl.

"Oh, c'mon. You and I both know the kid's got devil juice running through her veins. Don't get me wrong...I like her, but...yeah, she's a handful. We pulled out another tie, by the way. Would you like me to show you the plumber's bill now or later?"

"Another one?"

"Well, to be fair, we think it was part of the original batch she sent whizzing down our pipes, but it got stuck and the plumber managed to fish it out. Something tells me you aren't going to want it back."

"Ah...sorry about that. Send me the bill. I'll cover it."

"Oh, it's on your bill," she assured him with a smile. "At this rate, the plumber is going to send you a fruit basket in appreciation."

At his sharp look, her grin brightened and he faltered, clearly not quite sure what to think of her. She didn't hold his confusion against him. Most people didn't know what to think of her. It was part of her charm. At least, that was how she liked to think of it. He recovered after a moment and returned to his original train of thought. "Listen, my daughter seems to have taken a shine to you...."

"Yeah? That's cool. I take back what I said about the devil juice. She's obviously a kid with a great judge of character."

"Uh...yeah, about that," he continued, uncomfortable. "Here's the thing, I'm just going to give it to you straight—"

"Great. I hate when people blow smoke up my ass. Makes me burp."

At that he almost laughed and she was struck by how handsome he could be when he wasn't acting like a stiff jackass. She regarded him with as much seriousness as she could muster. She was already bored with the con-

versation—mostly because she had a feeling whatever
he was struggling to tell her wasn't going to make her
feel all warm and fuzzy inside—and she wanted to get
it over with.

"You have to understand, my daughter is very impressionable and it's not personal, really, but—"

"Oh wait, this sounds like a 'it's not you, it's me'
conversation, which is funny because we're not even
dating. Also funny because *I'm* usually the one deliv-
ering that line."

He flushed and shot her a short look as if to say, *will
you stop interrupting so I can finish this difficult conversation?* But she was way ahead of him and simply
said with a sigh, "I get it. You don't want her hanging
out with someone as ultracool as me—an almost famous celebrity—because you wouldn't want to set her
up with an unreal expectation of what life can be like.
I get it. It's okay." She patted him on the shoulder. "But
honestly, Gabe— Can I call you Gabe? Okay. Good.
Here's the thing. I think we should give kids a high bar
to reach for. You know? So they can rise to the occasion. But that's just me. You do what you feel is right.
She's your kid."

And with that, she left him, staring with his jaw open
slightly and a serious *what-the-eff just happened?* look
on his face. And Lindy tried not to laugh.

Lindy left a lot of people with that very same expression. She suspected one particular director had pegged
it precisely: she simply didn't accept anything she didn't
want to hear and therefore created her own reality.

Now that she thought about it, maybe she had more
in common with Pops than she realized.

Huh. Interesting.

But she had to admit Gabe Weston was not hard on

the eyes. Not at all, she thought as she grabbed her beach towel and sunscreen.

Too bad she didn't date guys with kids. That was a deal-breaker in her book.

No matter how hot they were.

No matter how much she *kinda* liked the kid.

No. Matter. No. How.

Rules were rules, which ordinarily she delighted in breaking, unless they were her own rules, then she stuck to them religiously.

Yep. She was funny like that.

She spied Lilah and waved. "Hey, wanna hit the beach with me?"

"You bet. Gimme a sec." Lilah grinned with a nod before disappearing to grab her own towel and beach bag.

While she waited for her sister, Lindy's gaze strayed in the direction of Bungalow 2 for just a minute, then she sighed.

What a tragedy.

Rules sucked.

GABE WAS FAIRLY certain the hot woman had just bamboozled him.

Worse, he wasn't sure how it'd happened or how he'd allowed it to happen.

He supposed that was the foundation of a good bamboozle—the element of surprise.

Gabe was still thinking about Lindy when Carys came into view. She looked adorable in her pink bathing suit and for a moment he let his guard down. It didn't matter how she infuriated him, the love he felt for this kid was beyond comprehension. She'd been their miracle child, part of the reason she was an only child. Charlotte had struggled to get pregnant and they'd gone through several IVF cycles to finally conceive. They used to joke that Carys had been their million-dollar baby because when it was all said and done, the medical bills had been astronomical.

"She better be the next president," he'd joked a few months after Carys had been born and another wave of bills had come through. Charlotte, her blond hair tucked in a messy knot at the back of her head, simply graced the sleeping baby in her arms with an adoring smile and he forgot all about the dollar amount it'd taken to get their bundle of joy. All that had mattered was the love they all felt for this tiny person who'd come into their lives on a cloud of hopes and dreams. He'd pressed a kiss to her downy head, inhaling the soft sweet scent at her crown. "She's worth every penny," he'd admitted to Charlotte. Charlotte's eyes had watered and she'd lifted her mouth to his, sealing their lips with an emotion-filled kiss.

"You're an amazing husband…and an even more amazing father," she'd murmured. "I love you."

Gabe closed his eyes, wincing against the hurt that always followed when he thought of Charlotte. It'd been a year since she'd died. Sometimes it felt as though it were yesterday. He shook himself free of the pain wrapping itself like a band around his chest and forced a smile for Carys's benefit. "Hitting the beach?" he asked.

"Yeah," Carys answered, for once giving him a straight answer instead of one laced with sarcasm. He took that as a good sign. "Wanna come with me?"

Doubly pleased that she thought to include him without his prompting, he agreed quickly. "Let me just go get my BlackBerry and—"

"No phone," she returned with a faint scowl. "Can't you go two minutes without your emails and whatever?"

He hesitated but he could see she was waiting for him to choose her over his work. It was an easy choice if a choice was given but that was the thing…he was the boss. He had to know what was happening at all times. A lot of lives depended on him making all the right decisions for the company. He knew this was a concept an eleven-year-old girl couldn't possibly understand, but someday he hoped she might and forgive him for being a workaholic. "It's not that simple, honey," he said finally, hating the disappointment in her face. "But I tell you what, tonight at dinner…no phone at all. It'll just be me and you. I promise."

Carys regarded him with a knowing expression that bordered on distrust and it cut him to the core. Finally, she shrugged and started walking. "Whatever," she added over her shoulder and he swore under his breath. He should've just agreed to leave his phone behind. What was an hour or two incommunicado? But it was too late now and he was expecting an important phone call, besides. He sighed and walked to the bungalow, his heart heavy. Things had to change. But how was he supposed to make it change if he couldn't even spend the afternoon with his daughter without it devolving into a fight? He didn't have an answer.

That was the problem. Lately, when it came to Carys, he never had the answer.

He missed his wife—her smile, her easygoing nature, her way of smoothing over the rough spots—but most of all, he missed the way his daughter was when Charlotte was alive.

Just as he'd been unable to prevent Charlotte from dying, he felt incapable of stopping the downward slide in his relationship with Carys. Soon, she'd leave behind the preteens and head straight into the dreaded teenage years and everyone always said those were worse. He groaned softly. He couldn't even imagine.

He grabbed his phone and saw a missed call from the very person he'd been waiting for. "Damn," he muttered and quickly checked his voice mail.

This call couldn't wait. There was a three-hour time difference between here and California, which was where his office was located. With one final glance toward the beach, where he saw Carys setting up her beach gear, he quickly dialed his associate. He'd make it a brief call. Ten minutes tops.

Forty-five minutes later, deep in a tricky contract negotiation, Gabe knew all hope for time at the beach with his daughter had evaporated.

And it made him sick to his stomach. He made a mental promise to make it up to her at dinner.

Somehow his guilt felt like Charlotte's disapproval. He was a poor substitute for a mother.

CHAPTER SIX

LINDY AND LILAH headed down to the beach, chatting as they went. It felt good to reconnect with her twin; sometimes Lindy forgot how deeply she missed their unspoken connection until they were together again.

"So tell me about life in Hollywood," Lilah said, smiling. "Your emails are always so short."

Lindy made a face. "You know I hate writing. If you'd get a cell phone with text capability…"

Lilah grimaced with the same intensity. "That's all I need. I hate the concept of being at anyone's beck and call. The idea of a cyber tether makes me squirm." However, she shrugged as if she might actually consider the idea. "But if it meant I could stay connected with you easier, maybe I'll think about it some more."

"That's progress," Lindy remarked with a smile and stopped to spread their beach blanket on the soft sand. "So what's new, Li?" she asked as they both settled on the blanket. "It seems like something's bothering you."

"Why would you think that?" Lilah asked.

"Well, Pops mentioned something and I thought if something were bothering you, you might open up to me if you were inclined to open up to anyone." Lilah nodded but remained silent. Lindy tried again, saying, "Of course, you don't have to, but I hate the thought of you being in pain over something when I might be able to help."

Lilah's sad smile said it all. Lindy's heart sank a little. She'd been hoping everyone else was just imagining things, but the proof that her hope had been misplaced was currently staring off into the distance, with a bleak light in her eyes.

"What's wrong?" Lindy asked, concerned.

"It's hard to describe in a way that you could understand," Lilah answered.

"Try me."

Lilah sighed. "Have you ever felt that you just don't have a place in life? That no matter what you do, you're still standing on the outside looking in?"

Lindy shook her head. "No."

"I didn't think so," Lilah said with a short cynical smile. "You're the kind of person who walks into a room and all eyes are drawn to you because you shine with a light that's hard to ignore. When I walk into a room, no one notices."

"That's not true," Lindy protested. How could Lilah see herself like that? How could Lilah not see that she shone with a different kind of light, one that was soft and gentle and kind? "You have an ability to see the good in people, for smoothing over the rough spots in a person's personality… I mean, that's a true gift."

"Some gift," Lilah muttered, clearly not impressed. "Hardly useful if you ask me."

"You're being too hard on yourself. It's difficult being sandwiched between Lora and me. We're both in-your-face type of personalities but that doesn't mean that you don't stand out in your own way."

"It's not just that, Lindy," Lilah admitted softly. "It's that I don't seem to have anything that I'm good at." As Lindy started to protest, Lilah held up her hand with a gentle admonishment. "No, wait. Let me finish. It's all part of that knowing-your-place-in-the-world feeling that I was describing earlier. You're an actress. Lora is a businesswoman. What am I? The flighty sister who can't be trusted to handle tough jobs, the one who breaks under pressure. Not exactly the most flattering picture of myself, you know?"

"You're an amazing artist," Lindy interjected firmly, not willing to buy into Lilah's assessment. "Teachers always said you had an uncanny way of knowing how to bring emotional depth to your work, even without much formal training. If that's not talent, I don't know what is."

"What teachers said in high school certainly doesn't do much good now. I was adequately talented with art. And now that Heath isn't able to fire the glass for his glass fusion pieces, I've been filling in, but I'm just following his template. Any monkey could do what I'm doing."

"That's not true. Lora can't do it. Heath told me that he loved the woman but if she tried to fuse another glass piece it might ruin their relationship."

At that Lilah smiled. "Okay, you're right. Lora isn't any good with artistic mediums but she's such a sharp businesswoman, she doesn't need another talent. I'd like to be good at *something*. Anything."

Lindy didn't know what to say. It hurt her heart to hear her twin so candidly admitting how lost she was and it hurt worse knowing that Lindy couldn't fix Lilah's feelings about herself. She bit her lip, almost unable to believe the words were going to leave her mouth given her low opinion of therapists, but she knew her sister needed someone to help her through this. "Maybe you ought to see, like, a counselor or something," she said, wincing at the words. "Or I don't know…maybe read a self-help book?" she suggested, floundering for ideas.

"I'm fine," Lilah said, shaking her head. "It's my problem and not a new one. I'll get it figured out… eventually."

They were the right words, but Lindy sensed not even Lilah believed what she was saying and it scared Lindy. What scared her worse was that bleak expression on her sister's face, the way she seemed resigned to…what? Giving up? Fading away? Lindy didn't like any of those choices. "Move to L.A. with me when I go back," she said impulsively, almost desperately.

"You and I both know that's a terrible idea. I wouldn't even know how to begin to fit in there. I'd slowly die inside without my island."

"It kinda looks like that's what's happening now," Lindy risked murmuring, shooting Lilah an uncertain glance. "You're not happy."

"What's happiness?"

Lindy rolled her eyes, mildly irritated. "Don't go all philosophical on me. You're deflecting because you don't want to think about what's happening."

"That's all I do is think about it. I'm tired of thinking about it," Lilah returned a bit sharply. "I'm sorry. I didn't mean to snap but you're wrong. It's not like one day I woke up feeling melancholy and lost. It's a feeling I've had for a long time and it's just gotten worse."

"You sound depressed," Lindy blurted out, panicked by the utterly calm face of her twin as they discussed her situation. Shouldn't there be tears? Or anger, or something? Lindy had once read that suicide victims often knew weeks in advance of the day they were going to kill themselves and when they did finally do it, they were very peaceful about their decision. Lindy suppressed a shudder of dread as the horrid thought seized her mind. "Don't walk into the ocean and just disappear!"

Lilah did a double take, with a strange look. "What are you talking about?"

"Well…you're acting so…like the people who are about to kill themselves and I couldn't take the thought of you doing that so I figured I ought to throw it out there so you know that I'm not okay with that plan. You know?"

Lilah chuckled and the laughter actually reached her eyes, for which Lindy was inordinately grateful. "I can promise you I'm not interested in killing myself. I'm sorry to have put that idea in your head. I'm just sad, okay? Not suicidal."

Lindy let out a deep breath. "Oh, thank God," she said, feeling a weight lift from her chest. "Sad I can handle. Suicidal tendencies I cannot."

Lilah chuckled and as her gaze traveled farther down the beach, she frowned. "Isn't that the little girl in Bungalow 2?"

Lindy followed Lilah's gaze and indeed, saw Carys walking down the beach, her feet splashing in the surf in a sullen manner. Lindy sighed. "Yeah," she said and stood up. "I better go see what's going on."

Lilah nodded and Lindy walked to Carys. "What's up, kid? You trying to ditch your dad again?"

"No, he was supposed to meet me down here but he hasn't come yet. I guess he changed his mind."

Inside, Lindy winced at the forlorn tone couched within the thinly veiled sarcasm. This kid was hurting. Couldn't Gabe see that? How could he be so blind? She propped her hands on her hips and made a split-second decision. "Come hang out with me and my sister Lilah. She's cool—you'll like her. I promise."

Carys's gaze lit up hopefully but she held back, unsure. "I don't need a babysitter."

"I didn't say you did. I just thought you might like to hang out with the cool kids, you know? But if you've got something better to do…"

"No," Carys said quickly, smiling. "That sounds fine with me."

"Great," Lindy said, returning the smile as they walked back to the blanket where Lilah was sunning herself. Lindy stole a glance at Carys, troubled by the fact that she cared more than she should for this kid. She wasn't the kind of person who adopted people or causes. That was Lilah's gig. Lindy preferred her relationships easy and superficial. But for some reason, she couldn't turn a blind eye to Carys's pain. So how could Carys's father not see that his daughter was clearly losing the battle against her grief and sadness? *Stop it,* she ordered herself. Gabe was the kid's father; he'd figure it out. But what if he didn't? That same voice she was trying to silence was irritatingly persistent.

And Lindy didn't know what to do about it.

CARYS DIDN'T WANT to admit it, but she was grateful Lindy had invited her to hang out with her. Even though Lindy had promised to be available if Carys needed her, Carys was a little shy about actually hitting her up on her promise. But Lindy and her sister Lilah had happily dragged her along as if it weren't a huge inconvenience to have a kid hanging around and it made Carys feel good inside.

"Lindy said you guys lost your mom when you were young?" Carys prompted, sipping at the coconut-and-pineapple smoothie Celly had created for them as they sat on the Bells' private terrace.

Lilah and Lindy shared a look and Lilah nodded. "Yeah, and then our Grams died when we were teenagers. But Pops doesn't remember that, so we try not to remind him."

Carys frowned. "Huh?"

"Pops is losing his memory and it's easier on him to think that she's still here," Lindy explained, her expression dimming for just a moment. "So if he tries talking about Grams just try to pretend that he's making sense."

"That's weird," Carys said. "Can't you take him to the doctor or something?"

Lindy sighed. "I wish it were that easy. You can't fix dementia." Then she glanced at Lilah quickly. "You can't, right?"

Lilah shook her head. "No. The doctor said the damage to his brain is irreversible. All we can do is manage his care, and since all of us agree that we are not going to put him in a home, that means he's here with us. We just have to do what we can to keep him safe."

"Kinda like babysitting, but for old people," Carys said.

Lindy laughed. "Yeah, I guess so. But I ain't on diaper duty, that's for sure. That job can go to Lora."

Carys's expression mirrored Lilah's as they both said *ewwww* in unison.

"I can't believe you went there," Lilah said, fighting a laugh. "God, Lindy. You're so gross."

"Hey, you were thinking it, too. Don't give me that," Lindy said.

Carys grinned at the warmth between the two sisters, wanting to bask in that sensation for as long as possible. Grieving for her mom was hard, but the loneliness sucking at her insides felt worse. Being around Lindy and her quiet yet mysterious twin seemed to ease that awful feeling inside. "Do you miss your grams a lot?" she asked.

Lilah's expression turned wistful. "Oh, yes. Sometimes it's a weird comfort to pretend that she's just around the corner or at the store or something like that so I don't have to acknowledge the fact that she's gone."

Carys considered that for a minute and slowly came to understand. "Sometimes I close my eyes and pretend that my mom is in the other room, in the kitchen or something, making dinner or washing dishes. For a second it makes me feel better, but then I remember she's gone and then I feel worse."

"Well, imagine if you got locked in that feeling before you realized it was all in your imagination," Lindy said. "That's where Pops is at. He's locked in that feel-good place, and when we remind him that she's gone, it kicks him into the sad place but the sad place scares him because he doesn't understand. Ultimately, it's just better if we leave him to whatever he believes. It's not hurting anyone and frankly, it seems a small concession to keep things running more or less smoothly."

Carys nodded. Her dad would have a fit if she constantly wandered around having conversations with her dead mother. It might be the straw that broke the camel's back, as her mom used to say. "What was your grams like?" she asked.

At that both Lindy and Lilah shared a smile, but it was Lindy who spoke first. "Well, she was a kick in the pants. Strong like Lora, feisty like me, talented like Lilah. I guess we all got a piece of her personality." Lindy cast a speculative look Carys's way. "She would've loved you. You have just the right amount of piss and vinegar that Grams found amusing."

Carys grinned. "Really?"

Lindy nodded vigorously. "Oh, yes. Grams had a habit of gravitating toward extremes. She said love or hate them, they were never boring. I think the only thing Grams found more tedious than boring people was when others insisted she do things their way."

"Yep. The quickest way to get Grams to do the exact opposite—"

"—was to insist she do it whatever way she didn't agree with. She could be a little contrary," Lindy said, adding with a slight lift of her brow, "I guess I come by it honestly."

Lilah laughed. "Yes, well, you take it to another level. Even Grams agreed, you were just downright difficult by nature."

Lindy pretended to take offense but Carys could tell they were just joking. She giggled at the sisters and wished for the umpteenth time she hadn't been an only child. It probably would've sucked less if she'd been able to share her grief with a sister or brother, even. But she'd never know because her mom was dead and it wasn't as if her dad was in a hurry to get married again—thank God.

"So what was your mom like?" Lindy asked, swinging the conversation back around to Carys. "Was she like you?"

Carys shook her head and grinned. "No. She was nice."

Lindy cracked up and playfully slapped Carys on the arm. "Not bad, kid. There's hope for you yet. So, seriously, tell us about your mom. We've got time to kill before dinner, right, Li?"

"Sure," Lilah said, sipping at her smoothie. "I'd love to hear about your mom."

Carys took a deep breath and cast a nervous look Lindy's way. She'd never really talked about her mom to anyone before. It was something she kept locked away in a private place where no one else could judge, or touch. Oddly, she trusted Lindy and her sister Lilah. Somehow she knew they were genuine, unlike the dumb shrink her dad had hired right after Carys's mom had died. Dr. Dippity-Do, as Carys had privately named him when she'd seen how stiff his hair was from all the product he'd gooped on, had been a complete and total idiot as far Carys was concerned. He'd always spoken to her in a low, monotone voice that she supposed he thought was soothing, but really it made Carys want to bounce a basketball off his head. So, yeah, that hadn't ended well. The doc had diagnosed Carys with a personality disorder and had prescribed medication. Thankfully, her dad had agreed the doc was off his rocker and hadn't insisted on any more shrinks.

"My mom was supersupportive of everything I wanted to do, even if it was stupid," Carys admitted a bit shyly. "I mean, she never rained on my parade by saying something negative. I always knew I could tell her anything and I miss that." She glanced at the sisters. "Was your mom like that?"

Lilah frowned and Lindy answered with a sigh, "Not really. Our mom was…I don't know, timid. She was quiet and reserved, from what I remember. We were really young when she died. Lora might remember something different about her, but for us she always seemed sad."

"Why?"

"Well, our dad left and it was hard for her to take. It really threw her for a loop. I don't think she ever recovered from it."

"Oh," Carys said. Her father would've never left her mom. At least, she didn't think he would. He worked too much to spend time looking for anyone else, at the very least. "I'm sorry."

"Ancient history, kiddo," Lindy said brightly, though Carys heard the fake happiness in Lindy's tone. Lilah must've caught it, too, for she sent her sister a quick look. But Lindy had moved on, saying, "It sounds like even though your time with your mom was cut short, at least you had some quality time with her, right? You have great memories to hold on to."

Carys nodded but it was hard to be grateful when there was so much she still needed her mom to be around for. "She'll never see me get married. Or go to college," Carys said quietly. "I won't have anyone to call when I need, you know, advice about stuff. I mean, it's not like I can ask my dad about girl stuff. When I asked my dad if I could get a training bra he turned six different shades of red and then said I didn't need one yet. How does he know? My friend Yasmine said if you don't get a bra right when your boobs start growing, they'll sag like an old lady's. I don't want old lady boobs!"

Lindy didn't even try to hold back her laughter and let loose with a huge guffaw. "Old lady boobs! Ha! I remember thinking that, too." After a few more chuckles, Lindy said, "Listen, hon, your boobs are going to be fine. But if you really want a training bra, I think I could take you out shopping for one, though it might give your dad a heart attack if he knew. But take it from me, bras are a pain. Which is why I rarely wear one."

"And why your boobs are going to hang down to your knees by the time you're thirty," Lora said, surprising them all when she announced her presence behind them.

"They will not." Lindy sniffed as if offended. "For

those of us who weren't cursed with porn star cans, we don't have to worry about gravity as much, so there."

"Lucky you," Lora remarked drily. "Hey, while you ladies are out here enjoying the sunset, Celly's been busy making dinner. If you're hungry, dinner will be served in the formal dining room."

"Ohh, the *formal dining room*," Lindy said in a pseudo-British accent that made Carys giggle. "So *fancy* these days! In my apartment, I have a formal dining *recliner* that also serves as a guest bed for when friends crash for the night."

Lora grimaced and rolled her eyes while Lilah laughed, too. "Sounds divine. Dinner is ready in five."

"You hungry?" Lindy asked Carys. "Cuz there's always room for one more in the Bell household."

Carys nodded eagerly even though that smoothie had filled her up. She wasn't going to pass up an opportunity to hang with Lindy and her crazy family. It was far more interesting than anything happening back at her place, where her dad would spend all night on the phone or on his laptop doing whatever it was he did aside from pay attention to her. "I'm starved," Carys said, grinning. And it didn't even matter what was on the menu.

GABE SCRUBBED HIS face and tossed his phone, tired and frustrated by the turn of events. A simple phone call had turned into a major time-suck and now it was much too late to take Carys to the beach. Likely, she'd already returned and was now hiding out in her room, like an angry little chinchilla just waiting for the right opportunity to snap his fingers off.

Even worse, though, was he had a feeling she'd given up on him way before he'd given her the chance to believe he'd keep his word.

But damn it, it wasn't so easy to just drop everything when you were the boss. Livelihoods were balanced on his ability to make profitable decisions for the company. He wished he could make Carys understand. Ahhh, hell. Justifications, that's all they were. He'd let her down—again.

Time to face the music.

He went to her room and knocked. "Carys, honey? You hungry? Want to grab a bite? You name the place."

No answer.

He sighed. Not this again. The silent treatment was getting old. He tried again. "Carys, come on. You know I can't always control how long a business call lasts. Trust me, if I'd had my choices, I'd rather have spent the time with my feet in the sand with you." More silence. He frowned and cautiously opened the door, only to find it empty. He swore under his breath. Now what? He returned to the living room and grabbed his phone from the sofa where he'd tossed it. He dialed her phone. With a spike of alarm, he heard the muffled music of her ringtone sound from somewhere in her room. Damn. She didn't have her phone. Don't panic. She was probably…with Lindy.

Somehow, intuitively, he knew his daughter had sought out the company of the one person he'd rather she steered clear of.

"Carys…if you're with that woman I'm going to tan your little hide," he muttered, though it was an idle threat. It was likely why she was such a holy terror. He and Charlotte had never spanked Carys; it hadn't been their parenting style. And now, with hindsight being twenty-twenty, he wasn't above admitting maybe if he'd given her a little *wap* on the butt to put the fear of God into her when she'd been younger… Now it was too late. "Charlotte," he said to the ceiling, hoping his wife was up there, watching, listening. "I need a little help here…. She's twice as stubborn as I ever was. How did you handle it?"

"And here I thought only my pops talked to people who weren't there."

The voice at his back caused him to jump. He saw Lindy framed in the open doorway with a smirk on her face.

He had the grace to blush. She'd caught him in a vulnerable moment. It wasn't often he prayed or pleaded with the divine. His mouth tightened, hating that Lindy seemed to see right through to the raw wound inside him that he did his best to cover, and his voice came out sharper than he intended. "Where's my daughter?"

"You know, she's much too young to be left to her own devices," she admonished him instead of answering his question. He frowned and opened his mouth to offer a rebuke but she kept talking, eclipsing his opportunity. "Here's the thing—she's your kid, I know that. But it seems to me that you don't have a clue as to what you're doing and that kid is hurting. Big-time. And if you take a kid with a great big emotional wound weeping inside of them and pair that with an absent parent… disaster is only one dirtbag with a creepy smile away. You get me?"

Oddly, yes, he did, but he chafed at the idea that Lindy plainly saw what he didn't want to see. "She's my daughter. I would appreciate it if you minded your own business."

"Yeah, that's the smart thing," she agreed, as if irritated at herself for her part in this drama, which he found baffling. "But I've never been accused of doing the smart thing. I'm an actress, for crying out loud. Doesn't that tell you something about my decision-making process? Don't answer that, it's written all over your expression. Your daughter is with my sister Lilah. She's got a knack for lost things—cats, kids, dogs, birds…you name it. Right now, they're helping Pops set the table for dinner, which brings me to why I'm here right now."

"Which is?" He had to admit, he was curious as to what would drop from her mouth next. The woman was oddly fascinating…and it didn't hurt that just looking at her made him momentarily forget that he wasn't interested in dating.

"I'm inviting you to dinner. I think Carys, even though she denies it, would like you to be there."

Dinner…with the Bells? "Why?" he asked, openly confused. "Do you always dine with your guests?"

"Sometimes," she answered with a blinding grin that showcased a set of pearly white teeth that would make a dentist proud. "But the truth is we invited Carys to stay and I thought you should be there, too. She needs you. Even if you're too busy to forgo a business call to spend it with your kid."

At that, her voice hardened just a touch and he felt chastised, which immediately caused him to be defensive. "You don't know my business so I suggest you stay out of it," he reminded her coolly.

"True enough, but I do know that you're about to lose Carys," she said without hesitation. "I guess it's up to you to decide whether or not that matters. Hell, I don't know, maybe you don't care a fig about anything but turning a profit, but something tells me that you do care. And I'm banking that instead of being a stuffed-shirt prig about the fact that I'm trying to help you, you're going to accept my dinner invitation with the grace your mother tried to teach you back when you were a kid."

Gabe stared, caught between the urge to go get his daughter and give her a stern reprimand for hanging out with strangers, and giving in because Lindy had a point about Carys wandering around unattended. "I didn't leave her to her own devices," he said defensively. "I took a business call and I was going to meet her at the beach."

"Yeah, I heard. Except you forgot about the part where you're actually supposed to follow through when you offer to meet someone somewhere."

"My call went longer than I expected." He scowled.

She waved away his excuses. "Whatever. Don't care. For reasons beyond my understanding, I kinda care about your kid, though. We got off to a rocky start but now that I don't want to wring her little neck, I've realized she's actually a cool girl. Reminds me a bit of myself."

"Thanks," he said. "I think."

"So what's it going to be? Either way, we're about to eat and your daughter is eating with us. So make your choice."

The woman, for all her seemingly laid-back ways, was pretty damn bossy, he wanted to grumble, but he didn't. She had a point. He could see that she was trying to help. And even if it made him uncomfortable, he wasn't above admitting when he'd just fallen flat on his face.

He choked down something that felt like pride and said, "I'd be honored to join your family for dinner if you'll have me."

Lindy's face lit up with an approving—and possibly relieved—smile and she surprised the hell out of him when she hooked her arm through his as she said, "Excellent! This day might just be salvageable yet."

"Oh?" he couldn't help but inquire, curiosity getting him again. "I'm flattered…?"

"Long story. It involves my sisters. You don't want to know. Let's just say, if you think your problems with Carys are big…you ought to thank your lucky stars Carys wasn't a twin."

Carys a twin? He shuddered at the thought. That surely would've been the death of him.

CHAPTER SEVEN

LINDY WALKED INTO the expansive dining room that looked out onto a beautiful open-air patio. Whenever all the Bells were home—which wasn't often these days—Pops always opened up the dining room. The front windows were actually giant partitions that slid away, completely exposing the dining area to the glorious view of the ocean. Grams had said it'd cost an arm and a leg to remodel but it'd been worth every penny. Lindy had to agree. Judging by the obviously impressed expression on Gabe's face, he thought it was damn spectacular, too.

"Not bad, huh?" Lindy asked, smiling.

"Gorgeous," he murmured in appreciation. "The architecture of the entire resort is impeccable but this is really something else."

"Thanks. This was added after my grandparents bought the resort. My grams said she'd always wanted a place without walls but seeing as that wasn't entirely feasible, even on an island, Pops had this created. He found the design in a magazine featuring a restaurant in Fiji."

Pops and Lindy's sisters walked in with Carys in tow. It was hard to miss the animation in Carys's expression, and the surprise in Gabe's eyes was dimmed by something else that Lindy couldn't identify but it seemed vaguely sad. For some reason she wished she could fix whatever had caused it. She shook herself, wondering where that notion had sprung from. She wasn't the fixer…of anything. "Carys, why don't you introduce your dad to the crew?" Lindy suggested, somewhat discomfited by her reaction. She covered well, moving to her seat and gesturing for Gabe to sit across from her with Carys to his left.

"Sure," Carys chirped with a smile. "Everyone, this is my dad, Gabe. He and I are guests at Bungalow 2."

"We're happy to have you," Lora said in welcome, shooting Lindy a subtle questioning look that Lindy chose to completely ignore. Lora smiled at Heath, her boyfriend, and murmured her thanks when he pushed her chair in for her.

Lindy resisted the urge to giggle at the insane change that had come over Heath and Lora. They hadn't always been so lovey-dovey. Once Lora had done her level best to pretend Heath didn't exist at all. That had changed when Lora caused Heath to fall from the roof of the resort when he'd been trying to repair a leaky tile. He'd fallen and cracked his noggin open, scaring the life out of all of them. Lindy supposed it'd been a life-changing event for them both because when he'd finally woken up, Lora had realized she'd fallen in love with him somewhere along the way and Heath had admitted he'd always loved her. Go figure.

At first glance, it was a saccharine-sweet story that could give a person cavities at the telling, but anyone who knew Lora would know that it was impossible to feature her at the center of any story that could be deemed *sweet*. Heath had always been like a brother to Lilah and Lindy so when Heath and Lora had finally hooked up, Lindy's first concern had been for Heath. But they truly seemed to be in love. And Heath brought out the best in Lora now that she was all softened up, so Lindy was all for that.

But now, Lora was giving her looks that plainly said she was dying to know why the father of the kid Lindy had christened "the demon spawn" was suddenly sitting at their dinner table and Lindy was getting irritated. Lilah was always bringing home strays and no one thought to question. Why couldn't she?

The savory smells coming from the kitchen made Lindy's stomach growl. In Los Angeles, she ran with a crowd that rarely ate more than a poppy seed in one sitting and although Lindy loved to eat, she wasn't one to eat alone so she'd gotten used to the liquid diet of her peers. But now that she was home, her stomach was gleefully reminding her how much she used to love to eat.

"Oh my word…is that…?" Lindy gestured to the steaming plate Celly had just brought in.

"Boiled bananas," Lora supplied, grinning. "Even better than the ones at The Wild Donkey. It's Celly's one saving grace," she added, earning a scowl from Celly before she swished from the room, her multicolor sarong fringe dusting the floor as she went.

"Don't be getting after Celly," Pops warned good-naturedly. "She'll send a *jumbie* after you for talking bad about her. She's real island folk, you know."

Lindy grinned and started piling her plate with braised pork with a squeal of open delight. "I've missed this!"

Gabe accepted the boiled bananas from Lilah and tentatively put a little on his plate, clearly unsure about the dish, but he seemed intrigued by Pops's warning. "A *jumbie?* What's that?"

"A ghost," Heath answered around a hot bite, smiling

at Gabe's look of open disbelief. Heath shook his head in warning. "Locals are real superstitious about certain things, like their legends and myths. You'd be surprised how many stories are out there. You know the islands have a dark past."

"Like what?" Carys asked, suddenly captivated.

Heath smiled, loving that he had an audience and Lora simply rolled her eyes at his love for telling stories. Lindy chuckled and Lilah listened intently. "Well, my friend Billy Janks, his family goes all the way back to the slave days. His grandmother, a little woman with grizzled hair that used to stand on end as if she'd stuck her finger in a light socket, was a full-blooded Carib whose family had been brought to the island as slaves to work the sugar plantations. And she used to tell us all sorts of stories about *jumbies* and zombies roaming the jungle at night."

"Zombies?" Carys's eyes widened and Lindy wondered if she'd be able to sleep tonight after Heath had finished scaring the life out of her. "Real ones?"

"There's no such thing as real zombies," Gabe interjected, shooting Heath an exasperated look that said, *C'mon, man, ease up on the zombie angle otherwise she's going to be sleeping with me tonight.* "But it makes for a good tale, right, Heath?"

"Right." Heath winked and continued. "But there are definitely *jumbie* running around *dis* place, for sure."

Lindy suppressed a giggle at the way Heath slipped into a Crucian accent for the story. It was a wonder he wasn't the one pursuing an acting career, thought Lindy wryly.

"I was on a hike on Reef Bay Trail near the old sugar mill and I swear I saw the *jumbie* of a boy killed back in the days when they used slaves to process the sugarcane. It was a gruesome way to die, for sure," Heath said solemnly.

"What happened?" Carys asked, so absorbed in the tale she'd completely forgotten about her dinner. "What happened to the boy?"

"I don't know if I should tell you…. It's not exactly dinner conversation…."

"Too late now," Lora quipped and Pops grinned, gesturing for Heath to continue.

"It's a great yarn. Finish! Don't leave our guests to wonder. That's rude, my boy," Pops said, chewing his pork with great relish. Pops loved a good story as a complement to good food. "Go on… The boy…his name was…Maunie…something like that…."

Heath nodded. "Maunie Dalmida."

Carys clapped her hands to her mouth as she suppressed a delighted squeal of shock. "This was a real person? You know his name?"

"Everyone on the island knows the story of Maunie Dalmida," Lilah said with a small smile. "It's one of the best ghost stories around. They tell it on tours of the island."

"Ohhh," Carys said, shuddering, but the light in her eyes was something to see. Lindy smiled, enjoying her reaction. It reminded Lindy of herself when she was young and new to the island and all its mysteries. "What happened?"

"Well, unfortunately young Maunie met a terrible end. He was crushed between the cogs used to mill the sugar. But anyway, I was hiking the trail and there he was…." Heath paused for dramatic effect and even Lindy was engrossed. She couldn't recall ever hearing this particular story. "Standing there plain as day. Except his clothes were that of a slave boy circa 1700s. He looked right…at…me."

"What did you do?" Carys asked, her voice barely a squeak.

"The only thing I could do," Heath said solemnly before breaking into a grin. "I squealed like a little girl, ran like hell and never looked back."

Everyone broke into laughter, including Carys, and Lindy grinned, enjoying the unexpected warmth in her chest as she returned to her exquisite island dinner. This felt good, sharing a meal with her family and Gabe and Carys. It felt…natural. She wasn't sure why, and figured she shouldn't spend too much time dissecting it for fear she might not like what she found, so Lindy simply took it for face value and left it at that.

She stole a look at Gabe, struck again by how attractive the man was when he wasn't glowering hard enough to scare small children. Sure, there was an austere quality about him most times, but now, with his guard down, the lines in his face relaxing with intermittent smiles, he had star quality. Kind of like George Clooney, Lindy mused.

Lindy shook herself free from that particular train of thought and returned to the dinner conversation, which had continued without her.

There was something happening here. She just wasn't sure if it was something she should encourage or flat-out ignore.

GABE WAS SURPRISED to find dinner with the Bells had been unexpectedly enjoyable, even with the ghost story that was likely to give Carys nightmares in spite of her assurances to the contrary. As they walked to the bungalow, Carys ahead of them, Gabe felt compelled to invite Lindy to stay for coffee but didn't know if he should.

To be honest, any excuse would've worked—he wasn't picky—but some part of him was telling him to bid her good-night and put an end to the day.

In other words, move on.

Lindy was a wild card in a game with stakes too high for his comfort. If he were single and carefree, he wouldn't hesitate to slide his hand along her bare waistline and pull her to him, planting a slow and deep kiss on that totally kissable mouth, but he wasn't single.

He was widowed with an impressionable daughter and the last thing she needed to see was her father casually messing around with every attractive woman that happened to walk by.

Sound advice. Too bad his libido, which had been suppressed to the point he felt like a monk in training, was kicking to life, mentally removing each article of clothing on Lindy's perfect body with its teeth. His breathing quickened and he was thankful for the darkness, which the tiki lights did little to dispel on the walking trail.

"Dad, can we have ice cream?" Carys asked, completely oblivious to the awareness snapping between him and Lindy. She looked to Lindy with a smile. "You want some? We have chocolate and strawberry."

Lindy shot a look at Gabe as if asking his permission, and he appreciated her consideration. Saying yes seemed a small thing, even though he knew it wasn't. Being around Lindy complicated his thoughts and crowded his conscience with too much carnal imagery to control.

Sensing he wasn't going to agree, Carys pulled no punches, pleading with that sweet, innocent voice that always tore at his heart and guaranteed his capitulation.

"Pleeease, Daddy?" Carys asked, clasping her hands in front of her as if she were absolutely desperate to eat ice cream with Lindy and he couldn't help but give in. It was just ice cream, right?

"I don't want to horn in on your family time," Lindy murmured, quietly communicating that she understood his dilemma. "Dinner was great. Thanks for spending it with us."

Carys moaned in disappointment and started to pout as Lindy turned to go the way she came, and suddenly Gabe was blurting out an invitation that he wasn't even sure he'd said out loud until he heard Carys squeal and start to run for the bungalow door.

"Yay! I'll go get the stuff ready. Do you like sprinkles?"

"Of course," Lindy said as if there was no other way to eat ice cream. "I like two scoops, one of strawberry and one of chocolate." She slid a sexy look Gabe's way, adding, "I don't like to miss out on anything."

He swallowed and his Dockers shorts tightened, making him grateful, yet again, that it was dark outside. Damn, she was a sexy woman. And he was horny as hell.

CHAPTER EIGHT

LINDY WASN'T SURE why she was pushing the envelope with Gabe. He didn't want to start something with her and she sure as hell knew for certain she didn't need to start something with him.

However, she'd never been good at following her own advice, which clearly explained why she desperately wanted to kiss the man when she had no business doing so whatsoever.

Maybe that was part of the allure.

Her former therapist had said something about her always needing the thrill of the chase—not so much the relationship—and even though Lindy had thought the woman had been a quack and definitely not worth the $125 an hour she'd been charging, Lindy had grudgingly admitted there'd been a certain amount of truth to that assessment.

The thrill was the chase.

And the more unattainable the quarry, the better.

But once she had them? Meh. Her interest level waned quickly.

"I want to kiss you," Lindy said bluntly, curious to see his reaction. With any luck he'd tell her he'd rather eat an eyeball sandwich than swap spit with her. Not that that was likely but a girl could hope.

His mouth firmed in a deliciously aggravated line, then he said, "I want to kiss you, too. Which is a bad idea," he added, though his eyes had fastened on her mouth as if he was already tasting the mango juice she'd had with dinner. A dark thrill chased her spine. "I don't do casual," he warned her.

"And I don't do relationships. At least not well," Lindy amended with a subtle frown. "So what do we do?"

"Nothing."

"Nothing? I don't think that's going to work. We're both dealing with some hefty attraction, right? I mean, I know I'm not in a one-sided situation in this. So... maybe we should just kiss and get it out of our system and see what happens."

"I know where kissing leads," Gabe said, his brow lifting in a sexy, yet sardonic arch that Lindy found insanely attractive. "Don't you?"

"I have an idea," she murmured, biting her lip against the surge of arousal that followed his silky statement. "And that's bad?"

"I have a daughter to think about."

At the mention of Carys, Lindy flashed on the kid's face and how devastated she'd be if Lindy were to come and go from her life as she was likely to do if Lindy and Gabe started hooking up. The kid didn't need more people abandoning her. The knowledge was heavy enough to snuff the desire that had begun to kindle. Lindy took a step away, putting some distance between them. "You're right." She drew a deep breath to settle her nerves and then fixed a bright smile for his benefit. "Hey, tell Carys I'll take a rain check on that ice cream. I just remembered my sister wants to have a family meeting to discuss some resort business so...yeah, I'll catch you later."

"Lindy..."

She stopped. "Yeah?"

"It's just ice cream."

"Maybe," Lindy acknowledged. "But we both know ice cream could lead to…I don't know, dangerous places. So, it's better to just…not eat ice cream."

"Yeah, I guess you're right." He exhaled, disappointment in the sound. "So…thanks for dinner."

"Sure." *Keep walking, Lindy,* she told herself sternly, fully planning to execute that directive, but her feet seemed to have a different plan because she spun on her heel and launched herself at Gabe, connecting with his lips before either of them could come to their senses.

His lips moved against hers, eager, almost desperate, and his tongue sought and found hers with unerring accuracy, sending an immediate wild thrill arcing through her body, causing Lindy to momentarily forget all the good reasons she wasn't supposed to want him.

The sound of Carys returning, her young voice happy and excited, caused the two of them to bounce apart as if scalded. Lindy's hand trembled as she wiped her mouth, shocked and appalled at the same time how much she wanted to continue doing exactly what they shouldn't be doing, and judging by Gabe's expression he struggled with the same impulse.

"I should go," Lindy whispered, her voice an embarrassed wobble.

Gabe jerked a nod, true distress in his eyes replacing the haze of lust. "Carys…" he started, as if needing to explain but Lindy didn't need an explanation. She got it. Oh boy, if anyone got it, Lindy did. Carys didn't need a flake like Lindy in her life, not like this. Not now.

"Tell her I'll take a rain check," Lindy reminded Gabe with a forced smile, eager to get the hell away. Shame was setting in for her lack of control, her dangerous need for the hunt no matter the cost and Lindy knew she couldn't let Carys get caught in the cross fire of her emotional damage. Not trusting herself to say more, she split without looking back.

GABE TRIED CALMING his wildly beating heart but it was still racing when Carys poked her head from the door. She frowned when she saw Gabe was alone. "Where'd Lindy go?" she asked, looking beyond Gabe into the darkness.

"She had to go. She forgot about some resort business," Gabe answered, adding when Carys's expression fell, "but she said she wants a rain check. She truly wanted to stay but there were other things she had to attend to." Gabe's mind was spinning—had he just been in Lindy Bell's mouth? Their tongues twining like vines with one another? He suppressed a shudder of pure desire at the memory. Yes, that definitely had happened. Oh hell. So much for shutting down the libido before it got him into trouble. He pushed the thought away and focused on Carys. "But how about me? I'm still up for a scoop or two."

"Okay," Carys said, but plainly she was still disappointed. "Do you think we can hang out with Lindy tomorrow?"

Definitely not. "I don't know, sweetheart. She probably has plans. I'd hate to be an unwelcome houseguest who doesn't know when to do their own thing, you know? It was real nice of the Bells to invite us to dinner but ultimately, we're just guests at their resort. We can go shopping, though, if you want. How about we check out that new shop in the plaza, the one with the bracelets you liked?"

"Sure, I guess," Carys said, sighing, casting one last

look toward the main house. "Well, we'd better eat our ice cream before it melts."

Gabe refrained from commenting on how Carys's preference for Lindy's company hurt his feelings. It'd been a good night. He wasn't about to ruin it by picking a fight.

For the first time in months, he'd heard Carys laugh and act like a normal eleven-year-old and not some petulant, spoiled brat.

And he wasn't above savoring the moment.

He wasn't sure how long it would last.

Carys's disappointment over Lindy changing her mind at the last minute didn't seem to dim her enjoyment of her ice cream and she finished two scoops in record time while Gabe was still savoring his. His cell phone buzzed to life on the counter and both Gabe and Carys stared at the phone. His first instinct was to reach for it, but he sensed Carys was waiting to see what he would do. It felt as if something important was balancing between them and one wrong move could tilt their relationship in the wrong direction. In spite of the fact that his brain was screaming at him to answer the phone, he deliberately ignored the buzzing and continued to enjoy his ice cream.

His reward was a small smile from his daughter and it felt pretty good to earn it.

"So, tell me what you're looking forward to about the upcoming school year," he said, trying to spark a normal conversation. "Big fifth grade coming up. Before you know it, it'll be sixth grade and then junior high. Times flies when you're having fun, right?"

"When does the fun start?" She surprised him with a dry quip.

"You don't enjoy school? I loved school," he said.

"Times change. The teachers are mean and the kids are jerks. I hate my school. Well, I don't hate everything about my school but it's such a drag because the teachers are always in your business and I'm like, whatever."

"Teachers who care should be in your business," he reminded her. "I had an economics teacher I was sure hated me because he made me work hard. He made my life miserable my senior year but I passed the class with an A, and it sparked an interest that would propel me to the right classes in college so I could start my own company. So sometimes the classes you have the hardest time with are the ones you learn the most in."

"Maybe. But I'm pretty sure I'm not going to go into any field involving algebra."

He laughed. "I know math's not your favorite subject. But someday that might change. Don't give up just yet."

Carys grinned. "Now you sound like Mom."

"Yeah?" He smiled. Maybe he was headed in the right direction. "Well, your mom was a smart lady so if she said it, it must be pretty good advice."

"Dad, tell me how you two met."

Gabe sighed and rubbed his forehead with a rueful smile. "Well, it was in college and I was on a water polo scholarship and your mom was pursuing a degree in art history. But as it happened, I needed a tutor in this art appreciation class that I was totally failing and she agreed to help me out."

"Was it love at first sight?" she asked.

"Yeah…it was," Gabe answered, smiling in memory. "She was the most beautiful woman I'd ever seen with the most perfect smile that lit up her whole face. And, of course, she was wowed by my perfect physique—"

"Eww, Dad," Carys groaned, giggling. "You can skip

that part. I just like hearing the nondisgusting parts, okay?"

"Okay," he agreed with a grin. "Only nondisgusting parts of the story will be told. How about the romantic parts? Such as when I hired a limousine to pick up your mom for her birthday because she'd never ridden in a limo before."

"Actually, Mom told me that story. She said you guys went to the beach and had a picnic dinner on a blanket on the sand because you'd spent all your money on the limo and couldn't afford to take her to a restaurant." She cracked a yawn and peered blearily at Gabe.

He chuckled, his cheeks heating at the memory of that night. "Yeah, that's true. But it was one heck of a picnic, though. Top shelf all the way."

"I know. Mom said it was the most romantic thing you'd ever done. She also told me that's how I'll know if it's love or just a crush because someone who loves you will get to know you and go out of their way to make something ordinary in your world special. She said you always managed to do that for her. That's how she knew."

Stunned, Gabe stared at his daughter, momentarily knocked speechless by the revelation. He'd never known that about Charlotte. A sweet pain unfolded in his heart and he pressed a soft kiss to Carys's crown. "It's getting late, sweetheart. We'd better call it a day."

Carys agreed and slid from her chair. Gabe smiled as she walked down the hall and disappeared into her room.

He'd been reluctant to talk about his life with Charlotte because he didn't want to prolong the pain of her loss, but even though it hurt, it felt good, too, to share those special memories with Carys. Maybe Lindy had been right—talking about a loved one when they were gone helped.

Maybe.

The pain was there, but the sparkle in Carys's eyes as he'd shared those special moments had been worth it.

LINDY BOOKED IT back to the main house, intent on bypassing the business meeting and going straight to her room, but Lora intercepted her.

"Lindy, did you forget we have a family meeting?"

"No," Lindy answered with a grimace. "I have a headache. I think I'll sit this one out."

"Take some aspirin," Lora countered, not giving her an inch. "We need you. This is important."

"It can't wait one night?" Lindy snapped, not in the mood to go over business plans and strategy for the resort. It wasn't that she didn't care; she just didn't think she'd be of much use tonight. Her head was a mess and she had that blasted therapist in her mind, going on about her self-destructive patterns. Argh! "Lora, I'm really not feeling up to it, okay?"

"Lindy, suck it up," Lora said, starting to get irritated. "This is serious. You agreed to the meeting tonight and everyone else is ready to start. Celly has Pops occupied and we need to take advantage of the window."

"You're such a jerk," Lindy muttered, glowering at her sister. Her fictitious headache was beginning to manifest in real pain that throbbed at the center of her forehead. "And a dictator."

"Yeah, yeah, flattery will get you nowhere, now c'mon." Lora turned and expected Lindy to follow, which she did with no grace at all.

They entered Pops's office and saw Lilah and Heath waiting for them. Pops was absent. The fact that they were talking about the resort without Pops seemed wrong, but Lindy knew it was probably best.

She dropped into the high-backed chair with over-size cushions and tried not to scowl at everyone. But she was in a foul mood so she doubted she was successful.

Lora began, pulling a chart she'd no doubt created with no small amount of glee to aid in her presentation and Lindy wanted to sink in her chair and disappear. "Larimar is about thirty thousand in the hole. We were able to knock down half the amount owed by liquidating some assets we found Pops owned in and around the island that he'd never miss. Both Lindy and I were able to pool our resources and make a substantial payment, as well, which staved off the immediate seizure of the resort by the IRS but it was just a Band-Aid fix. Bottom line, we need more income and we need it now."

"It's hurricane season. Not exactly the busy tourist time," Lilah said, worried. No doubt her stomach was grumbling with anxiety. Lindy sent a smile Lilah's way to let her know it was going to be okay. Lindy wasn't sure *how* it was going to work out, but she had to believe that it was. "How are we supposed to drum up guests when there aren't any?"

"Well, Heath and I have been thinking and although Lilah is doing a good job re-creating his designs, we both agree that we need to do a lot more to recruit to the area. I think we need to market ourselves to corporations as a business retreat. Executives with deep company pockets would love Larimar, with a few adjustments, of course."

"Adjustments?" Lindy asked, hooking onto the word with distrust. She didn't want Larimar to change at all. It was perfect just the way it was and if a bunch of stuffed shirts thought otherwise, they could pound sand. "Larimar doesn't need any adjustments."

"You need to stop thinking about this with nostalgic attachments," Lora warned, immediately ticking Lindy off with her admonishment.

"Why not? Isn't that why we're trying to save Larimar? We all have nostalgic attachments to this place," Lindy retorted. "And I know Pops would flip his lid if you tried to fill this place with a bunch of necktie-wearing idiots. It's not Larimar's style."

"Larimar needs a new style, then," Lora suggested, her gaze narrowing. Lilah shifted in her chair, uncomfortable with the sparks flying between her sisters. For the sake of Lilah's persnickety tummy, Lindy dialed back her next comment and instead focused on throwing out an idea of her own.

"Listen, I know Larimar needs money. We ought to start marketing to the movie and commercial business. That's quick money for not a lot of time."

"Aren't movie shoots hard to come by?" Lilah asked, confused. "And they take months, sometimes years, to coordinate. I don't think Larimar has that kind of time."

"True, but a producer friend of mine is shooting over in St. Thomas. I might be able to persuade him to lodge some of his above-the-line people here at Larimar instead of in St. Thomas. We could fill the resort during the off-season when typically we're empty. That should give us an influx of cash, at least for now."

Lora contemplated this suggestion. "Well, that would be great but it's a twenty-minute ferry ride to and from St. Thomas. Wouldn't that be a bit inconvenient for the crew?"

"Well, the above-the-line folks are the executives and

whatnot and they like luxury. I think it would appeal to their sense of entitlement."

Lora chewed her lip. "It's a long shot but we might as well try everything. Can you call your producer friend tomorrow?"

"Sure," Lindy said, cracking a yawn. "Is that it? I'm beat."

"We should have a plan B," Lora said and Lindy groaned.

"Can't we just see if plan A works before assuming it will fail? Sheesh."

"Putting all our eggs in one basket is never a good business plan," Lora said. "In the meantime, I'm going to continue to market to the top-level corporations. In fact, I think Sears Holdings Corporation is in the market for a new corporate retreat location. It would be a coup to land that account."

"Account," repeated Lindy, amused. "Boy, you are in your element, aren't you?"

Heath chuckled at the black look Lora shot Lindy and stepped in, saying, "Listen, both ideas have merit. Let's see what shakes out and go from there. Okay? In the meantime, Lilah will continue to man the front desk with Celly, which will save us money in overhead, and we should consider letting a few of the maids go and doing the work ourselves."

"Make beds and stuff?" Lindy asked, not liking that idea at all but not wanting to sound like a prima donna. When Heath nodded in answer she shrugged as if it was no big deal. "Fine by me. I know how to make a bed."

"Really?" Lora quipped drily. "You'd never know it by your own bed. Grams was always getting after you to do it. In fact, your room was always a pigsty."

"Oh, shut up," Lindy muttered, no longer interested

in being in this meeting. Her head was in a jumble; the last thing she wanted to discuss was marketing strategy and business plans. Frankly, she never wanted to discuss those things. "Are we done yet?"

Lora opened her mouth but Heath stepped in again, likely saving them both from a nasty verbal spat. "I think so," he said, shooting Lora a warning look before she said something to the contrary. She didn't look happy about it, after all, she'd made a flowchart using poster board and hand-drawn tables, but she must've trusted Heath enough to follow his lead.

A smirk threatened as Lindy mused, *my, how things have changed.* Love really did a number on a person. However, in this case, it was a positive thing. "I'll work up a maid schedule, if that's all right with everyone," Lindy offered.

"We should also discuss the possibility of letting Celly go," Lora suggested, but Lilah looked appalled at that idea.

"Just because you don't like her doesn't mean we should let her go. Besides, Pops loves her."

"I'm just saying, if we're trying to save money, there's no reason to keep Celly on when Lilah can take over her duties."

"Why is it automatically assumed that I don't have a life?" Lilah asked, clearly annoyed. "I don't mind helping out but I like to have some time off, too. Celly has been here, she understands about Pops and she doesn't take any of your crap. I say she stays."

"I agree with Lilah," Lindy said, happy to agree with anything that put Lora's teeth on edge. "Celly is cool. And she makes kick-ass boiled bananas."

Lora clamped her mouth shut, her blue eyes flashing,

and Lindy was tempted to stick her tongue out. So much for maturity. She smiled instead. "Are we done yet?"

"If you're not going to be helpful," Lora answered, clearly angry, but Lindy didn't care. At this moment, she didn't much care about anything. She was in a piss-poor mood and it wasn't doing much for her spirit of generosity. Lora made a sound of disgust and waved Lindy away, dismissing her. "Fine. Go. I don't know why I thought you'd bring more to the table. You and Lilah are two sides of the same coin."

"Okay," Heath said, trying to stop the train that was barreling toward them. "We're all tired. It's been a long night. We've made some good progress. Let's just call it a day."

Lora shook her head and muttered, "Whatever." And stalked from the room.

Heath didn't try to stop Lora but the expression on his face was one of disappointment when he turned to face Lindy. "You picked a fight with her," he said.

"No. She picked a fight with me," Lindy said.

"Really, Lindy?" Heath challenged, not buying her defense in the least. "You know, she's under a lot of pressure. She doesn't sleep well she's so busy worrying about how she's going to save this resort. The least you could do is be helpful, instead of a pain in the ass."

Lindy blinked in surprise at Heath's rebuke. Heath never spoke to her like that. "Wow. That was harsh," she said.

"And deserved," he replied, scowling. "I expected better of you. In case you haven't noticed, your sister has worked really hard to change and be more accommodating but you haven't budged an inch. In this respect, you're being a hypocrite and I never thought I'd see that in you."

"I think that's going a bit far," Lindy said, feeling immensely uncomfortable with Heath's judgment. Well, that was her cue to exit. "Right. Whatever, Heath. Just because you're sleeping with my sister doesn't give you a pass to start acting like her. I told her I wasn't in the mood to talk business and suggested we do this tomorrow night but no, she had to push the issue. So, this is what she got. End of story."

"No, it's not the end of the story. Your schedule isn't the only one she's working around," Heath countered hotly. "Do you realize how difficult it is to get your pops out of the house so we can have these types of discussions? No, you don't," he answered for her, causing her to glare. "The thing is, we all have to work together to survive and right now, it seems you're more interested in working your own agenda nitpicking at your sister than being helpful. If that's the case...go back to L.A."

Lilah's eyes were round as saucers and Lindy's own eyes stung with moisture. Had Heath just told her to get the hell out of Dodge? She'd never seen him so angry. Stunned, all she could do was stare as Heath left the room in a disgusted huff.

"What just happened?" Lindy asked Lilah, still reeling from the shock. Heath had been so...mean!

"I think he's just frustrated," Lilah answered hesitantly, clearly choosing her words carefully. Lindy glanced at her twin with open confusion. "It's just that you haven't really been...open to helping much since you got back," Lilah finally admitted with great difficulty.

"What?"

"Well...yeah..."

"Oh, great. Now you, too? It's a damn conspiracy. If that's the way you feel, maybe I will just go back to L.A."

Lilah jumped up, tears filling her eyes. "No, please don't go, Lindy," she pleaded, making Lindy feel like a toad for making the threat. As fragile as Lilah was these days, it was right stupid of Lindy to make those kinds of threats if she didn't mean to follow through, but her mouth was stuck between pissed off and hurt and she wasn't in much control of what fell from it.

"I'm sorry, Li," she said, trying real hard for Lilah's sake to dial back the locomotive of anger that'd jumped the tracks. Lilah would never say anything to deliberately hurt Lindy, so knowing that was true Lindy knew that there had to be some truth in what Lilah was saying, which plain sucked. "I'm not going anywhere. I'm just frustrated, too."

"I know," Lilah conceded, wiping the tears from her eyes. "But we need to work together."

Lindy nodded, drawing a deep breath. "I'll talk to Lora tomorrow. And Heath."

"Thanks," Lilah said, letting out a relieved exhale as if she'd been afraid to breathe. "I'm beat. That's about all the excitement I can handle for the night. You going to bed?"

"Yeah," Lindy answered, rubbing at the ache in her head. All she wanted was some aspirin and quiet. And maybe some peace of mind. She wasn't likely to find the latter. Not with the state of her thoughts being the way they were at the moment. Maybe some rum would help. She hugged her twin tightly. "Get some sleep, Li. It'll all work out."

Lilah nodded and they parted, splitting off to their individual rooms.

Lindy went straight to her room, closed the door and collapsed on her bed, hating how badly the night had ended on all accounts. She'd kissed a man she had no business kissing, and she'd attacked her sister for doing what they all wanted her to do: organize some sort of defense to save the resort. And both Heath and Lilah agreed she was being a selfish brat.

She sighed. Somewhere in that jumble of cause and effect, the truth lurked and it didn't look pretty.

Yeah…right about now, a shot—or two—of rum sounded really good.

CHAPTER NINE

GABE COULDN'T SLEEP—big surprise.

He stifled a groan and rolled to his back. The sound of the tide attempted to lull him to sleep but his mind was moving in too many directions to give in.

Lindy Bell.

Somehow she'd sneaked into his brain and awakened a part of him that he would've preferred to remain comatose.

After Charlotte had died, he'd been pretty sure his heart had died with her. The need for female companionship didn't even register any longer. It was as if the switch had been snapped off and there was no fixing it even if he'd been of a mind to try.

And that'd been okay.

His work had kept him occupied enough for two people and then with Carys…well, he'd been grateful he wasn't trying to find someone else to fill his off-time; the hassle hadn't seemed worth the reward.

But now?

One kiss and suddenly he'd been turned into a raging animal of lust and desire, eager to get his hands on the one woman who was so ill-suited for a potential relationship that it was laughable.

He turned to his side and glanced at the bedside clock and stifled a groan. Midnight and still wide-awake. He tossed the light sheet aside and rose from the bed. He checked on Carys and found her fast asleep, one foot dangling over the side of her bed like she used to do when she was a baby. Smiling, he closed her door. He double-checked the windows out of habit and then went to the private patio to watch the waves.

Larimar was a beautiful place with an enviable beachfront. He didn't regret picking this place for their sabbatical but he had to wonder if the timing of his awakening libido had been inevitable or if it had everything to do with Lindy.

He was a red-blooded man, after all. He had to assume that he would've started thinking about the opposite sex and all that it entailed eventually…so maybe he needed to address some issues before he went any further down that road.

The beach called to him and since it was only a few feet from his door, he felt secure enough leaving Carys to put his feet in the water for a few minutes.

The water was like bathwater, even at midnight. Charlotte would've loved this place. She'd always been after him to take more time off so they could go someplace tropical. He smiled sadly. God, he wished he had brought her here before it'd been too late.

Out of the corner of his eye he caught movement and he strained to make out the lone figure walking the beach. He could tell it was a woman but he couldn't tell anything beyond that. She was lost in her own thoughts, her feet splashing in the water as she walked the shore, and she didn't realize Gabe was there until she'd almost bumped into him. It was then he realized, it was Lilah, Lindy's twin.

"Oh!" she said, startled as she murmured an apology. "I didn't see you there…."

"Are you okay?" he asked, peering at the woman

with concern. He wasn't sure she should be wandering the beach alone at this hour. He glanced past her in the inky darkness. "Are you with someone?"

"No. I like to walk the beach at night. Clears my head when I can't sleep."

"Is that safe?" he asked. Her enigmatic smile gave him pause. There was something melancholy about Lilah, something so distinctly different from her sister. "It's pretty late…. You never know who could be out at this hour."

"I grew up on this beach," Lilah said by way of an answer or perhaps a gentle way of telling him to mind his own business. "Can't sleep, either?" she asked.

He smiled with a chagrined sigh. "Appears not. I'm not usually an insomniac but tonight seems to be challenging that statement."

Lilah regarded him openly, and he saw Lindy in that stare even though they weren't identical. "You two are real close, huh?" he asked, not even needing to identify who he was talking about; Lilah just knew. She nodded with a smile. "Must've been cool to be a twin," he mused, wondering how he might've been different if he'd shared a womb with another. As an only child to distant parents, he'd often wished for a sibling. It hadn't been his and Charlotte's choice to make Carys an only child; fate had made that decision.

"It's hard to describe," Lilah said, glancing out across the water. "She likes you." She returned to Gabe. "More than she wants to, I think."

"That makes two of us," he murmured under his breath, shocked he'd even said it out loud, to Lindy's sister no less. He grinned, somewhat embarrassed at letting the comment fly, and exhaled sharply as he gestured to the bungalow. "Well, I'd better get back. I don't want to leave Carys alone for too long. Are you going to be okay? I feel uncomfortable leaving you alone this late at night."

"I'll be fine. I've been taking midnight walks on this beach since I was seven. Good night, Mr. Weston," she murmured and went on her way, walking in the surf as if he'd never been there. *What an odd woman,* he thought to himself. As different as night and day from Lindy. Or was she? They were twins, after all. Maybe he was just seeing the surface of who Lindy was.

Well, one thing was for sure, he didn't have the luxury of discovering what lay beyond the surface. Lindy was not the woman for him.

And as such, he ought to keep his distance.

It was a good plan...but it left him feeling let down, as if he'd just agreed to miss out on something amazing for the greater good.

He rolled his eyes at his own mental theatrics and locked the door behind him.

He wasn't the kind of man who pined.

And he wasn't about to start.

LINDY CRACKED ONE eyelid and groaned at the early-morning light attempting to stab her in the eyeball. She squeezed her eyelids shut and rolled away from the offending window. In her memory, Grams's voice sounded.

"Get up, sleepyhead. You're going to sleep your life away, child."

Lindy had been thirteen and even then, not a fan of early rising. "I don't want to get up," she'd whined and pulled the covers over her head.

"Okay, but you'll miss fresh mangoes and pancakes with blueberry syrup."

"And sausage?" Lindy had asked from beneath her blanket, her stomach grumbling.

"And apple sausage," Grams had confirmed. Lindy had appeared from beneath her blanket, her hair standing on end from the static electricity to see Grams retreating from the room with a handful of laundry she'd scooped from the floor of Lindy's bedroom.

"Apple sausage," Lindy murmured, back in the present. "Boy, Grams, I'd do anything for your apple sausages just one more time." She sighed and her gaze roamed her floor, smiling when she saw clothes dropped where she'd left them. Not much had changed, except Grams was no longer around to tell her to pick up after herself. Damn, she missed Grams. When she was in L.A., there was always so much to do or see that she didn't have time to remember how it hurt that Grams was gone or that her family had scattered like dandelion seeds on a stiff breeze. Lora had run off to Chicago; Lindy had run off to Los Angeles; and Lilah…well, she may not have run far, but she was just as unreachable.

Grams had tried to get them all back together again but each one of them had made excuses until it was too late.

She wished she could spend just one more hour with her grams. Grams had been their voice of reason and lately, she sorely missed that element in her life.

Grams wouldn't have much nice to say about the crowd she ran with right now. Nothing but a bunch of superficial *clungs*. Maybe that wasn't fair but sometimes Lindy caught herself wondering why the hell she hung out with those idiots. Life wasn't all about the movie business.

At least, that's how she used to feel.

Now? She didn't know how she felt about anything.

Damn, maybe Lilah was right. She shouldn't have fired that therapist. Maybe she'd been onto something when she'd stated Lindy had some issues to work through.

Isn't that a lovely thought? *Hello...you have issues.*

Eh. Didn't everyone?

Not about to continue with that mental argument, she sighed and climbed from her bed. Hopefully, there was coffee brewing. If she had to be up this early, at the very least there ought to be some very dark, very strong coffee available.

If she knew Lora, there would be. In Chicago, the woman had existed on coffee, adrenaline and hard candy alone.

She bit back the sigh when she saw Lora sitting there with her mug in hand, reading the newspaper. Well, now was as good a time as any to eat some humble pie.

"Hey," Lindy said, going straight to the coffeepot and pouring herself some of the dark brew. "So...last night..."

"No need to rehash the past," Lora said brusquely, focusing on her paper.

Lindy withheld the snappy comment that came to mind and took a measured sip of coffee before saying, "Yes, normally I would agree, but I seem to be suffering from an attack of conscience this morning and I feel compelled to apologize. You need to just sit there and listen for a minute so I can get this over with."

Lora's brow lifted but she remained silent and for that Lindy was grateful. One thing she had in common with her older sister was her difficulty in admitting when she was wrong. At least Lora knew where she was coming from.

"I was out of line last night. I came in with a bad at-

titude and I crapped all over your good intentions. I'm
sorry. There. Short and sweet. You can return to your
regularly scheduled programming."

Lora nodded, but there was an expression of satisfaction on her face that was hard to miss. "Will you be
able to speak to your producer friend today?" she asked,
deftly switching subjects.

"I should be able to. He drunk-texted me around three
this morning. He obviously wants to see me."

"That sounds like a booty call."

Lindy shrugged. "I didn't say how I knew him."

Lora grimaced as if she didn't want to know that
kind of information about her sister and chose to let it
go. "All right. Let me know how it goes. I've made a
few calls to friends in Chicago, planted a few feelers."

"How do you think Grams would feel about all of
this?" Lindy asked.

At the mention of Grams, Lora's expression dimmed
but there was a determination in her eyes that would've
done Grams proud. "I've wrestled with that for a while
and I've come to the conclusion that Grams loved this
place and she would've done anything to keep it if it
were ever threatened and so that's how I've had to look
at this. Pops isn't going to get better—he's going to get
worse. We need to get something going now before all
of our energy is needed to take care of him."

Lindy rubbed at her eyes, swamped by sadness.
"Most times he seems just like he ever was," she said.
"But then he'll say something off and it reminds me
that we're slowly losing him. It's hard to take, Lora. It
hurts so much."

That quiet admission was about as much sharing as
Lindy had ever done with Lora and it felt foreign but
as much as she fought it, Lindy needed her older sister.

"I know," Lora acknowledged hoarsely. "We just have to take each day as it comes. Celebrate the good days and accept the bad."

"I hate that plan," Lindy groused with complete honesty. "But I suppose you're right. I still hate it, though."

"Me, too."

Lindy shared a look with her sister and they both smiled in understanding. After several minutes of puttering around the kitchen to find something for breakfast, Lora casually asked, "So, what's the deal with inviting Gabe Weston and his daughter to dinner last night?"

Lindy had hoped not to have this particular conversation but she supposed that hope had been a fruitless one.

"He's having some issues with his kid and I thought dinner might help them reconnect. It's no big deal," she said defensively.

"I didn't say it was," Lora said. "I was just asking. It seemed a little odd given the fact you were ready to hang the twerp only yesterday."

"Her name is Carys and I didn't realize at the time that she was just acting out. She lost her mom a year ago to cancer and her dad doesn't seem to want to talk with her about it. And she really needs to be able to talk about her mom because it's festering inside. I know how that feels."

"I can't remember you ever being silent about anything," Lora quipped wryly, at which Lindy shrugged.

"But maybe I wasn't talking about the right things. I never had anyone but Lilah to talk to about losing Mom and then Grams. It took its toll on me just as it did with you and Lilah."

"Lilah seems to be the only one without any serious issues from her childhood. Honestly, that girl flits through life like a butterfly on a breeze. I wish I had her life sometimes," Lora said, chuckling.

But Lindy didn't find her comment funny. She knew Lora was oblivious to what was happening with Lilah but it still made her prickly to hear her talk about her twin like that. Lindy chose her words carefully because she didn't want to start a fight but she wanted Lora to know all was not well with their baby sis. "I think Lilah needs help."

"What do you mean?" Lora asked, her smile fading. "Has she said something?"

"No. Not really. It's a feeling. I mean, we had a conversation the other day that made some alarm bells go off in my head even though she assured me she's fine, which I don't believe at all. I think she's depressed."

Lora waved away Lindy's concern with a sigh. "That's not surprising. All this pressure to save Larimar would depress anyone. If I didn't have Heath to tell me that it's all going to work out, I'd cry myself to sleep every night."

"It's not just Larimar," Lindy said, shaking her head. "It's something deeper. I'm really worried."

At that Lora paused, taking Lindy's real concern into consideration. A flash of guilt crossed her features as she admitted, "I've been harsh on her lately. Maybe I should talk to her."

"No, not yet. She'll feel attacked and she'll withdraw some more. Let me think about it and I'll figure something out."

"Okay," Lora agreed, and Lindy quietly took note how Lora was trusting her to know what was best for her twin. Lora was really changing and it wasn't just surface deep. Did that mean there was hope for Lindy to change, too? Wait, did she want to change? The question hovered in her mind, branching into all manner of confusing thoughts in different directions. Her life was a hyperactive jumble of constantly changing scenarios, yet oddly, everything had started to feel the same. Same people, same parties, same old drama. When did she stop enjoying all that? This was stupid, she thought with a flash of irritation. Now was not the time to get all introspective. She loved her life. And frankly, there were plenty in the biz who would gladly take her spot. Enough said. Lindy shook herself. Way too deep a conversation for this early in the morning. She grabbed her coffee and a banana. "Well, I'm off to shower and meet up with my producer guy."

"If you feel compelled to sacrifice your dignity for the sake of Larimar, at least know that it's for a good cause," Lora joked, sipping her coffee.

Lindy barked a laugh. "I'm an out-of-work actress in L.A. I don't have any dignity left to sacrifice!"

CHAPTER TEN

LINDY WALKED DOWN the marina and hailed Billy as she approached. His grin lit up his eyes when he saw who was coming aboard.

"Yah come to make me a happy mon?" Billy teased as Lindy kissed him on the cheek.

"I need a ride to St. Thomas. You busy?" she asked.

"I'd do anyting for yah—yah know dat," Billy answered. "What's in St. Thomas?"

"A friend." Even as she said the word, she had to amend it. "A work acquaintance. He's shooting a film in St. Thomas and I'm trying to convince him to lodge some of his people here at Larimar."

Billy scowled. "Why yah bring does Hollywood people here and spoil our island? Leave dem be in St. Thomas. Good place for dem."

"Now, Billy…a lot of those people have deep pockets. Don't you want some of that green in your pockets?"

"I have plenty of green," he retorted but he nodded just the same. "Well, whatevah. I bring yah there. Anyting for yah, Lindy."

"I knew I could count on you." Lindy grinned and went to the front of the boat, settling into a nice comfortable spot with her face to the sun. This was what she missed most about living on the island. All the high school kids were ferried to St. Thomas each day and she loved the ride. As she got older, she found friends who used their parents' boats to go island-hopping. It'd been a privileged experience, for sure.

They were on their way when Billy asked, "Everyting all right with Li?"

His question rang a chord of concern inside Lindy that clanged more loudly when coupled with her own misgivings. She regarded him apprehensively. "Why do you ask?"

"I see her walking late at night…way too late for her to be safe," Billy said, his voice grave. "She need to be more careful. Bad people come to de island, too. It's not like it used to be when we were kids."

"How late are we talking?" Lindy asked.

"Sometime three, sometime two. Never the same. But late."

"When was the last time you saw her?"

"Last night. I saw her walking de beach."

"Last night?" Lindy asked, confused. "Are you sure? I was with her until eleven and she said she was pretty tired and was going straight to bed."

"I know what I see. It's Lilah."

She didn't bother disputing what Billy knew. Larimar was a long walk to town. Why would Lilah walk so far, so late? It didn't make sense. Worse, the knowledge created a cold knot of fear in her stomach. What the hell was going on with Lilah?

"Thanks, Billy. I'll check it out," she assured him and he looked relieved enough to return to the business of sailing, but Lindy wasn't relieved at all. In fact, she felt the overwhelming urge to tell Billy to turn the boat around and head back to the marina.

But even as the impulse was strong, she knew she

had to follow through with this meeting or else they might lose an opportunity to help Larimar, at least in the short term.

CARYS FOUND HERSELF alone and bored, again, as her father tended some *pressing* detail that couldn't wait another second, and when she'd gone looking for Lindy she'd been disappointed to learn she'd gone to St. Thomas for the day. Carys pouted. Lindy had promised a rain check on the ice cream, but now she was nowhere to be seen. Typical adult behavior. Make a promise and then find a way to wiggle out of it.

The urge to break something or plug the toilet was strong but when she considered how disappointed Lindy would be, she corralled the impulse and decided to hit the beach instead.

But as she started down the path, she heard a whole bunch of racket and decided to detour. Whatever was making that noise had to be more exciting than what she had planned.

She found the source: Lindy's grandpa, and he was banging around in the garage behind the main building, appearing frustrated as he tossed tools around.

"Damn it," he muttered, slamming a tool down on the small workbench and causing the rest of the tools lying around to jitter. "Where is my ratchet set?"

"What's a ratchet?" Carys asked from the doorway, curious.

The man—Lindy called him Pops—jumped at the sound of her voice and smiled, motioning for her to enter. "There you are, sugar bird. I can't seem to find my favorite ratchet set. I know I left it somewhere in here but I can't remember where exactly that is. Would you mind helping me look around?"

Carys hesitated. He'd called her a sugar bird…what was that? "Sure," she said, sliding into the room, curious. He seemed a nice enough old man. "What are you building?"

"Your grams has been after me to fix her birdhouse and I'm going to do it if it kills me. Have you seen Grams this morning?"

Carys stared at the older man with a quizzical expression until she remembered what Lindy had told her about her grandfather's memory. He must've thought she was one of his granddaughters. It was on the tip of her tongue to correct him, but she figured there was little point. He'd probably just freak out, like Lindy said he did when anyone intruded on his fantasy. And to be honest, Carys kind of liked the idea of belonging to this crazy family, if even for pretend, so she played along. "She went…to town," Carys lied with a smile.

He looked at the ceiling and pretended annoyance as he muttered, "That woman and her need to shop. You'd think by the way she comes home with bags and bags of stuff on each shopping trip, that there'd be nothing left to buy on the whole island."

"Well, you know Grams," Carys said with a sigh, secretly delighting in this charade where she belonged with the Bells. It's funny, her own grandparents—on her dad's side, of course, because her mom's parents had died before she was born—were stiff and stale as old pancakes. They sent her an obligatory birthday and Christmas card with a crisp twenty-dollar bill, and it was a rare occasion that she was invited to visit. They were nothing like this adorable old coot and Carys already liked him far more than those people who were actually related to her. "So, Pops…what's with Grams and the birdhouse? I mean, is it special or something?"

His eyes turned warm and he chuckled, getting that look on his face that told Carys a story was coming and she gleefully settled in to listen.

"Your grams, bless her heart, is a bit of a nut, which I'm sure you've already figured out by now. And she's always had a thing for birds. So when we moved here to the island and saw all the bananaquits bouncing around, she just fell in love. It's also why we nicknamed all you girls sugar birds. It's our connection to the island and our connection to you girls. It just seemed right. Anyway, a regular birdhouse simply wouldn't do for the bananaquits because they love sugar."

"Is that why they're called sugar birds?" Carys asked, intrigued.

"You got it." He winked before continuing. "As I was saying, the regular birdhouses didn't have a wide enough base and opening for a small bowl of sugar water. So your grams had me make special birdhouses so she could see her sugar birds every day. Kind of like hummingbirds, you know?"

Carys nodded, smiling. "You sure do have a lot of birdhouses around Larimar," she noted.

"That's what I said," Pops said drily. "But your grams said we needed one more. So I made her one more. Then we had a monster storm come through and it fell and broke to pieces. Oh, your grams was mad." He chuckled at the memory. "You'd have thought someone came along and broke all of them. She insisted I fix it. And to be honest, I've been putting it off. But…well, I don't think I should put it off any longer."

There was something about his voice that caught her attention. She glanced up and noted the laughter had faded from his eyes and he seemed to stumble on something in his mind.

"What's wrong, Pops?" she asked.

The older man paused to stare at Carys, a look of confusion on his aged face as if he couldn't quite decipher what she'd just said, and then returned to his tinkering with a slightly quivering lip. "She's real sick, sugar bird. Real sick. But I'm going to fix this birdhouse for her, don't you worry. I just need the right tools."

Carys nodded, feeling sad for this man. She'd hate to relive what her mother went through. It'd been bad enough the first time around. "What does the tool you're looking for look like?" she asked, glancing around the messy garage.

The old man blinked and concentrated on his answer, forming the words with difficulty as if pulling the memory from molasses. "Well, it's a circlelike thing, and it fits like this." He pulled two pieces of wood and held them up. Carys saw a bolt of some sort on the one piece. Carys started looking for a tool that might fit, like a jigsaw puzzle piece. She spied something on the shelf above her and reached for it. "Is this it?" she asked, handing him the tool.

His aged face, browned from the sun, lit up with a smile. "Hot damn. I believe that's the one I'm looking for. Good job, sugar bird. What would I do without you?"

Carys smiled, warming under the praise. Her grandparents never gave her pet names or spoiled her like some grandparents did. If and when Carys saw them, they always called her by her proper name and rarely spoke to her beyond superficial questions that required little more than a polite response. She wondered what it would be like to have a grandparent who was in her business, in a good way? One who cared about her grades, her friends, and wanted to spend time with her, just be-

cause they liked her company. She swallowed the lump
that had risen and called out a quick goodbye, making
a hasty exit before any tears started to fall.

LINDY PASTED A bright smile on her face for Paul's benefit and accepted the hug and kiss on the cheek when
she arrived on set.

Paul Hossiter, a man who was known for throwing
lavish parties in his Malibu mansion with his plastic-
perfect wife, Danica, was also a consummate man-
whore who slept around as much as his wife—
sometimes, unknowingly with the same people. He'd
been trying to get into Lindy's pants for a year now and
she'd always sidestepped his offers, preferring her one-
night stands to have less frequent-flier miles. Because
of her refusal, Paul had taken on what he'd perceived
as a challenge to get her into bed.

"Honey, you look amazing," he said, openly admiring her body from head to toe. "The Caribbean agrees
with you. Now tell me why you and I haven't spent some
quality time at some ridiculous expensive resort explor-
ing each other's bodies?"

"Because you're married," she reminded him by way
of an excuse, but honestly, she would never sleep with
Paul. Rumor had it, he had a penchant for filming his
escapades and holding on to the footage for blackmail
purposes later. And there was no way in hell she'd risk
that, not for anything in the world. But as she glanced
around she couldn't quell the pang of envy at the lavish set and the top-notch costuming for the adventure
movie. It was a multimillion-dollar production and they
were sparing no expense to get the right look, hence the
exotic locale.

"Such a stickler for the rules," he teased, though his

eyes had lit up with lecherous zeal. "And what if I invited my wife along…. Would that help change your mind?"

Eww. She faked a sweet smile. "I'm not into chicks. Sorry."

He exhaled in disappointment and said, "All right, I tried. So, I have to say I was surprised when I got a call back. Usually, you ignore my texts unless you're pestering me for a part in something."

"Which you never give me because I don't give it up," Lindy quipped, daring him to disagree.

Paul shrugged, as if to say *guilty*. "Hey, I'm just a man and you have a body that would tempt the Pope."

"Somehow I doubt that," Lindy said drily. "Listen, I wondered how things are going with the lodging here in St. Thomas for your above-the-line people. Everything good?"

Paul shrugged. "It's nice. It's not Fiji, but it'll do. Why?"

"You may not remember this, but my family owns an upscale resort in St. John and I thought if you wanted to get a real feel for the islands, you ought to come check it out. We have five-star accommodations and a private beach."

"I'd love to, baby, but we've already locked down the hotel accommodations for this shoot. But…I'd love to see it. Would you give me a personal tour?"

Lindy quickly sifted through Paul's seemingly innocuous query for any hidden meaning and came up with a moderate suspicion that Paul wanted a personal tour of her bedroom and nothing more. "Listen, St. Thomas is the port of call for every major cruise ship out there. How are you going to keep your actors free from prying eyes with all that exposure? Didn't I hear that you were trying to keep this production hush-hush because it's running neck and neck against the new Michael Bay flick and you don't want the press making unfair comparisons?"

At the mention of Michael Bay, Paul's face darkened. "Don't even get me started…"

"Larimar could give you the privacy you're looking for," she interjected before he could get ramped up about his current scuffle with the Hollywood A-lister. "Think about it."

He wavered, which gave her hope, but ultimately he shook his head. "Listen, gorgeous, I'd be happy to spend some quality time with you at your resort but we're committed and locked into where we're at for this production. Our hotel is a short drive from the location and everything we need is easily accessible. You know what I'm saying?"

"Yeah," Lindy said, disappointed. If she thought it would make a difference, she was almost tempted to take one for the team and let Paul finally get what he wanted, but just the thought made her skin crawl. "If you change your mind, just let me know," she said, covering her sharp frustration with false cheer. "I'll be here helping my family out for a little while longer so I'll be around if you need anything."

A speculative light entered his stare, and she wagged a finger at him, saying, "No, no, you perv. Keep it PG-13."

"Bah. Where's the fun in that?" he asked just before a production assistant who looked like he ate antacids for breakfast came to him with a look of pure panic. He listened for a moment and then, Lindy forgotten, Paul followed the assistant, bellowing orders as he went.

"Damn," she murmured, watching him leave. There went her big chance at being the hero. Back to square one.

She called Billy, letting him know she was on her way back to the boat.

And to please, please, have some rum ready.

CHAPTER ELEVEN

LINDY DIDN'T WANT to admit defeat just yet, putting off the inevitable discussion with Lora until she had no choice. Plus, by the time she'd returned to St. John and then Larimar, she'd consumed quite a bit of rum and wasn't up to talking to anyone.

She'd safely made her way past the front desk lobby and was headed for the main house when she ran smack into Carys and Gabe. Lindy wanted to groan and run the other way, but her legs were a little wobbly and she doubted she'd manage a brisk walk much less a run.

"Lindy?" Carys said, frowning. "Are you…drunk?"

"You shouldn't even know what drunk is, kid," Lindy said, pointing at Gabe. "Geez, Gabe, what are you exposing your daughter to?" Then she giggled and tried to move past them but she stumbled and nearly landed in a bush. Gabe's firm hand kept her from getting a faceful of tropical foliage and for that she was grateful, but even in her inebriated state she knew this was a terrible mistake letting Carys and Gabe see her like this. "In my defense…I've had a shitty day," she said, deciding a good offense was the best defense.

"Dad, I think she needs to go to bed," Carys said, watching as Gabe hoisted Lindy into his arms.

"I think you're right," Gabe agreed grimly, settling Lindy's pliant body more securely in his arms.

"You're surprisingly strong for a suit-wearing kind

of guy," Lindy remarked, happy to lay her head on his shoulder for just a minute. "I never saw that coming...."

"Maybe we should just take her to our place, Dad," Carys suggested and Gabe must've agreed because they were heading in the wrong direction for Lindy's room.

"You don't have to do that," Lindy said, sighing. "But I think you're right.... I don't really want to deal with my sisters right now. Or Pops. Or Celly. Or anyone associated with Larimar. Frankly, I think I just want to go back to L.A. where everybody in my circle is simply a superficial fame-whore—Carys, don't repeat that—who would sleep with their own mother if it got them ahead. And don't get me started on the whole eating thing. I think I've gained five pounds already."

Damn, it felt surprisingly good to be nestled in Gabe's arms. It felt...right.

No, it had to be the alcohol fuzzing her brain. She hated this kind of intimacy. It was too...*intimate*. She wasn't a cuddler by nature and yet, this was pretty close to cuddling and she was so comfortable her eyelids were fluttering shut.

"Gabe...has anyone ever told you, you have a great chest hidden beneath those hideous Hawaiian shirts? Just perfect for this..."

And then she was asleep.

GABE PUT LINDY in his bed and then closed the door behind him to talk to Carys.

"Is she okay?" Carys asked, concerned.

"Yes, I'm sure she just needs to sleep it off. Sometimes adults overindulge—"

"Dad, please," Carys interrupted with a condescending expression. "I'm eleven, not five. I know what happens when people drink too much. I go to a public school, remember? You'd be surprised what I know."

That statement didn't make him feel better…if anything, it made him want to homeschool her for the rest of her school career and then enroll her in a nunnery for college.

"Oh…okay," he said, biting his lip as he wondered how to proceed. "Well, let's keep it down while she sleeps. Or better yet, maybe we ought to leave the bungalow and do some sightseeing. She might be a little embarrassed when she wakes up, and seeing us will be the last thing she wants to do."

"Why would she be embarrassed?" Carys asked, intrigued. "Lots of people drink. Miranda Potter's mom drinks every night. She was passed out cold the last time I spent the night at Miranda's house. It was cool, though, because then we had the run of the house and we tried on all her jewelry."

That uncomfortable feeling earlier was just eclipsed by the more uncomfortable feelings he had now. It was obvious he needed to pay better attention to the types of people his daughter was hanging out with. "Where was Mr. Potter when all this was going on?" he asked.

Carys shrugged, but then she grinned with a mischievous light in her eyes. "But according to Miranda, he was probably sleeping with his secretary, which is why her mom was drinking so she could forget."

Gabe resisted the urge to clap a hand over his face in total chagrin. He had no idea the Potters were so dysfunctional, but then he only saw them when they were on their best behavior. One thing was for sure, he wasn't too keen on letting Carys continue to have sleepovers at their place. "Okay, well, that's gossip and we don't traffic in gossip," he admonished, hating this conversation. "If it's not true, it would be very hurtful if the other person heard it. And if it is true…well, it's still hurtful because they're obviously going through something painful in their marriage."

Carys nodded. "Yeah, Miranda acts all like she doesn't care, but I think she does," she said, pausing a moment to regard Gabe with serious eyes. "Dad… did you ever sleep with your secretary when Mom was alive? Miranda says all dads do it because they're pigs and can't help themselves."

Even though he remained standing, the question knocked him on his ass. He floundered, unable to fathom the kind of conversations his preteen was having with her girlfriends, but worse, he was flabbergasted that Carys would even think that he'd do that to her mother. He took her hand and held it firmly between his and stared her straight in the eye as he answered solemnly, "I don't know how other people live, Carys, but I can tell you with complete honesty, your mother and I didn't have that kind of relationship. We had our problems, but fidelity wasn't one of them. I believed in my vows and never took them lightly. That's the way it should be."

Carys's eyes watered and he gathered her in his arms, surprised at the sudden show of emotion. "I miss her, Dad," she whispered, and he hugged her more tightly.

"I know you do, sweetheart. I miss her, too."

Gabe held Carys for as long as possible before letting her go. His own eyes pricked with moisture. This was why he didn't like to talk about Charlotte; it sucked up all sorts of muck that he didn't have the time to wallow in.

He hadn't lied; he'd never cheated on Charlotte.

But there'd been a time, right before she'd gotten sick, that he'd been sorely tempted.

And the question that lurked deep in his heart was would he have strayed if Charlotte hadn't gotten sick?

The question nagged at him.

He hated to think he might've but he remembered the illicit thrill, which had contrasted so starkly with the staid complacency of his marriage and he feared that eventually, he would've succumbed.

And he never wanted Carys to know that.

Ever.

LINDY SLOWLY OPENED her eyes and grimaced at the sticky taste in her mouth. Damn rum. She rose and saw it was dark outside. She looked around and realized she was not in her bed. A moment of disorientation followed the uncomfortable feeling that she didn't know where she was. She flashed to a party in the Hollywood Hills where she couldn't rightly remember all of the details but was pretty sure things had happened without her express permission and she fought the rising disquiet that followed when she thought too much about that night. She swung her legs over the side of the bed and waited for the dizziness to go away.

It was then she realized she wasn't alone in the room.

She opened her mouth to scream but realized a heartbeat later Gabe was the dark form lying uncomfortably in the chaise lounge by the window. He was still clothed, wearing board shorts and a hideous magnolia shirt, and his dark hair, which was usually so orderly and perfect, was disheveled and mussed as if he'd spent the night raking his hands through it during a crisis. It shouldn't have been sexy given the circumstances, but it was.

The knowledge that he'd slept in an uncomfortable

chair so a drunken stranger could sleep in his bed, oddly enough made Lindy want to cry. It'd been a long time since she'd met any decent men. Of course, it would stand to reason that the first time a decent man came into her life, she'd have to run like hell in the opposite direction.

Irony was a bitch.

Lindy read the time on the digital clock: 1:00 a.m. Had she really slept that long? Man, she must've hit the rum way too hard. She exhaled softly and rose from the bed with the intent to slip out unnoticed, but Gabe awoke as she reached the door.

"You're awake?"

She turned, biting her lip. "Yeah...sorry about all this. I'd forgotten how quickly rum hits me." She thought of the impression she must've made on Carys and she cringed, hating how everything had unfolded. "I'm so sorry.... I never meant for you or Carys to see me like this. I'm not usually so..."

"Irresponsible?"

"No, I can be terribly irresponsible," she retorted with a weak smile. "What I was going to say was, careless. I never would've wanted Carys to see me like that. It's not my style to be drunk around kids, just so you know," she felt compelled to add.

He let that go and she was grateful; her head was pounding and she needed water and aspirin immediately. "Are you okay to walk to the main house?" he asked solicitously.

"Yeah," she answered, her cheeks heating. Why did she feel as if she'd been caught with her hand in the cookie jar? She was a grown adult. She straightened. "Anyway, thanks."

"I'm thinking it would be best if we checked out and

found a different resort to finish our stay in St. John," he said, and she turned to stare at him. It was difficult to discern his expression in the dim moonlight but the tone of his voice was clear: she was a bad influence on his daughter.

Lora was going to kill her. Lindy licked her dehydrated lips and her mind fought to think fast, though all that materialized was the overwhelming urge to apologize profusely and beg—two things she wouldn't do.

"I've heard the Worchester is nice," she said stiffly. "Ask for Darla. She'll give you a good rate."

And then before she could do something stupid or rash, further mucking things up, she let herself quietly out of the bungalow and walked on unsteady feet to her room.

Each step was punctuated by the very real fear she'd just screwed Larimar with her stupidity.

But there was something else that gnawed at her that she was reluctant to look at too closely.

Gabe was leaving because he thought she was a bad influence on Carys, and after last night maybe he was right. What business did she have being around an impressionable kid? Hell, last year, she'd partied so hard at the Playboy Mansion, Hugh Hefner had hinted that she had an open invitation to join the house bunnies if she was willing to play nice. Of course, she'd politely declined. It was one thing to run around without a top in the heat of the moment, quite another to run around topless as an everyday thing. She bit back the unhappy sigh, surprised at how much it hurt to think she might've damaged her relationship with Carys for her stunt. Worse, she knew how Gabe felt about her, too. It'd been written all over his face. She was nothing but a boozehound with loose morals. Her cheeks heated. The sad part, back in L.A. she'd really started to feel the same.

Lindy pushed open the gate to the private area and went straight to her room, each step making her queasy stomach that much more agitated.

Face it, a voice told her, *you hate that he thinks that about you.*

Yeah…she hated it a lot.

And that scared her more deeply than anything she'd ever known.

She shouldn't give two figs what Gabe Weston thought of her. He was a Larimar guest. Nothing more.

Right?

CHAPTER TWELVE

GABE WASN'T LOOKING forward to this conversation but he'd booked them a room at the Worchester and he had to break the news to Carys they needed to pack.

"Morning, Dad," Carys chirped with unusual good cheer that morning as she grabbed a banana from the fruit bowl and peeled it open to take a big bite. "Somehow the bananas here taste better than the ones at home. Have you noticed that?"

"That's because they're fresh, whereas the bananas at the grocery store in the States have been picked green and ripen later."

"That's stupid. Why would you pick something before it's ripe?"

He smiled. "Because if they didn't, by the time it reached the store it would be rotten. Did you know apples are picked six months ahead of schedule and then slowly ripen in cold storage?"

Carys wrinkled her nose and grimaced. "That sounds gross."

"Well, apples still taste pretty good."

"Not as good as this fresh banana," Carys quipped, taking another bite for emphasis. "So, we should see if Lindy is feeling better today. Maybe she'll be up to some ice cream for that rain check."

Here it goes...the dreaded conversation. "About that... You know, with everything that's been going on,

I think it might be best to switch resorts. I've booked us an amazing suite over at the Worchester and I know you're going to love it."

"I don't want to leave Larimar," Carys said mutinously, her brow furrowing darkly. "I like it here."

"You tried to kill the plumbing," he reminded her.

"That was before. Things have changed."

"Yes, and although I'm grateful you've seen the error of your ways when it comes to malicious mischief, I have to question whether or not this is a good environment for you."

"You wouldn't know a good environment for me if it came and bit you on the nose!"

His cell phone trilled to life at his hip and he groaned at the ill-timed interruption. He paused a minute to check the caller ID and then cursed softly when he realized he couldn't send it to voice mail. "Listen, I have to take this call. This isn't up for discussion. I need you to pack your things."

"No." She folded her arms across her chest.

He did a double take as he answered the phone. It was Vincent Burchell, the attorney representing Weston Enterprises' most recent acquisition bid. "Weston," he said, then covered the phone with his hand to warn in a fierce whisper, "Carys, I'm not going to argue with you about this. Now go!" Vincent asked if he'd received the relevant documents. Gabe, believing the matter with Carys finished, returned to his conversation, answering, in a normal tone, "Yes, I received the acquisition documents but I told you I wasn't going to go a penny over twelve million for that property. You and I both know it's in distress. The market value simply isn't there to support a higher offer." Suddenly, he was startled by his daughter's angry shriek.

"You never ask me how I feel about anything!" She stomped her foot and clenched her small fists. "You just tell me what I'm doing and where I'm going and you never ask how I feel about it! You never change! You promised me you'd listen but you aren't listening to me now. You'd rather talk on the phone about your stupid business stuff than talk to me! I hate you!"

"Everything okay?" Vincent asked, overhearing Carys's enraged scream.

"Vincent, I'm sorry, I'm going to have to call you back. I've got something I have to deal with here," he said, gritting his teeth at the image of the attorney on the other line smirking. "I'll call you back in five minutes."

"Take all the time you need. My client isn't going to accept your offer as it stands. It's an insult."

"Vincent, let's get real here," Gabe started, holding his finger up to Carys for her to wait until he got off the phone, but she wasn't going to give him another second. Her face reddened at being put on hold and she ran out the door. Damn it. "Not again," he muttered, closing his eyes for a brief second before muttering a hasty good-bye to Vincent. He quickly dialed his own attorney and barked into the phone, "Vincent Burchell is saying he's not going to accept my offer. I need you to show him the error of his ways. I don't want to talk to that man again until he's ready to do some real business. This is bullshit and a waste of my time."

"I've been trying to call you all day. I received the news first thing this morning that Harris Montgomery was having a change of heart. He wants more money and believes he can get it."

"He's a doddering old fool who's holding on to a company for nostalgic reasons and not ones grounded in good business sense. Make him see reason. I'm not about to lose out on this deal because Harris is feeling sentimental."

"I'll see what I can do. You might have to walk away from this one," his attorney warned, but Gabe wasn't in the mood to hear that.

"I've already invested too much time and energy into this damn acquisition. Make it happen, Warren," he fairly growled into the phone. He clicked off without saying goodbye. The situation wasn't improving his already raging temper. And now he had to go find his hotheaded daughter while the biggest deal his company had ever brokered was starting to go down in flames, as well.

He cursed long and hard, irritated by the whole situation—Carys, the deal, and more importantly, Lindy.

The last time he'd felt so out of control of everything was when Charlotte had gotten sick.

Was it too much to ask for calm waters instead of all this chop? Maybe it'd been a bad idea to take a month away from the office. Hell, maybe he'd been fooling himself into thinking that it would make a difference with Carys. Charlotte was gone; no amount of fun in the sun was going to change the fact that she'd died, and he'd been stupid to think that a change in scenery would salvage his relationship with Carys. So far, that harebrained notion had been a gigantic bust.

A part of him was tempted to let the kid run, but the moment the selfish and angry thought entered his brain, shame followed and kicked his feet into motion.

He chased her all the way to the main house where she'd run straight into Celly's arms.

Oh criminy, he thought, feeling as if he'd just crossed into the path of a lioness guarding her cub. He sighed as he caught his daughter's impassioned sobs.

"I hate him," she cried into Celly's ample bosom, earning a black look from the Crucian front desk woman.

"What yah do to dis chile?" she demanded, stroking Carys's hair and murmuring soft accented words that Gabe couldn't begin to make out. "She all upset and quaking."

"He wants to move us to the Worchester," Carys answered for him, spitting the words as if they were dirty and Celly's resultant look was just as expressive.

"Bah on de Worchester. Plenty good here."

"It's not that…" he started, then stopped, wondering why he was explaining himself. "If you please, this is a situation between me and my daughter. Carys, come with me. I will not entertain this emotional manipulation. Now let's get packing."

"You go. I'll stay."

He stared. "Excuse me?"

"You heard me. I like it here and if you drag me out of Larimar, I'll just find a way back."

And he didn't doubt that for a goddamn second. "Carys! Enough."

But Carys merely turned away from him and clutched at Celly harder as if she were afraid that Gabe might do something terrible to her and Celly was her only hope for safety. He'd never wanted to grab his little heathen by the neck and shake her silly more than he wanted to at that moment but he held himself in check by the narrowest of margins.

"The chile don' want to go," Celly said unnecessarily as if that were the end of it.

"Well the child is not in charge," he said tightly. "If you please, Celly…you're not helping."

"Don't you be mean to Celly!" Carys shouted, glaring at Gabe. "She cares about me, which is more than

I can say for you! You couldn't even miss one stupid work call to talk to me. You always choose work over me. Always!"

Celly patted Carys's back and crooned to her softly, clucking her tongue, chastising Gabe with a short look. This was getting ridiculous.

Why couldn't they just get along? They used to, but now it seemed she lived to make his life more difficult. He wasn't about to carry on this conversation with an audience of one judgmental and intimidating hotel receptionist. "Carys…let's talk about this in private."

"No."

"Dis chile is more than yah can handle," Celly observed, chuckling when he scowled at her candid observation. Then she surprised him by waving him away, saying, "Yah go and do something.… I talk wit her."

Gabe hesitated, caught between the urge to simply grab Carys by her arm and drag her out of there or go back to the room to cool off. "I can handle my own daughter," he said, freshly pissed off that the woman was right.

Celly arched one brow as if she found his statement absurd and then said, "Yah stubborn mon. Chile don' fall far from de tree. You force her to go…she come back. Yah decide. Either way, de same."

Hell, she was right. He choked down a bitter pill of resignation, and said tersely, "I'll be back in an hour. Be ready to pack or I will pack for you."

"I hate you!" Carys screamed at his back and he flinched but kept walking.

LINDY WALKED INTO the lobby and found Celly talking to Carys in soothing tones that Lindy didn't think the

older woman was capable of, which made Lindy realize Carys was crying.

Immediately forgetting her own mental stuff, she
went to Carys with open concern and asked, "What's
wrong?"

"My dad wants to leave," the girl answered with a
sad hiccup.

Lindy took in the puffed and swollen eyes and the
runny nose and felt sick to her stomach. This was no
act. There was no hiding the genuine distress written
all over the little girl's face. Lindy winced. This was her
fault. "Let me guess…the Worchester?" she supplied,
to which Carys nodded.

Lindy sighed and straightened, forgetting her headache and minor complaints to concentrate on how to fix
this immediate problem. Aside from the obvious fact
that Larimar needed the money, she knew if Gabe took
Carys away it would cripple his chances of ever repair-
ing his relationship with Carys. Even if he didn't see it,
Lindy knew it in her bones. If only she'd swallowed her
damn pride and apologized for being such an idiot. And
then begged him to stay.

Would it have mattered? She didn't know but if she
didn't at least try, what leg did she have to stand on with
her excuses?

Lindy wiped away a tear from Carys's cheek and said
to Celly, "Why don't you ask Lilah to cover for you and
you two go to the kitchen and raid it for some ice cream?
I think Pops always has chocolate on hand. And while
you're doing that, I'll go talk to Mr. Weston."

"Good idea," Celly agreed, holding out her hand to
Carys. Carys sent her a pleading look, as if to say, *please
fix this,* and then went with Celly in the direction of the
kitchen.

Lindy blew out a short breath. *Here goes nothing...*

She walked to Gabe's bungalow and gave the door two solid, confident knocks, even though her insides were quivering and her brain was chattering with all sorts of unhelpful crap. She'd really screwed up on this one. Somehow, she had to fix it. The pressure was more than she was accustomed to but she was determined to repair the damage. She wouldn't allow her mistake to mess with Carys. The kid had enough on her plate.

Gabe opened the door. She wished she could say she saw pleasure in his eyes, but no, she didn't.

"Can I talk to you?" Lindy asked.

He hesitated but good manners dictated that he open the door for her to enter. "Can I get you something?" he asked.

"Water would be great," Lindy answered, smiling gratefully when he handed her a cold bottled water from the fridge. After she'd guzzled half the bottle, she said, "Listen, I know why you're leaving and I can't say I don't understand but let me plead my case before you make that decision."

He spread his hands in a gesture that said *go ahead* but the look in his eyes told her this was going to be a waste of time. She was tempted to say *forget it,* but the memory of Carys's tear-streaked face wouldn't let her.

"I'm sorry about last night," she started, preparing herself mentally to be brutally honest and hope that it did some good. "I don't usually drink like that but I'm under a lot of pressure and I got news that wasn't exactly what I'd been hoping for. My friend Billy owns his own charter company and he ferried me to St. Thomas for some business, and when my business concluded badly he consoled me with what used to be my poison of choice. I'd forgotten how quickly rum goes to my head and before I knew it, I was stumbling out of the cab. I never meant for you or Carys to see me that way, I promise. And if I could take it back, I would in a heartbeat. Carys is a special kid and I'd never do anything to give her a bad impression of me."

"I understand that, but, Lindy, I can't erase what happened just because you didn't *mean* for it to happen."

Lindy scowled. "I know that but people make mistakes, okay? If we own up to our mistakes, it shows that we're willing to learn from them, right? And, if I were a parent, I'd want my kid to soak up that lesson instead of some hypocritical hogwash that kids see right through."

"Well, it sounds good in theory, but when you're an actual parent, you'll have a different perspective."

She bristled. "Oh, because I don't have kids, my point is invalid?"

"No, I didn't say that," he said.

"Sounded like it to me."

Their stares collided and locked. Lindy couldn't believe what a narrow-minded jerk he was being. By his expression, he was irritated, as well. *Great way to patch things up, Lindy.* She might as well throw kerosene on this blaze because her good intentions were already going up in smoke.

"I think we're done here," he said.

Oh, hell no. "Not yet," she retorted stubbornly. "I get that you're the boss of your company and you're accustomed to getting your way and calling the shots but you're going to have to remember that you're not always right and in this instance, I think it would be a big mistake for you and Carys to leave."

"You've made your point. I disagree."

"Well, if you weren't being such a pigheaded tool, you'd see that I was right," she spat, half wondering why she wasn't simply throwing her hands in the air and declaring the situation beyond her control. That was her usual MO for dealing with difficult situations. She wasn't a fixer. Never had been, and frankly, the idea had never appealed but even as the impulse was strong to quit, she just couldn't bring herself to do it. She was going to make him see reason even if she had to conk him over the head with the fruit bowl and tie him to a chair until he saw things her way. She squared her shoulders. *Let's try this again.* "So, let me get this straight… You never make mistakes?"

He scowled in open annoyance at her direct query. "Of course I make mistakes."

"Well, then why is it so hard to let me have a do-over in this instance?"

"Because I don't allow do-overs with my kid," he shot back. "She's all I've got and I'm doing my damnedest to see that she has a childhood that isn't spoiled and ruined by the bad choices of the adults in her life."

"I hate to break it to you but in case you haven't noticed, Carys knows more about life than you do at this point. She's a savvy kid, almost precocious, if you ask me. She doesn't need you treating her like a baby. She just needs you to listen to her and what she's saying to you in the plainest terms is that she doesn't want to leave."

Gabe stopped short and glared. The heat between them fairly snapped with sparks and electric energy. Lindy could tell he was struggling with her statement. Something must've hit a chord. Either he was going to flat-out ignore what she was saying, or he'd let it sink in. She held her breath as she waited. He didn't look ready to concede his point. He grudgingly shook his head and said, "I know she doesn't want to leave but I have to do what's right for her, even if it's not the popular choice. I just don't know how admitting to an eleven-year-old girl that you got slobbering drunk because you were disappointed is a good lesson. Certainly not the one I'm comfortable teaching on vacation."

Lindy's cheeks burned. "All I can say is I'm sorry," she said from between gritted teeth. "It won't happen again."

"I know it won't," he said. "Because we're still leaving."

"Are you always this difficult?" she asked. He was being deliberately pigheaded. Something else was happening here, too. She could feel it. "Don't bother answering that. I have a better question for you. Is there something else that's eating at you? Take Carys out of the equation because honestly, let's get real. If you think she's never seen someone she knows drunk, you're living in a fantasyland. What else is happening that's got your towel all twisted up?"

He stiffened. "This is about me trying to protect my daughter."

She narrowed her stare at him in open speculation and then when she still didn't buy it, she called him on it. "Bullshit."

"Nice language," he said caustically. "You see? This is what I'm talking about."

"What? Carys isn't here and we're two adults having an adult conversation. Is that too much for you?"

"No."

"Well, then as my ex-therapist would say, stop deflecting for a damn minute and just tell me what the hell is really upsetting you."

CHAPTER THIRTEEN

GABE DIDN'T KNOW why he wasn't telling Lindy to mind her own business. He didn't have to answer to her, or anyone. He was the CEO of a highly successful corporate raiding company that he started from the ground and turned into a fierce, hard-to-evade force in his field. He made lesser men quail and women were constantly making themselves available to him even when he didn't give off any (known) signals that he was available or interested.

And yet…two females, an eleven-year-old and a—hell, he didn't even know how old Lindy was—grown woman were chopping him off at the knees at every turn.

If he hadn't acknowledged it before this moment, there was no denying it now. Lindy was the exact opposite of Charlotte.

Charlotte had been sweetly supportive, that quiet guiding force that had always been his moral compass when he wavered. He could always count on her to be the calm in the storm of his complicated life.

And, at times, it was a bit boring. His cheeks colored at the shameful private admission and he realized his mind had wandered. He rubbed at his forehead as he stood conflicted, buffeted by thoughts from the past that seemed to have awfully inconvenient timing. Maybe this was a latent form of grieving he hadn't yet experienced. Hell, it didn't matter, either way. Lindy was right.

He was dealing with more than just parental concern for his impressionable daughter. He leaned against the counter and looked away when he couldn't hold Lindy's gaze any longer for fear she'd see right through him.

"I'll listen," she said, losing some of her edge. The sincerity in her voice loosened his lips when he otherwise would've remained stubbornly silent.

"I'm trying to be both mother and father to a child I don't even know anymore," he said softly, hating the honesty of his admission. "When Charlotte died, Carys changed. She turned into…a little spoiled brat. I can't tell you how many nannies and tutors and maids we've gone through in the last year. It's gotten to the point where I can't get any of the referral agencies to take my calls. No one wants to be around her. That's why we came here. I'd hoped a change in scenery would help things. That maybe she'd work through this stage and we'd get back to normal when we returned."

"What's normal?" Lindy asked, mildly baffled by the term. "The kid lost her mom. There's nothing *normal* about that, and you shouldn't expect things to return to the way they were because they won't ever be without Charlotte."

"What am I supposed to do? I can't bring her mother back from the dead."

"You find a new normal."

"I've been trying," he said. "Every attempt has blown up in my face."

Lindy took a deep breath as if considering her next comment carefully, then said, "Gabe…she doesn't need nannies or tutors or fancy vacations. She needs her dad. That's all she wants. Ask yourself how many times you've blown her off for work?"

"I have to make a living," he said stiffly. "She has to

understand I can't be at her beck and call whenever she snaps her fingers."

"Of course not. But my grams used to say you have to have balance in life. All work and no play makes Gabe a dull boy, you know? I've only known you a short while but it seems to me that you're way out of balance. Plainly speaking, you're a workaholic."

"Yes, I work hard and I've got a thriving company to show for it."

"And a daughter who's miserable and doing everything she can to get your damn attention," Lindy countered, exasperated. "Even I can see that. Surely you can't be that blind?"

"What about you? Where's the balance in your life?" he asked, throwing an emotional mirror in her face. "From what I can see, you're a party girl who's no stranger to the L.A. club scene. Play all night and sleep all day, just to get up and do it again the next night. Do you call that balance?" She stared at him in wounded, surprised silence for his sudden attack. He didn't want to admit he'd looked her up on Google and found some tabloid pictures of her with a few well-known celebrity hard-core partiers. He'd planned to keep that information to himself—because frankly, he'd been embarrassed that he'd even gone looking—but it seemed a valid point to make seeing as she was pulling no punches herself. "Forgive me if I find your stance just a little hypocritical."

She swallowed and seemed to pale a bit but she rallied quickly, saying, "My choices are not affecting anyone but myself. If I had a kid, it'd be different. I'm trying to help you salvage your relationship with your daughter before it's too late, but if you'd rather throw stones at me for my choices, then I'll help you pack myself."

Heavy silence settled between them as Gabe wrestled with the demon snarling inside him and the voice that fairly screamed at him to heed this woman's advice. The thing was, he knew Lindy was right but his ego was demanding a chunk of her hide for daring to hold his feet to the fire. God bless her, Charlotte had never been so blunt in her attempts to get him to see reason. He supposed he'd gotten accustomed to her gentle manner, not that he hadn't flat-out dismissed her advice at times. Lindy made a sound of disgust and said, "Forget it. I'm done. Do what you want and have a good life."

"Lindy, wait," he called out, but she'd already slammed the door behind her.

He was two seconds from running after her but he stayed instead. What could he say? Her points had been valid but his pride hadn't allowed his mouth to admit it.

He tried to remember a time when Charlotte had called him out on anything but he came up empty. Surely, there'd been instances, but his memories of Charlotte were becoming tangled with his grief. He didn't want to remember Charlotte as anything but the loving wife and wonderful mother she'd been. Maybe that's why he shied away from talking about her too much. He didn't want to risk tarnishing the memories, even if they were beginning to morph into an amalgam of what was true and what he wanted to be true.

Charlotte had been a good mother. He wasn't disputing that, ever. She'd been a good wife, almost too good. She'd put up no resistance when he'd pushed. He'd told himself he appreciated that quality in a woman, that it'd given him the freedom to be the man he needed to be in his type of business.

But at its core, it was bullshit.

Lindy had hit the nail on the head.

The fact was, if Charlotte hadn't gotten sick…he might've left her eventually. It'd been getting to that point. His heart ached to admit it. His stomach twisted in knots at the painful realization that his wife getting sick had saved him the heartache of a lengthy, drawn-out divorce.

Tears sprang to his eyes and he wiped them away. "I'm sorry, Charlotte," he whispered, hating himself for admitting this ugly fact about himself. He'd loved Charlotte, but he may have fallen out of love with her some time ago. He didn't know anymore. Everything was a jumbled mess in his head. All he knew was that Lindy excited him in a way that Charlotte never had and it was becoming increasingly difficult to keep his distance. The pressure of being the perfect parent to a grieving, demanding child was too great a responsibility to allow a wild card like Lindy into the mix. How was he supposed to instill good values and strong morals in his daughter when the woman Gabe most desperately wanted to feel beneath him was the worst kind of example he'd ever want to give his daughter?

The answer was staring him in the face but he hated it.

He wanted Lindy. It wouldn't really matter if he left the island and went home. She was under his skin. And Carys adored her, which was a different type of complication.

Even worse, Carys had attached herself to Larimar in general. She already had free rein of the place as if she'd been adopted by the Bells and he knew that wasn't a good sign.

There was one thing that stuck in Gabe's mind that rang truer than anything else.

He had one shot to fix this situation with Carys, and if he wasn't careful, he'd blow it.

True, he'd always been a workaholic, but he'd always had Charlotte there to smooth over the rough patches. He'd been there for birthdays and holidays, some weekends and late nights, but Charlotte had always been the solid, dependable parent in their household. She'd excelled as a stay-at-home mom and had made his home an oasis where he was proud to hold dinners and gatherings without reservation. That had all been Charlotte's doing.

And he'd been happy to let her do it. But now that she was gone, he didn't know how to be a full-time dad when he'd barely been a full-time husband. Charlotte had given him a lot of rope. It was a damn miracle he hadn't hanged himself with it.

A memory stirred, an echo from the past that only served to drive the miserable point home.

It'd been a phone call from Charlotte on one of the many nights he'd stayed late at the office.

"Hi, honey." Her voice had sounded soft on the other end of the line. He'd taken the call, but only grudgingly. His head was on facts and figures, strategy and cunning, not the worries and cares of his wife. "It's getting late.... Are you coming home anytime soon?"

"I might just crash here," he'd answered, anxious to end the conversation so he could get back to work. He'd been single-minded in his focus to succeed. He had a wife and child to care for and a company to run. There was no end to the workday, and Charlotte knew it. Though it had seemed she'd forgotten that fact as of late. "Don't wait up."

"You've been sleeping a lot at the office." The reproach in Charlotte's voice had been hard to miss. "Your family misses you. *I* miss you."

He'd sighed in irritation, chafing at the neediness he heard in his wife's voice. "Sacrifices have to be made, Charlotte," he'd reminded her. "On everyone's part."

"I know," she'd said. "I just thought… Well, I didn't feel good tonight and wondered if you could come home."

Charlotte's voice faded in his memory but the sick feeling lodged in his gut remained. He hadn't gone home. He'd snapped at her and she'd backed down.

They hadn't known then but Charlotte had been riddled with cancer by that point. She'd been so busy being the best wife and mother, she'd pushed aside her own aches and pains and growing fatigue.

He wished he hadn't been such a dick at times. She'd been such a good woman. He certainly hadn't deserved her love.

Funny how things got twisted and relationships changed the longer couples stayed together. At one time, he'd wanted to give Charlotte the world. It wasn't until she was gone that he'd realized she'd been *his* world. Several tears had fallen before he realized he was actually crying.

"Charlotte…you were better than I ever deserved. I'm trying to do you proud but I'm failing miserably. What am I doing wrong? I'm a damn mess."

Great. Now he was talking to an empty room. He wiped at his eyes and blew out a short breath to collect himself. The bottom line, as he was fond of saying to his employees, was this: he didn't know how to be different but he had to learn.

He'd do anything for his little girl, even if it meant doing a better job of keeping his priorities straight.

If Carys felt more secure here at Larimar, he wouldn't force her to leave. He'd find a way to deal with his feelings for Lindy without penalizing Carys in the process. He just had to keep his hands to himself and his thoughts on the straight and narrow. Besides, before long they would leave and Lindy and Larimar would become a memory.

Feeling somewhat more secure in his footing than he was only moments ago, he splashed some water on his face and then struck out to find Carys and Lindy, but as luck would have it, Lindy had returned for, judging by the determined look on her face, round two.

LINDY INTERCEPTED GABE just as he was leaving the bungalow and pushed on his chest. "Not so fast," she said, propelling him clear of the door and kicking it shut with her foot. "You had me ready to give up but I'm not about to do that to Carys—"

"We're staying," Gabe cut in, surprising her into silence for a moment. He took advantage and continued, "You were right. I was being hardheaded about it. I'm sorry for coming down so hard on you. All I can say in my defense is that I'm flying solo when I'm accustomed to sitting in first class sipping champagne while someone else does the flying. I don't have a clue what I'm doing, but I'm just trying to do what's right."

Lindy's steam evaporated at his honest admission. She'd been prepared to bury him with her conviction that she was right and he was wrong. She wasn't prepared for the white flag. "Oh…" she said, pursing her lips as she processed. "Okay. This is good news."

"Are you sure?" he asked, a faint smile lifting the corners of his mouth. "You don't seem so sure."

"No, no, it is…. I was just prepared to really lay into you," she said sheepishly. "Now, I feel as if the wind has been sucked from my sails."

He chuckled wearily, then said, "I'm sorry for being such an ass. Old habits die hard. You know, I told myself that coming here was for Carys's benefit but I needed it, too. Somehow, all this has forced me to take a hard look at myself. It hasn't been pretty."

Lindy could relate. She'd been doing a fair amount of that herself. "Caribbean magic," she said with a quirk of her mouth. She risked adding, "I'm glad you're staying."

He met her gaze and the heat between them kindled again. There was something about this man that did weird things to her insides in a way that no man had ever managed. He clearly wasn't her type but maybe that was the point.

"Thanks for not giving up," he said with a small smile that was much too sexy for a man who was supposed to be eating crow.

She nodded, not trusting her mouth at the moment. She wasn't sure how to handle this reversal or the ever-present and growing attraction she felt for Gabe Weston. If the situation were different and he wasn't a single father with a singularly awesome kid, Lindy wouldn't have wasted a second in getting him out of his clothes and into her bed. But that wasn't the reality, so she was left to play it by ear in a game where her rules didn't apply.

Gabe saved her from too much thought on that score by redirecting the conversation to safer ground.

"What was your business in St. Thomas?"

Grateful for the distraction, Lindy answered quickly, "I met a producer friend of mine who's shooting his latest action flick there. I was hoping to persuade him to lodge here at Larimar but it was too late. They'd already secured lodging and they weren't going to budge. So, basically I failed in the one task my sister had given me."

"Why is it so important to get more people here? Is the resort in trouble?"

She hesitated, not sure if she ought to share her family's personal struggles, but there was something about Gabe that made her want to lay her head on his shoulder and allow him to help bear the burden. She swallowed, knowing the feeling was irrational and that she ought to be evasive but she just couldn't. "Larimar is in trouble with the IRS. We owe gobs of back taxes because my grandfather didn't pay any for years. If we don't pay off the bill within the structured payment plan, my family is going to lose Larimar. That would kill my grandfather. He's got dementia and it's getting worse. If we let Larimar go, it'll put the final nail in that coffin and we just can't let that happen. So, yes, although my primary concern was for Carys if you left, I also had other reasons for wanting you to stay. Larimar, unlike the Worchester—which is owned by a big corporation that really doesn't need your money—is owned by the same people you shared a table with the other night."

He smiled at that. "Persuasive argument."

"I try."

"So, what's your plan B?"

She scowled. "Ugh. Now you sound like Lora. I didn't have a plan B, per se, but I'm still working on it."

He looked reluctant to offer advice on her situation, and she didn't want him to feel obligated to, either. She waved away his concern. "Listen, we'll get it figured out. My sister Lora is a beast when it comes to business management. Between all of us Bells, we should manage to find a solution." She reached out and cupped his jaw impulsively but the minute her hand connected with his skin, she knew it'd been a mistake. She withdrew as if scalded and started to apologize but Gabe simply captured her hand in his and drew her slowly closer.

"Since we're being honest…I have something to tell you," he said, his thumb rubbing a slow, lazy but sensual pattern on the sensitive skin of her wrist. "Something I've been struggling with personally."

With him touching her in such a manner, she found it hard to breathe. "Such as?"

"It's you. And me. That kiss the other night…" he said, causing her breath to catch in her chest at the memory. "It awoke something in me that I would've preferred stayed dead to the world."

She didn't know what to say; she'd felt something, too. "I understand," she murmured. "It's complicated."

"Not really." He chuckled with dark humor, regarding her with a stare that went straight through her. "I'm a man who has been stifling any and all sexual urges since the day his wife died for the sake of his daughter. And it was working until I met you. Now, after that kiss, all I can think of is how I want to do it again. Do you have any idea how hard it was to keep from climbing into that bed beside you last night? You were passed out cold and I still wanted to feel your body against mine. That's reprehensible! I'm not that guy, but with you, it's hard to remember that simple fact and I'm ashamed of where my thoughts go every time I see you. Just two minutes ago I was telling myself to keep my hands to myself but here I am…touching you and not the least bit sorry."

She blinked against his impassioned admission and her breathing quickened in response as her own gaze zeroed in on his mouth. She wanted him like a fat kid wanted cake. He was right; it wasn't complicated at all.

"Say something," he demanded.

"I can't." She licked her lips, suddenly helpless with the overwhelming awareness that they were two consenting adults locked away in a bungalow with an hour to themselves. "There's nothing I could say that would make this any better. I want you, too," she whispered, knowing that probably wasn't going to make things any less difficult to manage.

"Damn," he murmured, his eyes darkening as he clasped her to him. "I was hoping you weren't going to say that."

Her breath hitched in her throat at the openly lustful look in Gabe's eyes. She should say something to put a stop to this, but she was already trembling, desperately wanting to feel him against her, inside her. She was swamped by feelings that were wild and inescapable; it was all she could do to hang on for dear life and wait for the ride to end.

Gabe's arms went around her, cupping her rear and pulling her to him. She gasped at his firm grip, thrilling at the feeling of being manhandled. Gone was the conservative businessman who'd arrived on the first day looking stiff as hardened concrete; he was replaced by a man who was dedicated to satisfying his desire to touch and consume.

CHAPTER FOURTEEN

His mouth traveled everywhere; the column of her neck, the valley of her breasts, her lips, earlobes and down her belly.

He pushed her against the kitchen counter and she braced herself with her elbows as he jerked her sarong off to reveal her bikini bottoms. His growl of appreciation at the dainty scrap of material caused goose bumps to erupt up and down her body. He eased the fabric free from her hips and gazed at her most private of places.

"Open your legs for me, gorgeous," he instructed softly and she did, slowly, feeling as vulnerable as she'd ever felt with another person. It wasn't as if she'd never done this with another man; it was the way Gabe was admiring her body as though she'd cornered the market on female perfection. His stare devoured her and she could barely breathe from the way her heart was hammering.

His hands returned to her rear and cupped her cheeks to bring her to his mouth. His tongue delved into her hot folds on a seek-and-destroy mission, one he was determined to accomplish. She groaned as his mouth and tongue worked with the expertise of a man who knew his way around a woman's body and understood what to do to make her quake. Her knees felt ready to buckle as he gently but persistently worked the sensitive nub hidden within her very center until her toes were curling and her legs stiffened as an orgasm came barreling down her nerve endings, obliterating everything. "Gabe!" she gasped, threading her fingers through his hair, ready to collapse. "Oh! That's it!"

She shuddered and Gabe withdrew with a wolfish, almost feral expression. Before she could say a word, he'd lifted her into his arms to carry her to the bedroom. It was sweet and chivalrous, yet intensely sexy, given that she could smell her own musk on his skin and it was driving her wild.

"Do you know how many times I've dreamed of doing this very thing?" he murmured, nuzzling her neck. "Too many to count."

Lindy closed her eyes and he gently laid her across the bed. She started to untie her bikini top but he stopped her, saying, "Let me." He proceeded as if unwrapping a highly anticipated Christmas present, putting off the final reveal of her breasts until the last possible second. When she was finally free from the top, he leaned back and exhaled low and soft. Lindy lifted herself on her elbows and grinned. "See something you like?" she teased, knowing she had great breasts. They were small but perfectly pert and round, just right for squeezing and kissing.

"You have no idea," he groaned, moving to push her down with his body. He cradled her head as he moved his mouth over hers, leisurely but hungrily tasting her, and Lindy could feel the insistent press of his erection against her pelvis. The pressure was intoxicating and she moaned from the anticipation. He raised himself and slipped a nipple into his mouth, tugging and teasing with his tongue against the hardened tip. She arched, allowing him better access, and he responded by sucking the entire areola into his greedy mouth.

"So beautiful," he murmured against her skin in awe. "Your skin is like a soft peach."

Lindy smiled but didn't have time to respond properly for Gabe had moved to her other breast, laving it with the same attention as the first, and she was too busy drowning in the sensations that were spiraling from the tips of her nipples and pooling lower. Soon she was writhing, begging to feel him inside her. "Gabe," she pleaded, wrapping her long legs around his torso and drawing him closer. "I need you now! Please tell me you have protection!"

Gabe groaned and disentangled himself to stumble to his dresser drawer and yank it open. "I didn't imagine I'd need to use them but a buddy of mine insisted that I come prepared and I stuffed them into my carry bag," he said with mild embarrassment. His hands shook as he fumbled around, cursing when he didn't immediately find what he was searching for. When he exclaimed softly she grinned. He flashed the condom package and tossed it to the bed while he shucked his shorts. She took the opportunity to get a good look at his equipment and was delighted to find Gabe had been hiding an impressive package behind those boring khaki Dockers. "Gabe, I never would've guessed," she teased, causing him to blush as he slid the condom on. "If things don't work out in business, I know another industry in L.A. that would love to have you."

"Not in a million years," he said, coming over to her with a dark grin. "I'm a one-woman kind of guy."

"I like that," she murmured, wrapping her arms around his neck and drawing him to her. "Now show me what you can do with that bad boy."

"My pleasure."

Lindy's breath caught as Gabe's erection pressed

against her opening and slid inside. She clung to him as he pushed until he was seated to the hilt, his forehead resting against hers as he fought for control. She sensed a difference in him and gently directed his mouth to hers. Something told her he hadn't been with anyone since his wife and it humbled her beyond anything she'd ever known that he'd chosen her to take that step with. She kissed him deeply, sucking his tongue into her mouth, reminding him that he was here with her now, and nothing else mattered. For better or worse, this moment belonged to them and no one else.

Gabe withdrew only to bury his erection again deep inside. He whispered her name as he began to build a rhythm and sweat had begun to bead their bodies in the balmy heat. Lindy moved with him, matching him stroke for stroke, urging him on as they careened toward that magical moment, demanding from each other's bodies every sensation, every groan.

And then it happened.

Lindy stiffened as Gabe continued to rub and pound at a particularly good spot and every muscle tightened in a delicious contraction that had her gasping, panting, almost unabashedly squealing his name as a starburst of insane pleasure exploded throughout her body. She clamped down with her internal muscles and suddenly Gabe shouted to the ceiling and his eyelids squeezed shut as he found his own orgasm, and judging by the way he was shuddering, it was huge.

One final spastic thrust later, Gabe rolled off Lindy and collapsed beside her, his breathing as harsh as her own. They lay there, stunned and still rocking against the waves of pleasure coursing through them, and Lindy knew with a certainty that she'd be willing to bet her life upon that this was no average experience, for either of them.

This was big.

This was epic.

This was…bad timing.

GABE'S HEART WAS pounding so hard he thought it might jump from his chest and land on the hardwood floor. If he'd been in worse shape he would've been worried about having a heart attack. Feelings he'd shut down for a long time came rushing to the surface, and to his horror, tears sprang to his eyes. He squeezed his eyelids to prevent the moisture from seeping out but it was too late. The slow, inevitable slide of tears oozed from his eyes and he choked back the emotion that followed. Suddenly, he felt Lindy's touch on his chest and he opened his eyes to see Lindy staring at him with understanding.

"I'm sorry. I've ruined it, haven't I?" he asked in a chagrined tone, but she simply shook her head, surprising him with her empathy. He swallowed and wiped at his eyes, embarrassed. "I don't usually cry after sex. It's just that…"

"You haven't had sex with anyone since your wife died," she supplied with a soft, knowing look in her eyes.

He affirmed her supposition with a nod. "I just couldn't bring myself to look at anyone like that after she died. It felt like cheating even though she was gone."

"You don't have to apologize," Lindy said, moving to lay her head on his softly furred chest. She threaded her fingers through the crinkly hairs. "You loved her and you were grieving. That's only natural."

Gabe quieted and then admitted, "I wasn't always the best husband. I think after she died, anytime I started to feel any kind of attraction toward someone, I shut it down because the guilt was more than I could bear. In the end, it was just easier to ignore that part of my life and bury myself in work."

"I think your wife would've wanted you to be happy, right?"

"Yes. She was the most giving person I'd ever met."

"Well, then what held you back? What *really* held you back?"

"Carys," he answered, sighing. "I didn't want her to think I was trying to replace her mother with someone else so I just made sure there was never anyone else to contend with. In a way, it was easier because it was just Carys and me. But it was lonely, too." He tightened his arms around Lindy, loving the feel of her against him, but it troubled him. Just because they'd made love didn't mean anything had changed. In fact, likely it made things worse. "Lindy…" he started, but she must've sensed where he was going with this because she sat up and smiled, putting her finger against his lips.

"I know."

"You know?"

"Yes. I'm a smart girl," she quipped with a teasing smile that was a little sad around the edges. "You're worried about my influence on Carys because I don't fit the mold of what you deem appropriate for her. I get it. I'm an actress. I live in L.A. My lifestyle isn't exactly kid-friendly. Trust me, I get it."

"Does that hurt your feelings?" he asked, worried.

"I'm not going to lie—yeah a little, but I can't get too hurt about it. You make valid points. I'm not sure I'd want me around my kid, either." She chuckled, then sighed. "How about this…finish out your stay here and then when you go we'll both have wonderful memories and go our separate ways. I'll do my best to display nothing but appropriate behavior for Carys, and in the meantime, I'll help you to mend your relationship with her. Sound like a deal?"

"What about us?" he asked, his gaze trailing to her glorious bare breasts, already aching to touch her again. "I'm not sure I can stay away now that I've had a taste."

Her gaze darkened and fresh desire pounded through his veins as she murmured, "We'll just have to be discreet. You can do that, can't you?" Lindy brushed a teasing kiss across his mouth and he barely held back the impulse to pin her to the bed again. "Just say yes," she instructed softly and he nodded like a good boy hoping for a treat. He followed with a firm kiss against her lips, taking her tongue into his mouth to tangle with his own.

"No kissing, no touching in public," he said, punctuating the rules with another kiss. "No indication that we're seeing each other privately."

"Sounds good," she responded, climbing on top of him, positioning her hot heat right above his quickly awakening manhood. "How much time do we have before the hour is up?" she asked, breathlessly.

"Long enough," he growled, rising up to meet her with his mouth.

She wrapped her legs around him and pressed her breasts against his chest, murmuring, "Well then, let's see how good you are with time management."

"Challenge accepted," he said, moving to flip her onto her back, causing her to giggle. But soon her laughter turned to moans, followed by high-pitched cries, and by the end, he had scratches on his back to go with his satisfied smile.

Discretion…he wasn't sure how this was going to

work out, but he'd be a liar if he said he wasn't interested in finding out.

Lindy was like a drug in his system and he wasn't ready to detox.

The only thing that worried him was…would he ever be ready to let her go? He'd have to be. Lindy wasn't offering forever. For that matter, he hadn't offered it, either.

CHAPTER FIFTEEN

LINDY LEFT GABE'S bungalow, her mind moving in slow, lazy circles from sexual satisfaction, but soon enough questions began to ruin all those feel-good feelings.

Could they really be discreet enough to fool everyone? Her sisters would be hard to fool, particularly Lilah, but she wasn't really worried about them. Lora would simply frown and go on about fraternizing romantically with the patrons, and Lilah would probably warn her about getting hurt when the Westons left. It was Carys who worried her.

She didn't want the girl to find out. The thought of facing Carys with the news that she was shacking up with Gabe made her stomach roll uncomfortably. She doubted Carys would simply punch her in the arm like a girlfriend and say, "Good job!" Egad. What was she thinking? Lindy fidgeted with the fringe on her sarong. The memory of seeing Carys angry and grieving for her mother came back to scratch at Lindy's conscience. Hell, Lindy thought with real fear, the kid might end up hating her for messing around with her dad—and well she should. She had no business being with Gabe casually.

Of course, there was also an opposite problem to consider. What if—in a shocking reversal—Carys actually embraced the idea of Lindy hanging around in more than a friendly capacity with Gabe? Worse! Because neither Gabe nor Lindy were in it for the long haul and because of that, where would their arrangement leave Carys when they finally left St. John?

Crushed.

Lindy worried a hangnail on her finger and almost ran smack into Lora.

"There you are," Lora exclaimed with a hint of exasperation. "How'd it go with your producer friend?"

Lindy grimaced. Well, now was as good a time as any to get this over with. "It didn't go as well as I'd hoped. They're not going to budge from their current location. I'm sorry, Lora. I tried."

"It's okay," Lora said, smiling. "I knew it was a long shot. I made some inroads with Sears Holdings Corporation but it'll be a few weeks before I can get a meeting with their travel VP. In the meantime, we'll just have to see what we can scare up locally. I was thinking we ought to see which charter companies are looking to partner for a split profit. We've never done that before, but I think it might serve us well to diversify."

"Billy might be up to partnering with us," Lindy suggested, and Lora nodded.

"I'll have Heath talk to him and see if he wants to sit down and talk business."

"I'd suggest Heath do the talking. If you recall, you and Billy aren't exactly close."

"Right," Lora said with a resigned grimace as she muttered, "That man can sure hold a grudge."

"Well, before you got all lovey-dovey, you were a bit of a hard-ass, remember?"

"Is everyone going to hold that against me for the rest of my life?" she asked, irritated. "Geesh, what do I gotta do for a little forgiveness? It wasn't as if I drowned kittens or something equally awful in my spare time."

Lindy chuckled. "True. You ought to put that on your résumé."

"Hey, on a separate note, I heard that Mr. Weston and his daughter were moving to the Worchester?" she asked, worried.

"No, I think we got that smoothed out. It was a small misunderstanding."

Lora looked askance at Lindy. "Did *you* have anything to do with that misunderstanding?"

"Perhaps. But I also had something to do with the resolution. So I think I've been redeemed."

Lora exhaled in exasperation. "Lindy, don't go messing around with the patrons. We need them to leave happy and wanting to return or at the very least eager to give glowing reviews. Okay?"

"You worry too much," Lindy said, smiling. "Loosen up, sis."

"Argh. And you need to…oh, never mind. So he's staying? Good. At least that's one worry off my mind. Have you seen Pops? I need to talk to him about his birdhouse project. He has sawdust everywhere on the patio."

Lindy turned wistful, remembering when Grams was alive. "Pops was always making her birdhouses. And they were so awful, but Grams acted as if she loved every single one of them."

Lora allowed a short smile, but Lindy could tell memories of Grams were painful. "Yes. Pops could do a lot of things, but making birdhouses was not one of them. Not for lack of trying, though, that's for sure."

Each reflected for a short moment, lost in their own private recollections of Grams until Lindy remembered something she wanted to broach with Lora. "Hey, I'm still worried about Lilah."

"Why?"

"It's a gut instinct thing, but I think she's getting worse. She may be depressed. She might need to talk to a therapist or something."

"Yeah," Lora said, her tone conveying her concern, as well. "I've been wondering the same, but each time I try to bring up the subject, she shuts me down pretty quick. I didn't want to be the overbearing older sister so I've backed away, but it does worry me a bit. What have you seen?"

"Well, it's nothing overt, but Billy said he sees her walking late at night on the beach and that's just weird."

"She likes to walk the beach at night—that's not particularly strange," Lora disagreed. "Heath takes an early-morning swim before the sun comes up."

"This is different," Lindy insisted. "Maybe it's a twin thing, but something is off. I'm really worried. Billy said he's seen her at two and three in the morning, walking the beach. That's not a normal stroll after dinner."

"Two in the morning? You're right…that's not normal. Okay. We'll talk to her, but chances are she's just, I don't know, going through something that she doesn't want everyone poking their noses into."

"Maybe," Lindy allowed, but still her gut told her Lilah was hurting and no one was paying enough attention.

"In the meantime, we need to start brainstorming again. The next IRS payment will be due in November and it will be here before we know it. I don't want to be sitting around in October wringing our hands. I want a solid plan in action."

Lindy did a mock salute and said, "Yes, ma'am!"

Lora sent her a short look, muttering, "You're hilarious…." before heading off, leaving Lindy to go in search of Lilah.

GABE FOUND CARYS practicing painting with Lilah in the bright and sunny atrium. When Carys saw Gabe her expression dimmed and a pout started to form.

"Before you get all sass-mouthed again, we're staying," he informed her, then turned to Lilah and said, "Thanks for keeping her busy, but would you mind if we chatted in private?"

"No problem," Lilah murmured, gathering her supplies. "Feel free to take as long as you need. The atrium is available to all guests."

Lilah hustled out of the room and Gabe took a seat beside Carys with a grave expression. "We need to talk about your attitude, as in it has to improve."

Carys remained silent and returned to her watercolors until Gabe plucked her brush from her fingers with a stern look. "Carys…I mean it. You can't spew ugly words and a bad attitude every time something doesn't go your way. How would you feel if I did that to you? Or worse, how do you think your mom would feel if she saw you acting like that? I know we raised you better than that and it kills me when you act like a spoiled brat because, deep down, I know you're not like that."

"How would you know? You weren't around," she said dully. "Mom was always the one there for me and now she's gone."

Gabe took a deep breath. "You're right. I wasn't there enough. I can try to apologize a million different ways, but it won't change a thing. All I can do is promise to be better from this point forward."

"But what about your work?"

"It's true I work a lot, but maybe I need to start delegating more instead of taking on so much myself. Your mom made it so I could do that, but I realize now that I shouldn't have put everything on her shoulders. I thought what I was doing was what was right for the family by being a good provider, but somewhere along the way I took it to another level."

"Mom used to look sad," Carys said softly, glancing at him to catch his reaction. Gabe felt her statement like a punch to the gut.

"Really?"

"Yeah…she tried to hide it but I saw her crying sometimes when you worked late."

"Carys…I loved your mom but I could've been a better husband," he said. "I wish I could make it right, but I can't. That's something I have to deal with on my own. But your mom was a beautiful, gentle person and we were both lucky to have her in our lives for as long as we did."

Carys nodded, her eyes watering. "When will I stop missing her?"

"I hope you never stop missing her," he said, surprising her. "She's a part of you and that will never change. We will always miss her, but eventually it will stop hurting so much that she's gone."

Carys sniffed, then said, "Being here helps me to feel less lost. I like it here. Lindy and her family…they make me feel like I belong somewhere. They never shoo me away or tell me to find something else to do because they're too busy to deal with me."

"I'm sorry. I do that, don't I?"

Again Carys nodded and wiped at the tears leaking down her face. She stared at her fingers as she said, "I don't want to leave and you didn't even give me the chance to tell you why I wanted to stay."

"True. I should've taken your feelings into consideration. I apologize for that." She glanced up at him, startled at his admission. He smiled. "What? Dads can't admit to mistakes? Hell, I make plenty. But I also take responsibility for when I'm wrong," he said, sending her a meaningful look. "Is there something you'd like to say?" When Carys looked sheepishly away, he prodded her gently. "C'mon, it goes both ways when people are wrong to each other."

"I'm sorry," she whispered.

"That's my girl. Come give me a hug," he said, and she climbed into his arms like a spider monkey. He hugged her tightly and closed his eyes against the pang in his heart. He loved this girl more than anything in this world. He should've been better at showing that everything he did, he did for her benefit.

She pulled away and wiped at the tears dribbling from her pretty eyes. "Daddy…why'd you want to leave?" she asked.

"I guess I was being a little overprotective. I know you're a smart girl and you know what's right and wrong. Besides, this is a great place. I doubt the Worchester has half the cool factor that Larimar has," he said, teasing.

"Dang straight," Carys said, recovering with a watery grin. "And Celly said you can't swim at the Worchester beach cuz it's full of parasites from all the yachts. They just dump their poo right into the water! Ewwww…"

He grimaced. "That's pretty disgusting," he agreed. "Glad we're staying, then."

"Yeah, me, too." Carys smiled up at Gabe and then plucked her art from the easel. "See what Lilah showed me how to do? Isn't it pretty? It's a dolphin."

Gabe admired his daughter's handiwork with pride. "This is very good. Lilah taught you?"

"Yep. She's a real artist. You should see some of her art. It's amazing," Carys said, her eyes sparkling. "Oh, Daddy, you ought to buy some of her art for your office. It would totally look great above your desk and I bet she'd give you a good price. We should ask her."

"Maybe," Gabe said, not quite sure if that was going to happen. It was one thing to appreciate the artistic talents of someone who helped an eleven-year-old produce a nice doodle, but quite another to purchase art for his business. But he figured there was no harm in checking out Lilah's art for appearances' sake. "Is her art in the gallery here at Larimar?"

"Oh no, she doesn't let anyone see her art. She's very private about it," Carys answered solemnly. "She only let me see because I was so upset."

"Oh. Okay," he said. "Then how will I see it?"

"I'll talk to her," Carys said confidently. "Lilah is shy about her art. It takes a certain touch."

The way his daughter sounded so mature made him chuckle, but it also gave him pause. His daughter was growing up faster than he would've imagined. It made him sad to wonder what he'd been missing out on in his quest to bury his grief in work.

"All right, how about some food?" he suggested, to which Carys jumped up and suggested Sailor's. "Of course. I mean, you can never eat too many hamburgers when you're on vacation, right?" he teased.

"And we should ask Lindy if she wants to go, too!"

"Sure," he said with an easy smile, but inside he was hesitant. Would he be able to be around Lindy without giving away the fact that when he saw her, all he pictured was her without her clothes? Just the thought caused his heart rate to quicken and he ruefully wondered if he was on course for a disaster. He supposed there was only one way to find out.

CHAPTER SIXTEEN

GABE FOUND LINDY with the intent of inviting her to lunch with him and Carys, but it was hard to quell the sudden rise in body temperature when he saw her standing in the lobby, chatting with another guest.

It took everything in him to wait patiently and not sweep her into his arms and plant possessive kisses all over her body. She simply sparkled. There was something about her that drew people like moths to a flame or butterflies to a flower. He couldn't believe he hadn't seen it before. It was more than just beauty; she had that effervescent quality that stars possessed and he was struck by the overwhelming desire to casually walk over to her and sling his arm around her shoulders like some hormonal teen with his first girlfriend. Damn, he thought to himself, more than mildly alarmed at his gut reaction. How was he supposed to remain discreet if he couldn't even keep his hands to himself for two seconds? Thankfully, Carys took care of the immediate problem and didn't wait for him.

"Lindy!" she exclaimed with the natural exuberance of a child. "We're going to Sailor's. Wanna come?"

The guest drifted away and Lindy grinned at Carys. "I never give up a chance to eat at my favorite place, but I was trying to find Lilah." She glanced over at Gabe and he could've sworn sparks flared to life between them. Her cheeks pinked with high color and a small smile toyed with her lips as if she was replaying the same memory as he was. He coughed and looked away, breaking the spell.

"Maybe another time?" he suggested, and Carys reacted with visible disappointment.

"Why can't we just invite Lilah, too?" Carys asked.

"I don't know where she's at," Lindy admitted, glancing around the lobby. "I was hoping she was around so I could talk to her about something."

"Celly probably knows where she is," Carys offered helpfully.

"You're right," Lindy agreed, turning to Gabe. "If you wouldn't mind waiting for a few minutes for me while I look for Lilah…"

"Of course," he said, smiling around the giddy feeling that followed knowing she was going to lunch with them. "I'll go start the car."

"I'm going to help Lindy find Lilah," Carys piped up, and slipped her hand into Lindy's. The action surprised Gabe, but when Lindy smiled down at his daughter, something tightened dangerously in his heart. Things were happening at a terrifying pace. He'd never felt so wildly charged about another person. Seeing Lindy with Carys, so openly affectionate, made something else happen for him that he wasn't prepared for. He recognized the feeling, but he pushed it away. He'd never disrespect Lindy by thinking of her as a good-time girl or island booty call, but he had to keep reminding himself that neither of them were playing for keeps. He watched as Carys and Lindy disappeared down the main hallway, clasped hands swinging as they walked.

It was too easy to imagine Lindy in his life permanently. He knew he had to nip those thoughts in the bud. But he had no idea how to stop them from continually popping up.

LINDY AND CARYS found Lilah in the atrium, tending to Grams's many tropical plants. She didn't hear them enter and seemed lost in her own world.

Lindy's earlier conversation with Lora came to mind and immediately worry returned to her thoughts about her twin. "Hey, Li," she said, startling her sister into almost dropping the water can. "Sorry, didn't mean to scare you. Carys and I wondered if you'd like to go to Sailor's with us to get some lunch."

Lilah smiled at Carys and smoothed her hair but shook her head. "Thanks for the offer, but I'm really not hungry right now. Plus, I have to get the watering done or else these plants will wither away to nothing and I'd never be able to forgive myself."

"C'mon, Li, you need to get out for a while. When was the last time you just went and had some fun?"

Lilah sent her a strange look that caused a discordant tremble down Lindy's back and murmured that she needed to return to her watering.

Carys looked to Lindy with a question in her eyes, and even though Lindy could tell by the way her sister's shoulders were set that she wasn't going to change her mind, she tried anyway. "Li, you know you can't resist Sailor's...cheeseburger with fries...root beer..." she said, trying to tempt her.

Lilah sighed, the sound slightly irritated, and said, "I'm not hungry. I'm actually going to finish the watering and then maybe go take a nap. I haven't been sleeping well and I just want to lie down for a little bit, okay?"

"Oh," Lindy said, relenting grudgingly, but she

couldn't help but add quietly, "Maybe if you weren't walking from here to kingdom come every night till three in the morning, you wouldn't be so tired."

Lilah looked at her sharply and just when Lindy thought her twin was going to respond with something sarcastic for butting into her business, she shrugged and agreed with a nod. "Maybe so."

Lindy had been deliberately trying to bait Lilah to see if she could get some kind of response, but when her attempt fell flat, she simply felt bad for trying to goad her. "Hey, in all seriousness, I wish you weren't out walking the beaches so late. It's not like it used to be when we were kids. There are bad people roaming the beaches when everyone's asleep."

"You worry too much," Lilah scoffed gently with a smile as she returned to her watering. "I haven't run across anyone more disturbing than Cracky Dan and he's been around for years. I'm fine."

"Who's Cracky Dan?" Carys asked, curious.

Lindy glanced at Carys. "He's the local crack addict. He's harmless but really gone in the head. Sometimes he sweeps the floors at the local restaurants for scraps of food and a cup of coffee. He's older than dirt. I can't even believe he's still alive."

"He's not that old—he just looks like it," Lilah said.

"How do you know?"

"I asked him," she said simply.

"Lilah," Lindy gasped. "Why are you talking with crack addicts?"

"Why not? They're people, too," Lilah reminded Lindy. "Besides, the way I look at it, he's just a guy who took a lot of wrong turns in his life. Could happen to any of us."

Lindy supposed that was true, but it still made her

uncomfortable to know that Lilah was associating with people who were unstable. It definitely didn't reassure her about Lilah's mental health, that was certain. But seeing as Lilah was pretty firm about not going to lunch with them, Lindy sighed and said, "Okay, I hope you get some rest. Gabe's waiting for us in the car."

"Have fun," Lilah said, smiling.

As they left the atrium, Carys said, "Lilah is a fairy. It's like she drifts on the wind."

"Yeah…she's usually in her own world." More so lately, Lindy wanted to add but kept that private worry to herself. Switching gears, she said, "We'd better hustle. Your dad is probably wondering if we got lost. And I'm starved!"

"Me, too!" Carys said, grinning as they started to run toward the door. They found Gabe waiting patiently in the car, his face lighting up when he saw them emerge from the front doors.

She was struck by how devastatingly handsome he was, and that wasn't a term she used lightly. Previously, she'd only reserved that term for George Clooney, Sean Connery and that new actor who'd played Thor. Now she could add Gabe Weston to that list.

"No Lilah?" Gabe surmised as they piled into the car.

"She has other plans," Lindy answered, forcing a bright smile.

"She has to water plants and take a nap," Carys supplied as she buckled her seat belt.

Gabe cast Lindy a questioning look, which she ignored. She wasn't going to get into that conversation right now. Her worries were too personal and sharing them would clearly go against their previous arrangement to keep things surface deep between them.

"So, we're celebrating," Carys announced as they drove.

"Oh?" both Gabe and Lindy answered, intrigued.

"We're celebrating because Dad came to his senses and realized it was dumb to check out of Larimar and move to the Worchester. Did you know they have parasites in their water? Their beach is dirty!"

"You've been talking to Celly, I see," Lindy said drily. "Well, I'm sure their beach is nice but Larimar is just that much more special."

"You got that right," Carys agreed, leaning back in her seat, smiling.

Lindy stole a look at Gabe's profile and her breath hitched in her throat. She didn't know how he'd remained single after his wife had died. Surely women must've been chasing after him in droves. Successful, handsome, smart... Unless he had some really disgusting personal habit that he was hiding, he was a real catch. Any woman would be lucky to call him her man.

Even her. Lindy swallowed and looked away, hating where her mind had gone. She wasn't the kind of woman he was looking for, and he wasn't the kind of man who'd mesh well with her current circles. Good God, she could only imagine how annoyed he'd be by most of her friends.

"What was it like growing up here?" Carys asked.

"Most of the time it was amazing," she answered candidly. "But there were other times when it wasn't so great."

"Like when?"

"Like when a hurricane came through and one of my good friends in high school was killed by a piece of roof that had come free and hit him as he was trying to get his grandmother to safety."

"Oh," Carys said, stunned. "That's awful. Was his grandmother okay?"

"Yeah," she answered with a sad smile. "He gave his life for her, actually. She finally died many years later a really old lady in her bed."

"Wow. Do hurricanes happen a lot here?"

"At least once a year, but it depends on the severity. Sometimes it's just a bunch of wind and rain—other times, it's pretty gnarly. Reminds you that you're not in charge, that's for sure."

Realizing she'd just cast a pall on their lunch trip, she tried to brighten things up. "You have to take the good with the bad and this place is no different, except there's way more good than bad so that's a pretty sweet trade. For example, our prom was on the beach and we all wore flip-flops. How cool is that?"

"Pretty cool," Carys agreed, grinning. "What else?"

"Well, my first boyfriend got a boat instead of a car for his sixteenth birthday, and we all used to go out and sail the Caribbean on the weekends. That's pretty sweet."

"My friend Sara's older sister got an older Porsche for her sixteenth birthday but I think a sailboat is way cooler," Carys said. "If we lived here would I get a boat for my sixteenth birthday?" she asked her dad and Lindy thought Gabe was going to drive off the road.

"Let's not skip ahead—you're going to give me a heart attack," he said, causing both Lindy and Carys to break into a fit of giggles.

Gabe did a good job of finding a parking spot—no small feat on the island—and they walked into the tiny restaurant.

Lindy waved at the waitress and smiled, gesturing for two beers and a root beer and then they took a seat by the window. The place didn't have any air-conditioning so it was possibly warmer inside than it was outside, but Lindy was already acclimating to the heat. Gabe, not so much.

"I didn't expect this humidity," he admitted, wiping at his brow. "It surely didn't have this listed on the brochure," he joked.

Lindy wrapped her hair into a messy bun on top of her head and simply grinned. "You'll get used to it and by the time you're ready to leave, you'll hardly notice."

"I doubt it. I always feel wet here."

"I like it," Carys said. "It's so warm. I bet it never gets cold here. It's always freezing in San Francisco."

"Is that where you live?" Lindy asked, glancing at Gabe, surprised. "I didn't know you lived in California."

"You never asked," he countered evenly. "Yes, we live just outside of the city in Marin County."

Lindy digested that information, not sure why she didn't realize he was also in California. "I live in Los Angeles," she offered, to which he nodded.

"I knew that," he said. "The actress thing gave it away."

"Ah." She grabbed a menu and stared at it, though she didn't really need the menu. The menu at Sailor's hadn't changed in decades and she always ordered the same thing. Knowing Gabe lived in California, too, put a different spin on her previous comfort level with the short-term-fling idea. With him living in the same state, the opportunity to see each other would arise. Would they want to? California was a big state and they basically lived ten hours away from one another if they traveled by car. Only an hour and fifteen minutes by plane. But it wasn't as if she had access to a plane all the time and that could get expensive.

Why was she even considering this? They weren't going to continue their relationship beyond his stay at

Larimar so it was a moot point. She returned her menu to the table with a bright, strained smile. "I know what I'm getting. How about you guys?"

"Hamburger," they both said and laughed. Lindy smiled at how cute they both were.

"Lindy, tell me about what it's like to be a famous actress living in L.A."

"Hold up there, not famous yet," Lindy corrected Carys with a laugh. "But not for lack of trying. It's a hard field to break into and there are plenty who never make it. I just hope I'm not one of those poor saps."

"What was your biggest part so far?" Carys asked, her eyes sparkling.

Lindy thought hard about this answer. She had parts she wasn't entirely proud of. Naked Girl No. 3 came to mind, where she basically had to lie there with another naked woman and act like a rock star groupie who'd just engaged in the orgy of all orgies. Surprisingly, it wasn't soft-core porn—it was actually a big-name director who had directed the flick—but it'd had a limited box office release due to the NC-17 rating it'd received and Lindy hadn't gotten the bump in exposure, aside from that of her behind, that she'd been hoping for. She cleared her throat and answered, saying, "Well, I'm trying to think of something you might've seen…. Oh, I know. I had a bit part on a *CSI* episode. I was Sexy Blonde No. 2. Unfortunately, my character died and I had to spend two days lying on a slab looking dead. It wasn't fun. And the slab was cold. But I'd do anything for my art," she added theatrically, causing Carys to giggle and Gabe to smile.

"Do you go to Hollywood parties?" Carys asked.

Lindy met Gabe's curious stare and she was deliberately evasive. "Some. But they're not all that fun. A lot of self-important goobers chatting it up with other self-important goobers."

"Oh," Carys said, disappointed. "I thought it'd be more glamorous than that."

"Glamour is an illusion, kiddo. Don't buy into it and you'll save yourself a lot of heartache."

"I still think it sounds supercool," Carys said with a gleam in her eyes.

"Okay, let's order, shall we?" Gabe suggested and Lindy agreed. Time to change the subject. Making movies wasn't as sensational as it seemed, and for some it was downright devastating to their self-esteem, integrity and everything they held dear about themselves. She wasn't sure she'd encourage any child to go into the field, which seemed a little contradictory since she was still trying to break in.

"I have to go to the bathroom," Carys announced and popped from her chair to go to the small restroom at the back of the restaurant.

"I know, I know, don't fill her head with movie-star dreams," she said as soon as Carys was clear. Gabe surprised her by leaning over and kissing her. She leaned into his kiss, eager to feel him again. Her eyelids fluttered open when he'd pulled away. "What was that for?" she asked.

"Because I couldn't hold back another second."

She felt herself blush. Nice to know she wasn't alone in this struggle. "We're traveling the same wavelength," she admitted in a husky whisper. "But this could become a problem. You know…the *being discreet* thing?"

"Yeah," he admitted with a grimace but his eyes danced with open desire. "I'm getting the same feeling."

She tried not to let her mind wander into dirty places, but she couldn't help it. He must've read her mind because he chuckled and actually shifted in his seat as if he were having a problem down there. "Okay, think PG-13 stuff. No, I take that back. Let's talk about basketball and rocks. Anything that couldn't possibly remind us of what we'd rather be doing right this second."

"Ohh, that didn't help at all," she murmured, glancing up as Carys emerged from the restroom. "Here she comes. Back to your corner, mister."

"You're the sexiest woman I've ever met," he said in a low voice, sending shivers down her back.

"Shh," she said, just in time for Carys to plop back in her seat.

"Did you order?" Carys asked hopefully.

Lindy shook her head. "Not yet, but we all know exactly what we want so as soon as the waitress gets her butt over here, we'll order."

"Good, cuz I'm starved."

Lindy met Gabe's hungry stare and they both thought the same thing.

They were starved, all right.

But not for food, and Lindy almost melted at the smoldering look Gabe was covertly sending her way.

Holy hell, being discreet was going to kill them both, but what a way to go!

CHAPTER SEVENTEEN

"TELL ME WHAT it's like to be on a movie set," Carys said, before taking a big bite from her hamburger. Her eyes were lit up with anticipatory glee, and Lindy couldn't help but get caught up in her enthusiasm even though she knew whatever she said would probably only further glamorize the business.

"Well, when you're on a movie, it's like everyone is a family because you're all working long hours and you're on the set longer than you're at home. And a movie set is like a small city—everything you could possibly need is provided for you. And if you're one of the stars you get your own trailer, which is supercool."

"Have you ever had your own trailer?" Carys asked.

"No," she admitted. "But I've had some pretty neat experiences on the set nonetheless."

"Such as?" Carys asked.

Gabe cleared his throat and lifted his brow, as if to say, keep it kid-friendly, and Lindy grinned. "Okay, once I was on this B-movie set—it was the worst, let me tell you—but we were shooting at this supposedly haunted castle, and you know, I grew up with stories of *jumbies* and whatnot so I went in with a healthy respect. But my cast mates didn't and some freaky stuff happened to them while we were there."

Carys's eyes were round saucers. "Like?"

"Well, the lead actress, a total wench and a half by the

name of—well, I probably shouldn't name names—anyway, she was a *nightmare* to work with. The crew hated her, the director hated her—and I think he was *sleeping* with her but he still couldn't stand her so that goes to show just how wretched she was—and her fellow cast mates wanted to strangle her by the time the production had wrapped. We were all sitting around chatting, waiting for our call times, when she overheard us talking about the stories and ghosts that were documented in this castle. She happened to walk by and mocked all of us for telling stories, calling us nothing better than a bunch of sixth graders at band camp trying to scare one another. I tried to warn her that the *jumbies* were listening but she just scoffed at my 'backward island craziness' and went to her trailer." Lindy lowered her voice as if imparting a great secret as she continued, "Later that night, she ran shrieking from her trailer saying she woke up to find a man staring at her but when security searched the trailer and the surrounding area they didn't find anyone."

Gabe seemed intrigued as he asked, "So what happened next? Was someone playing a practical joke on her or something?"

"Well, when the woman gave a description of the man in her trailer, it was exactly the same as one of the apparitions that supposedly haunted the castle. Coincidence? I think not."

"Whoa," Carys breathed, audibly swallowing. "That's creepy."

Lindy laughed. "She deserved it. Trust me when I say we were all hoping she'd get a scare of some sort. She was annoying in her snobbery."

"On that note, are we finished with lunch?" Gabe

asked, gathering their trash and depositing it in the waste bin. "Because I'm ready for the beach!"

Carys whooped and bounced from her chair. "Let's go to Maho, it was less crowded than Trunk," she said and skipped from Sailor's straight to the car.

Gabe grabbed Lindy's hand and drew her to him. "Was that story true? Or just told with dramatic license?" he asked.

Lindy stared at him solemnly as she answered, "I wouldn't joke about a *jumbie*. It was one hundred percent true. It's one of my favorite stories." A smile found her mouth as she said, "Why? Are you scared? Will you need someone to hold your hand tonight when you go to bed?"

Gabe pulled her in for a quick, stolen kiss as he answered with a growl, "It's not my hand that needs holding."

Her breath caught and her cheeks flushed but she couldn't help the grin that followed. "Careful," she admonished in a silky tone. "Remember? Discretion?"

He reluctantly let go but the look in his eyes made her quiver. He exhaled a sharp breath and said, "This is going to kill me. I never knew keeping my distance would be so difficult."

She managed a shaky smile and murmured, "You and me both. Let's go cool off before we do something reckless."

"That's a problem. Being reckless is all I want to do when I'm around you."

The muttered comment sent a thrill skittering down her spine. Lindy knew exactly how he felt. And she agreed—it was deliciously dangerous.

GABE WAS REALIZING, with the certainty of a man facing death row, that keeping his hands off Lindy when she was right there in front of him was going to be a challenge.

For one, her body was like something out of his deepest, darkest fantasies and he couldn't help but stare. Second, thanks to their illicit tryst, he had crystal clear memories of what it was like to bury himself deep inside that gorgeous body.

And if that wasn't bad enough…he really enjoyed her company. She made Carys laugh and smile—something he hadn't accomplished in months—and she managed to get him to relax and forget about work for the time being, which was nothing short of a miracle given the turbulent times his company had been going through with this crap economy.

It was as if she were infused with some sort of island magic, if he were to buy into her Caribbean stories, and he was under her spell. He shook off the fanciful notion and grinned, observing Lindy and Carys laughing while they watched tiny fish flit between their legs as they kicked up the fine, floating sand.

"Lindy said we should go for a night swim!" Carys said, looking up with an excited grin.

"I don't know about that— There are sharks out there, remember?" he said, shaking his head.

"Yes, but they rarely eat chicken," Lindy quipped with a daring grin that made his stomach tighten with desire even though he wanted her to stop putting dangerous ideas in his reckless daughter's head. Then Lindy made chicken noises and Carys copied her.

"Very funny," he said drily. "Why would you want to go out at night? You can't see anything."

"There's something peaceful about the sea at night. It's hard to explain."

"Yeah, real peaceful…right up until the point when the great white rips into your torso. No thanks."

"Aww, Dad," Carys moaned. "Stop being such a worrywart."

"I'm serious," he protested, trying hard not to grin when Lindy went cross-eyed at him as she stuck her tongue out. "Oh, real mature, Miss I-Love-Danger," he said, barely able to hide the laughter in his voice. "All I'm saying is, perhaps for an eleven-year-old girl, a night swim probably isn't the best idea."

Lindy sighed and conceded the point. "Oh, okay. Your dad is mildly right," she said. "But when you get a bit older, that's definitely something you ought to give a try. There's nothing like it."

"I want to try it now." Carys pouted, shooting Gabe a dark look for spoiling all the fun.

Lindy caught the look and rushed to his defense. "No, your dad is right. I was just kidding. There are some things that go bump in the night and it's best to swim when you can see them in plain sight."

"Like what?" Carys asked.

"Sharks, stingrays, jellyfish… That's it mostly."

At Lindy's casual answer Carys's eyes widened and she seemed to lose some of her fire to go on a night swim.

"Oh," Carys said, pursing her lips in thought. "Hmm… maybe I'll wait until I'm a little older."

"Probably wise," Lindy said, laughing at Carys's expression as the girl grinned and disappeared under the water to pluck seashells from the seabed at her feet.

While Carys splashed and played in the surf far enough away for privacy but not far enough to cause alarm, Lindy swam lazy circles around Gabe, delighting in the knowledge that he was having a hard time keeping his hands to himself.

"So tell me about what you do for a living? What does a CEO do all day?"

"Everything," he quipped, sending a splash her way, which she avoided by going under. She reemerged with a giggle and he smiled warmly. "What do you want to know?"

"I don't know…. It sounds so…executive office-ish."

"It is," he acknowledged without arrogance or false modesty, either. "I'm the boss. I do all the hiring and firing of the upper management and I oversee every acquisition."

"Acquisition of what?"

"I'm a corporate raider, to put it simply. I acquire struggling companies with undervalued assets and then I break the assets apart and resell them at a higher value."

"Sounds mercenary," Lindy said with a grin.

"It can be," he said.

"My sister Lora would love you. She was a corporate marketing executive in Chicago before she came back to St. John to help out Pops with the resort. I can only imagine the *fascinating* conversations you two would have," Lindy said. "You might discover you have more in common with her than me."

"I doubt that. There's only one Bell sister who's caught my attention and she's right here in front of me."

Her heart rate sped up at his sexy admission. "When you say things like that it makes it hard to keep my hands to myself," she warned playfully, floating past him.

His brow arched and he said, "When you tease me with a look-don't-touch, you make *me* hard."

Lindy gasped at his bold statement and longed to curl

her hand around him beneath the waves. She'd never been so hot for one person. She deliberately looked away and submerged herself. When she popped up again, she asked, "How did Charlotte handle you being such a workaholic?"

At the mention of his deceased wife, Gabe's expression dimmed and she realized she'd hit a sore spot. She felt like an idiot for inadvertently ruining the playful mood between them. "I'm sorry.... I shouldn't have asked something so personal," she immediately apologized, but by the haunted expression in his eyes, Gabe looked as if he needed to confess something.

"I worked too much. I should've been home more," he said quietly. "She didn't tell me she was sick until it was too late to do much about it. I'd been too wrapped up in my deals and business meetings to realize I should've noticed something was wrong. She went through a lot alone."

"Oh, Gabe...I'm sorry," Lindy said softly, hating the real pain reflecting in his eyes. She bit her lip, wondering what to say to that admission without sounding trite and awkward. Gabe saved her the trouble.

"There's a lot I would take back if I could. Let's just leave it at that. Okay?"

"Yeah, sure," she said, nodding. A moment of silence followed until Lindy surprised him with a splash right in the face.

"What the...?"

She broke into a grin, and splashed him again, prompting him to lunge after her. She squealed and swam away but not before he caught her quickly and hefted her into the air with a roar and then tossed her into the waves.

They spent a good hour splashing around in the surf,

taking turns dunking one another or chasing Carys to throw her into the water. When the sun started to sink into the horizon, they reluctantly headed for the beach and started drying off amid laughter and chatter. It felt so good to share a day with them both. Lindy couldn't remember when she'd felt right at home with people other than her own family.

Lindy happened to catch Gabe's look and what she saw there almost took her breath away. Had any man ever looked at her like that? With one smoldering glance that took a nanosecond to absorb, Gabe managed to make her feel lost and found, hot and cold, scared and exhilarated.

And Lindy didn't think she liked it. It smacked of conversations that inevitably included words like *forever* and *I love you.*

Sure, there were plenty of men who had thought they'd been in love with her but she'd let them down quickly and abruptly. She wasn't the kind of woman who suffered that kind of tedious relationship crap. She was in it for a good time, not a long time. She swallowed and broke eye contact to scoop up her clothes and shake out the sand. "We'd better get back to Larimar. I'm sure my sister has some sort of odious task for me to do," she said airily, though truthfully, her skin was becoming prickly and she needed some space. It was then she realized she'd missed a call from Paul Hossiter. Thankful for the distraction, she quickly returned the call.

"Hey, Paul, what's up?" she asked, hoping for a miracle. "Did you suddenly realize you need my family's resort?"

"No, but I may need your hot little body," Paul answered back, causing Lindy to laugh and be thankful that Gabe wasn't hearing the other end of the conversation. Still, she angled away from Gabe and Carys and motioned for them to go ahead to the car. Gabe's brow furrowed but he gave her the privacy she needed.

"Aww, come on now, Paul. You know that's not going to happen anytime soon," she teased, enjoying the banter. "Why'd you really call?"

"No, I'm serious," Paul said and she could hear the smile in his voice. "Except you need to get your mind out of the gutter, little girl. One of our actresses got some kind of terrible flu and she dropped out when we needed her. You're perfect for the part."

Lindy bit her knuckle to keep from squealing but kept it together to ask, "Is it a speaking part?"

"Yeah, not a major speaking role but decent. Probably about a day or two of work on location with a few days scheduled once we're back in L.A. for ADR. You know the drill."

"Right," Lindy said, shaking out her hand where her knuckles still had bite indents. "What are we talking? I guess I should call my agent and run it by her."

"Aww c'mon, Lindy babe, it's a bit part," he groused. But then he sighed and said, "Oh, all right. I'll have my assistant send it over. But I need an answer by tonight or else the part goes to my No. 2. Got it?"

"You betcha," Lindy answered, unable to keep the grin from her face. "I'll call. I promise."

Paul chuckled. "You know, if this were a different day and age…a little gratitude wouldn't be out of order."

"Stop being a perv," Lindy said, still on cloud nine. She'd been wanting to get onto a Paul Hossiter film for years but he'd kept passing her over. She wondered what the part would be like. "I'll be in touch."

They hung up and Lindy ran to the car. She jumped in and said in an excited rush, "You're never going to guess who just called and offered me a bit part in his newest film...Paul Hossiter!"

Both Carys and Gabe stared as if that name held absolutely no meaning whatsoever, and Lindy had to remember that she wasn't in L.A. and she wasn't chatting up her fellow actors and actresses at some retrochic diner. "Paul Hossiter, you know, he makes those cool action flicks, such as *Dark Side of Dangerous* and *Fatal Flaw?*"

Carys still looked confused and then shrugged, saying, "My dad doesn't let me watch rated R movies."

Slightly deflated, Lindy realized Carys had made a good point. Neither of those flicks would've been appropriate for a kid. She looked to Gabe—surely he'd seen those movies? "How about you?"

"Sorry...I must've missed those ones. I don't get to the movies very often," he said, lifting his hands in apology. "Maybe I'll catch it on Netflix or something when I have a chance. I like a good action movie."

Lindy exhaled and shook her head, silently laughing at herself. "Sometimes I forget that the world doesn't revolve around what's happening in Hollywood. Anyway, yeah, so Paul offered me a small job."

"Are you going to take it?" Carys asked.

"Yes," she answered. "I'm having my agent take a look first but that's just a formality and Paul knows it. It's a small part, probably only a few speaking lines but that's okay. It's a paycheck and I could really use one of those. Plus, it helps keep my SAG membership good."

"What's a SAG?"

"Screen Actors Guild," Lindy said. "It's the actors'

union. It's complicated, kiddo. We'd be here all day if I tried to explain."

Carys accepted that but her expression had still dimmed. "What's wrong?" Lindy asked, looking to Gabe. "What happened? One minute it's all smiles and giggles and then after I get amazing news, it's all doom and gloom. Did I miss something?"

Gabe opened his mouth to answer but Carys jumped in first. "It's just that I was hoping we'd be able to go shopping together tomorrow and get ice cream."

"Oh," Lindy said, bothered to see that look on Carys's face, but she really needed this job. She bit her lip, not sure what to say. She looked to Gabe for help.

"Lindy is an actress…that's what she does for a living. Sometimes, grown-ups have to make sacrifices in order to get further in their career. Sort of like when Dad has to cancel dinner reservations or a movie date with his favorite kiddo," he explained, but somehow that didn't make Lindy feel better. Carys already knew that grown-ups bailed for reasons that sounded logical on the adult end, but to a kid, it was just being ditched for something else.

"How about this…want to come onto the set with me tomorrow?" she asked, impulsively throwing out the offer before truly thinking it through. Seconds after the words left her mouth she knew she shouldn't have offered. Paul's films were not exactly kid-friendly. But the light in Carys's eyes was worth the risk. That is until she caught the completely disapproving expression on Gabe's face.

Oops.

She sent a tentative smile Gabe's way. "It'll be fun?" she ventured.

He shook his head and exhaled a sharp breath as he muttered, "We'll see," and then pulled onto the highway.

CHAPTER EIGHTEEN

THE NEXT DAY Lindy fidgeted behind the wheel of the Jeep with Gabe and Carys in tow as they rode the car ferry across the channel to St. Thomas. She'd considered making some excuse so they stayed behind but she couldn't bring herself to utter the words for fear of crushing Carys.

So here they were. Riding to a movie set with jangling nerves. And Lindy felt ready to vomit.

"Your agent was okay with this role, huh?" Gabe asked in an attempt to start conversation. She shot him a brief look and then nodded. She wasn't about to tell him that she overrode her agent's opinion on the subject. In defense of her decision, Lindy knew that her agent didn't care for Paul Hossiter at all, so she basically stuck her nose up at any project attached to him, which frankly wasn't doing Lindy's career any favors. But that was a different conversation altogether. She tuned back in and realized Gabe was still talking. "Are you sure it's going to be okay for me and Carys to tag along?" he asked, sounding nervous.

"It'll be fine," she assured him. "Listen, I should probably warn you that the movie business is a lot of 'hurry up and wait.' I mean, my call time is noon but depending on how efficiently the takes are going, it could be anywhere from one to two hours later."

"This is so exciting," Carys said in a breathless whisper that oozed excitement. Lindy couldn't help but grin. The kid's enthusiasm was infectious. "Are there going to be movie stars, I mean, besides you, there?"

At that she smiled, then answered, "Well, according to the call time, there might be an actor or two you recognize."

"Like who?" Carys asked, jumping up and down in the seat. "Someone totally, amazingly famous?" she asked. "Like Selena Gomez?"

Selena Gomez? Lindy tried to place the name. "Is she the latest Disney kid?" At Carys's affirmative head bob, Lindy chuckled but shook her head. "No. Sorry, kiddo. This isn't a Disney flick. But there's going to be some pretty cool people nonetheless. I bet I could even wrangle a meeting with the director. Would you like that?"

"Ohhh, my Goood," Carys squealed, causing Gabe and Lindy to wince. "That would be *aaaa-mmmmaaaz-ing!*"

Lindy felt her chest muscles loosen up and she could actually breathe for a minute. She grinned at Gabe but he didn't look any less tense. "Are you okay?" she asked.

"Yeah," he answered, trying to shrug off any evidence of his discomfort. "I'm just not used to being in situations where I'm not familiar. I've never been on a movie set before…. I don't know what to expect. I don't like surprises."

"I love surprises," Lindy murmured with a smile. Boy, could they be more different from one another? "It'll be fun, I promise." She hoped.

GABE MADE A conscious effort not to appear as if he were scowling. Charlotte had once told him that when he was concentrating or focused on not doing something, he had a tendency to scowl. He didn't want to spoil the day for Carys or Lindy but he was distinctly out of his comfort zone.

The ferry landed in St. Thomas and Lindy drove off the ferry and onto the road. "Do you know how to get where we're going?" Gabe asked.

"Yeah, it's been a while but I used to drive around St. Thomas all the time. I went to high school here because there's no high school in St. John. The production is renting out a villa on the hill. It should be pretty high-end. The catering ought to be amazing. All-you-can-eat goodies," she said, winking at Carys in the rearview mirror.

Gabe smiled and tried to relax. It was no big deal. So Lindy was in the movie business. It wasn't the end of the world. It wasn't as if they were trying to be a couple or anything. He could be supportive in the short term. Besides, it wasn't as if he was trying to audition for a permanent role in her life. The reasoning should've been a comfort but it wasn't. The knowledge only served to make him grouchier and it was getting more difficult to hide it the more he thought about it.

They drove up a long, windy road that plateaued at the villa. Security stopped them before entering and Lindy gave her name, which was then cross-referenced on the guard's call times. They finally got through and Gabe joked, "With the security you'd think they were trying to protect the president's location."

"Well, Paul doesn't like when details about his production get leaked without his approval. He likes to dole out the information as he sees fit. He gets really peeved when reporters or those damn paparazzi get wind of his films."

"Like when stuff ends up on TMZ?" Carys piped up and Gabe did a double take.

"How do you know what TMZ is?" he asked.

"Dad, you'd have to live under a rock not to know what TMZ is," Carys answered with a roll of her eyes. "Right, Lindy?"

"Well, yeah," she admitted, her reluctant answer coaxing a smile from him. "But then with the circles I run with…it's kinda like our CNN."

Gabe nodded and grunted as if he understood but he felt more bewildered than ever, and the fact that his daughter seemed more hip to the outside world was a bit unnerving. Suddenly, he felt like that old guy desperately trying to hang out with the cool kids yet who was so clearly *not* one of the cool kids. "You know, I'm in pretty good shape for my age," he blurted, causing Lindy to do a double take. "I'm just saying, you know, I might not know about this TMZ thing but that doesn't mean I'm some old guy who needs a walker to get around."

At that Lindy burst out laughing. "Are you on drugs? Carys, did your dad smoke something before we left? Nobody is calling you old."

Carys hooted in laughter. "Dad, you're so funny."

Gabe's cheeks heated but a grin found his mouth just the same. He chuckled. "Yeah, I don't know where that came from," he admitted, embarrassed. "Forget I said anything."

"Sorry, buddy, it's logged and filed away for future reference," Lindy said, the tease in her voice matching the mischievous spark in her eyes that made Gabe want to put a kiss on her that would show just how fit and able he was. He forced himself to look away before his body language revealed everything he was feeling. Lindy parked the Jeep and they climbed out. "Ah, okay, follow me, guys," she instructed, striking off toward a fancy trailer. She climbed the short steps, knocked twice and then the door popped open. A man, probably a few years older than Gabe, stuck his head out and when he saw Lindy, a big smile wreathed his face as he gathered her in his arms without hesitation. Lindy laughed a bit nervously as if she sensed Gabe taking exception to this man's familiarity, and she disentangled herself quickly to point out she wasn't alone. "Paul, I'd like you to meet my friend Gabe and his daughter, Carys," she said.

The man descended from the trailer, all smiles and professional courtesy, but Gabe couldn't erase the image of how easily he had wrapped his arms around Lindy.

"Carys wanted to see what a real movie set was like, so I thought they could tag along. Is that cool?"

Paul stuck his hand out to Gabe with a cavalier smile, saying, "Any friend of Lindy's is a friend of mine. Gabe, is it? What do you do, my man?"

"CEO of Weston Enterprises," Gabe answered, shaking Paul's hand firmly.

"CEO, eh? Have you ever considered investing in a movie?" he asked, joking, yet perhaps not.

"Not really," Gabe answered ruefully. "Are you saying you need investors?"

Paul laughed. "Well, Gage—"

"Gabe," he corrected him with a smile, knowing full well the man was testing him. Businessmen ran the gamut, and that included too-slick-to-be-trusted Hollywood types, too.

"Right, Gabe, in Hollywood, you can never have too much money or too many investors." He glanced down at Carys, who was watching him with wide, fascinated eyes, and he said, "You ever done any acting, kid?"

"Not real acting but I was once in a school play," Carys answered in earnest.

"And you were the best darn carrot in the entire vegetable garden," Gabe said playfully, earning himself a scowl for bringing in the specifics of that production.

"How'd you like to be in a real movie?" Paul asked, and Lindy's attention shot to Gabe as if worried he'd overreact, but Gabe played it cool.

"She's probably a little too young for a Paul Hossiter film," Gabe said, putting his hand on Carys's shoulder. "But we'd be happy to just hang out and watch the magic."

"True enough, but it just so happens the scene that Lindy is in has room for a pint-size extra with a cute smile and tiny freckles dancing across her nose."

Carys's fingers strayed to her nose and she grinned. "I have freckles," she said.

"Which makes you perfect for the part. C'mon, Dad, how can you ever say no to this adorable little face? This is why I only see my kids on weekends and holidays. I'm such a pushover. What do you say?" he asked Gabe, but he was looking at Carys.

Gabe sent a look to Lindy, who seemed genuinely shocked by Paul's offer, and he realized he'd been put into a difficult position. If he went with his instincts and declined Paul's offer, he would put himself at odds with Carys again; if he said yes, he had a feeling Carys would never get the acting bug out of her system. Frankly, neither scenario appealed but he found himself grudgingly agreeing for the sake of peace with his daughter. "As long as it's not inappropriate…I suppose it's okay," he said, and Carys squealed and jumped into Gabe's arms.

"Thank you, thank you, thank you, Daddy!" she exclaimed, squeezing a reluctant chuckle from him in her enthusiasm.

Carys let go and Paul said, "If you and your dad would go over there—" he pointed to another trailer

"—you'll find all the necessary paperwork and whatnot that details all the legalese like pay scale and liability, blah blah blah. You know, all that unfun stuff."

"C'mon, Daddy," Carys said, grabbing his hand and pulling him along. Gabe spared one last look at Lindy before reluctantly allowing himself to be dragged off to sign paperwork.

PAUL WAITED FOR Gabe and Carys to be out of earshot before saying, "What's up with bringing the boyfriend along?"

"He's not my boyfriend," Lindy said. "He's just a friend."

"Oh, well, in that case," he said, pulling her into his arms, murmuring, "So, about that gratitude…" before his lips were covering hers. Under normal circumstances, she would've allowed the kiss but nothing more. If she were offended by every stolen kiss in this business, she'd spend half her life in lawyer depositions for the countless pending sexual harassment cases.

"Paul," she admonished, breaking away and putting distance between them. "You know I don't play that game. Either you gave me the part because you believed I could do it, or not. If you think that giving me a bit part is going to give you an all-access pass to my bed, you don't know me very well."

"Of course not," Paul said easily, not the least bit put off by her admonishment. "But you can't fault a man for trying."

"Yeah, well, try to keep it on a leash. Gabe is a friend and I don't want to make him feel weird."

Paul eyed her speculatively. "Friends with benefits, huh? I didn't think that was your style."

"It's not my style with you," Lindy quipped lightly. "Now, where is hair and makeup?"

Paul sighed and pointed to the appropriate trailer. "One of these days I'll either get you out of my system or I'll just have to marry you, Lindy Bell."

"Keep dreaming, Paul."

He chuckled and Lindy grinned as she walked away.

CHAPTER NINETEEN

AFTER GABE HAD signed all the appropriate paperwork and his eyes had bugged at the amount of money they were going to pay Carys for her tiny, nonspeaking role, he'd followed the girls into hair and makeup because he felt awkward just standing around.

Carys fairly beamed, her eyes alight with unadulterated joy as she sat in the makeup chair while the makeup artist made some minor touch-ups on her baby skin. Carys was just supposed to be a little girl on the beach with her family. All she would do was walk by the principal actors to provide a little beachy atmosphere. And they were going to pay her $250 for it.

"I think I'm going to go on a shopping spree," Carys said to Lindy from her chair. "Dad always puts the skids on the clothes I want to buy, but if I'm paying, then he can't say anything, right?"

"Nice try, sweetheart," Gabe interjected drily. "I still have a say even if you're buying, which you won't be because that money will go into your savings account."

"D-a-ad," Carys whined and pouted. "But this is the first money I've ever earned on my own. I want to spend some of it on something fun. C'mon, Lindy, help me out. Shouldn't I get to spend at least a little bit?"

"I have to side with her on this one," Lindy admitted. "A girl's gotta have her rewards or else what's the point of working hard? How about half goes into savings, the other half she can spend—within reason—on some fun stuff of her choosing?"

"Half?" Gabe repeated incredulously, then quickly countered with, "How about a quarter?"

"Gabe, seriously. When was the last time you went girl-shopping? You can't buy anything worth buying for less than $50. Give the girl half. She'll have earned it."

"Yeah, Dad," Carys piped up, then batted her eyelashes at him, saying, *"Please?"*

"No fair. I'm getting tag teamed here," he grumbled but he supposed half wasn't a bad deal. She deserved a little fun after the year they'd had. "Okay," he finally agreed. "But I better not find out you're shopping in some place like Victoria's Secret. I know what her secret is, and I don't need my eleven-year-old daughter figuring it out, too."

Lindy laughed and Gabe smiled. The makeup artist worked silently and quickly and before long both Carys and Lindy were ready. Carys looked like herself on a really good hair day; Lindy, in full hair and makeup, was stunning.

Then some production assistant came with their wardrobes and when both emerged from the dressing room, Gabe had to work to swallow when he saw Lindy.

She was dressed in an itty-bitty, hot-pink bikini that barely covered the right places and Gabe couldn't help but stare.

"Dad, you're practically drooling," Carys said, giggling, and he recovered with an embarrassed clearing of his throat as he looked at his daughter. She was wearing a bikini, too, but one that was age appropriate and cute. "How do I look?" she asked, twirling for him.

"You both look great," he said, smiling, but he didn't

trust himself to look Lindy's way again. She was hot enough to set his eyes on fire.

"Boy, this doesn't leave much to the imagination, does it?" Lindy said, twisting to check out her rear end in the mirror. "Geesh. I haven't worn so little on a film set since… Well, it's been a while," she quickly finished when she realized her story might not be appropriate for young ears.

"So what exactly are you supposed to do in this scene?" Gabe asked.

"Um, it's a bit of an action shot," she answered evasively. "And, well, it goes pretty fast. You'll see."

"Great. I can't wait," Gabe said.

Lindy flashed a small smile, and then Lindy and Carys went one way and Gabe went another as the production started to roll.

He was directed to sit near Paul Hossiter, who had his own executive chair set up in the shade of a tent with a clear view of where the action would be, and yet another production assistant rushed to get Gabe a chair, too.

"So how long you known Lindy?" Paul asked conversationally as they waited for the cameras to start rolling.

"Not long," he answered, his gaze searching for Carys. He found her waiting beside her fake parents on the beach. "We're staying at her family's resort, Larimar."

"Ah yes, she mentioned her family's resort. I'll have to check it out sometime. Lindy and I go way back. She mention me at all?"

"Can't say that I remember your name popping up, but like I said, we haven't known each other long."

Paul's sigh was filled with longing. "But she sure as hell has a way about her, doesn't she? The first time I met her I thought, holy hell, that woman's going to be a star. She had that certain something about her. Made you take notice."

Gabe couldn't disagree. "She's a special woman."

"And it doesn't hurt that she's probably one of the hottest pieces of tail to twitch past my nose in a long time and trust me, I've seen plenty."

Gabe shot him a look but otherwise ignored that comment. He didn't talk about women in that way and he wasn't about to start, even if some A-list celebrity producer had started it.

"So, you gotta tell me, you hitting that?" he asked, as if it weren't completely rude to ask. Gabe sent him a cool look and Paul chuckled. "I get it. You're not a kiss-and-tell kind of guy. I can respect that. Sometimes I spend so much time in the company of Hollywood players that I forget not everyone wants everyone else in their business."

Gabe nodded and returned his gaze to where he could see Lindy chatting and laughing with the actor who would play opposite her. He was a Tom Cruise type—hell, for all Gabe knew it *could've been* Tom Cruise—and he was bare-chested and sporting board shorts. There was a buzz of activity and suddenly everyone quieted as the director yelled, "Action."

The actor grabbed Lindy and jammed his tongue down her throat, causing Gabe to stare in growing discomfort as the kiss turned hot and heavy with plenty of the guy's hands roaming her backside. Gabe shifted and forced himself to look away, but found he couldn't stop watching. Lindy was hot enough to melt lead—so why should he be shocked that they wanted her for a sexy role?—but even reasoning things out, he still wanted nothing more than to plant his fist in the actor's face for daring to put his tongue where it didn't belong.

The appearance of jealousy was an unwelcome shock as Gabe had never considered himself the jealous type, but he was smart enough to recognize the telltale warning signs.

"And cut!" the director yelled and Gabe actually breathed an audible sound of relief. "That was great, guys. We're going to go again. Back to one."

"Again?" Gabe asked, surprised. "It looked pretty good to me. Did something go wrong?"

"Oh, no. Lindy did great. But the director likes to make sure he has what he needs when it goes to the editor and the only way to assure that is multiple takes. But it's no hardship to watch Lindy in action, that's for sure. I'd do anything to be able to trade places with the actor in this scene." Paul chuckled at his comment, seemingly missing the fact that Gabe hadn't appreciated his candid statement.

"Multiple takes?" Gabe repeated, feeling a bit queasy. He didn't know if he could sit there and watch Lindy getting felt up for even one more take. This was much harder than he could've imagined. "Whatever happened to being efficient or frugal," he half joked. "I mean, don't multiple takes cost money? Seems like an inefficient way to do business, if you ask me."

Paul chuckled. "Ahh, that's right. You're a CEO. Always looking for ways to improve the bottom line so the shareholders get their fair share, right?"

"Something like that," he said, trying not to stare at Lindy. "So, how do you know Lindy? You two go way back, you said?"

Paul shrugged. "Hollywood is an incestuous little circle. Eventually, everyone knows—and sleeps with—everyone else."

Gabe looked at Paul sharply, hating the idea that

Lindy may have slept with the guy, and Paul laughed as if reading his mind. "No, I've never been lucky enough to share quality time with Lindy. She's…particular."

That gave Gabe a modicum of relief but before he could take a breath, the director yelled *action* and the actor had his hands all over Lindy. This time, the actor gave her behind a firm squeeze as he kissed her like there was no tomorrow.

"Criminy," Gabe muttered, shifting in the chair and forcing himself to look away. Instead, he focused on Carys, watching as she skipped down the beach beside her fake parents. She looked truly happy, pretending to be someone else. He exhaled softly and wondered what Charlotte would have to say about all this craziness. She'd been a no-nonsense woman for all her seemingly gentle nature. The thought of her daughter wanting to become an actress would've distressed her. She'd always hoped Carys would go into the medical profession or perhaps be a lawyer or dentist. Certainly not the next Julia Roberts.

Ten takes later Gabe had to excuse himself. It was getting ridiculous and he couldn't take it any longer. He made some excuse about wanting to get some coffee and hustled away from the shooting area. He found the catering cart and was surprised to find custom smoothie preparation was available. He shook his head at the sheer strangeness of this alien profession and ordered a fresh strawberry coconut.

He was sipping at his smoothie when Lindy found him.

"There you are," she said, smiling, her eyes alighting on the smoothie. "Oh, that looks good. Can I have a sip?"

"Sure," he said, but then remembered whose tongue had just been in her mouth and he grimaced. "I'm trying not to be weird about this but…you were just pretty intimate with a complete stranger. Should I even ask what his hygiene was like? Hopefully he brushed his teeth before the scene started rolling. I mean, who knows what kind of stuff was floating around in his mouth."

Lindy laughed, mistaking his wry question for one based on humor, but he was serious. When she realized this, she paused and stared at Gabe, her smile fading. "What's going on?" she asked. "It was just a kiss, Gabe."

"No, a peck on the cheek is just a kiss. What was happening out there…that was a make-out session."

"Gabe." She sighed. "This is my job."

"Yeah, I know, but I don't think I want to come to any more shoots," he said, hating that he sounded like a prudish jerk, but he wasn't any good at pretending to feel something other than what he was feeling. And right now, he was seething with something he had no right to feel. The best course of action would be to remove himself from the situation.

Lindy looked hurt but she nodded. "I understand. I should've known this wasn't a good idea. I guess I wasn't thinking. I'm so used to everyone being in the same business as me that it never occurred to me that it might not be normal." She shot him a halfhearted smile and shrugged. "Occupational hazard, I guess."

"So, how much longer before you're released for the day?"

"A few hours probably," she said. "Sorry. If you want, you can take the Jeep back to Larimar. I'll bring Carys home later."

"How?"

"Paul will drive us. It'll be okay."

Paul? *No way.* "I can wait," he said, determined to suck it up for the sake of getting through the day without Paul weaseling his way into Lindy's affections. It was thinly veiled, but the guy had the hots for Lindy; Gabe was willing to bet his eyeteeth on it.

"Well, the good news is I think the kissing scenes are over. The next couple of hours should be a lot of running past the camera, looking scared because someone is after us," she said, trying to get him to smile. "No problems with that, right?"

"No," he answered, grudgingly allowing a smile. "Are you at least covered up a little?" he asked hopefully.

She shook her head. "No. It's a Paul Hossiter film, which means there's going to be a lot of things getting blown up, lots of action and hot, barely clothed girls. It's part of his winning formula."

"It's not going to win any Oscars any time soon," Gabe quipped.

"No, probably not, but he's winning plenty at the box office so he's laughing all the way to the bank, trust me. He doesn't care about winning a gold statue."

"I thought everyone in Hollywood cared about winning the gold statue," Gabe said. "Do you?"

Lindy gave him an enigmatic smile and simply lifted her shoulders as if to say, *maybe...maybe not,* and then said, "I have to get back. Try to stay out of trouble while I'm at work, darling."

She winked and sauntered away, her lovely behind swaying in an almost-obscenely sexy manner and he was nearly certain she'd given him the view on purpose. The woman was a moving violation in a hot-pink bikini—and he couldn't wait to tear it from her body with his teeth.

A flush stole through his body and he had to shift to avoid drawing attention to the quickly growing bulge in his shorts. "Fabulous," he muttered to himself as he walked away to will his libido to calm down. This was all he needed…a tent in his shorts like a randy teenage boy who couldn't control himself.

Geesh…what was happening to him?

It was as if he didn't even know himself any longer.

WHILE LINDY WAITED for the next scene to set up, she couldn't help but search out Gabe. He wasn't sitting beside Paul any longer, which made Lindy wonder if he'd run off to avoid watching her with Brandon, the principal actor.

"Want to get something to eat later? Check out the wild life?" Brandon asked casually while stretching his pecs for the upcoming scene. "I've heard St. Thomas gets crazy after dark."

She spared him a quick smile but wasn't interested in fielding date requests. "Sorry, I came with someone," Lindy said, wishing she knew where Gabe had gone. Carys bounded over to her and wrapped her arms around her, shocking Lindy with the sudden gesture.

"I'm having sooo much fun," Carys gushed. "This is the best day ever!"

Lindy grinned and hugged her back. "I've heard you're a natural," she teased, then added in a conspiratorial whisper, "How are we going to break the news to your dad?"

"This your kid?" Brandon asked, inserting himself back into Lindy's line of sight. In the blinding light of Carys's smile, she'd completely forgotten about Brandon and frankly, was irritated he was still trying to talk to her. "She's cute," he said, reaching out to touch Carys's hair. "I can see the resemblance."

"I'm not her mom," Lindy said. "Her dad and I are friends."

"Just friends or more?" Brandon asked as if Carys wasn't still standing there soaking up every word with keen interest.

Lindy forced a smile and said to Carys, "Can you do me a huge favor and get me a bottled water from the catering cart? I'm dehydrated."

"Sure, Lindy," Carys said, rushing off to do just that.

Dropping the smile, she turned to Brandon. "Listen, I get it. You're excited about being in a Paul Hossiter film and figure because you're the hot shit on campus that you can say or do whatever you want to whomever you want when you want. I'm not interested in going anywhere with you to check out the wild St. Thomas nightlife, which I'm sure is a thinly veiled attempt to get into my pants, and in the future, I'd appreciate if you could watch what you say around a child."

Brandon scowled. "No need to be a bitch about it," he said. "I get it. You're a lesbian. No harm, no foul."

"Yeah, I'm a lesbian because I'm not interested in banging you," she quipped wryly, freshly irritated at this idiot she was forced to work with—and worse— allow to kiss her. "Just keep it professional, will you?"

"Who the hell are you to talk to me like this? I'm the lead in this film. You're just a bit player. You probably don't have enough lines to support your SAG card. You ought to be thankful I thought enough of your body to even notice you. You can't tell me that you didn't get this part on your back anyway." He started to say something else but Lindy didn't give him the chance and popped him right in his snarky piehole of a mouth.

He went down like a girl.

And cried like one, too.

"One thing you should remember about island girls… We don' take any shit from *clungs* like yah," Lindy said in her best Crucian accent. "Piss off, yah donkey."

CHAPTER TWENTY

GABE HEARD THE commotion and headed over to investigate. He found the actor that'd been in the scene with Lindy clutching a bloody tissue to his nose as he cursed and cried while a production assistant fluttered around him like a frantic butterfly trying to evade a collector's net.

"What the hell happened?" the director yelled, coming over to glare at Lindy and the actor.

Paul, who also came over, looked directly at Lindy and then, seeing the smugly dismissive expression on her face, he blew out an exasperated breath.

"Lindy...did you do this?" Paul asked.

Gabe jumped in, ready to defend Lindy. "Hey now, let's not jump to conclusions," he warned, looking to Lindy for answers, too.

She chuckled and sent him a sweet smile that warmed him from the inside, then looked to Paul and said, "He was being a dick. I simply showed him how things were done here in St. Thomas. It's not my fault he's a puss."

"She punched me," the actor whined, groaning when the action caused his split lip to bleed fresh.

"You punched him? Our lead actor?" the director asked incredulously, then looked to Paul as if it were his fault he'd hired a crazy woman for his film. "That's just great. I can't shoot the next scene with my lead actor sporting a fat lip. Just great. Just great!" he shouted, then stomped off to rearrange the shooting schedule.

"Lindy, what the hell are you doing?" Paul asked, exasperated. "This is not going to look good. I mean, this is going to cost us money and heads will roll. Mainly yours, I suspect."

Lindy bit her lip and tried contrite on for size, but Gabe sensed her contrition was only skin-deep and frankly, he didn't care. The way he saw it, if Lindy saw fit to punch the guy, he probably deserved it. "Paul, I'm sorry. He got under my skin. I should've just ignored him."

"Yes, you should've," Paul agreed with an irritated expression. "Okay. Time for damage control. You can go for the day but *if* you get a callback, you'd better be on your best behavior.... No more punching people. You got it? Now, get over here and give me some sugar," he said, gesturing to his cheek.

"Thanks, Paul," she said and leaned in to kiss his cheek but he grabbed her at the last minute and placed a smacking kiss on her lips.

Gabe started forward, ready to rip Paul's head off, but he released her with a satisfied grin, winking at Gabe. "Worth the risk, buddy. Worth the risk."

Paul walked off, and Lindy stopped Gabe from going after him. "It's no big deal," she said, laughing. "I mean, Paul's going to take whatever advantage he thinks he's got. It's just who he is."

"I don't like him," Gabe said flatly, his blood still simmering. "He did that on purpose just to get under my collar."

"Maybe. But it's not going to do any good to call him out on it. Besides, if he can salvage the day after what I did to Brandon...I figure he earned the kiss."

"Oh sure, you get to punch someone but I have to rein it in?" he asked sardonically. "Doesn't seem fair."

"Yeah, I know. But life's not fair. And Paul doesn't want to sleep with you so you have no leverage."

He groaned, hating how cavalier she sounded about the fact that every single red-blooded male on this set likely wanted to have sex with her. He rubbed at his forehead to ease the pounding headache that had begun to pulse. "I'm not cut out for this shit," he admitted wearily. "I mean, it's like being plunked down in a country with a foreign language without a clue as to how to even find a bathroom and all the natives are hostile."

"It's not that bad," Lindy said, smiling, but he didn't agree. He was fairly certain his blood pressure had spiked to dangerous levels at least twice so far. She smoothed the scowl from his brow and her gaze softened. "You get used to it," she promised.

He shook his head. "Not me, Lindy. I'm not hardwired this way. I don't think most people are hardwired this way," he added ruefully.

Her chuckle sounded forced as she said, "You might be right but this is how I'm hardwired so I guess that tells you something."

Gabe gave her a short look and said, "Yeah, I think you need therapy."

Her expression screwed into a quizzical frown. "Why does everyone keep saying that?"

In spite of himself he laughed. "You're a train wreck but one helluva sexy one, that's for sure. Let's get out of here before they change your mind and I have to sit through another five hours of you getting manhandled right before my eyes."

NIGHT HAD FALLEN by the time they rode the car ferry back to St. John and the warm, humid breeze felt like a caress against Lindy's cheek. She longed to lean over and rest her head on Gabe's shoulder, but with Carys right there she didn't think it was a good idea. She cracked a yawn and Carys followed.

"It's hard work pretending, huh?" Lindy teased, and Gabe chuckled as Carys rubbed her eyes.

"Yeah, I feel like I haven't slept at all."

"It's the adrenaline," Lindy explained, settling against the seat and looking out across the inky black of the ocean. "I remember my first time on set. I don't think I slept for days. It was wild. I was so excited and I didn't even have a speaking role."

"What was your first part?" Carys asked.

"I was Patron No. 2 in a diner for a film you've probably never even heard of. It was an indie flick that was the worst production ever, but I didn't know enough to realize how terrible it was so I had a great time. I'm not even sure I got paid now that I think about it. It's hard to remember that far back."

"How old were you?" Gabe asked.

"Eighteen," Lindy answered, thinking back to that time. Talk about a train wreck. She'd sure made her share of mistakes. There was nothing like landing in Hollywood with nothing but a suitcase full of dreams and a head full of naive ignorance.

"You didn't go to college?" Gabe asked.

She shifted in the face of one of her private regrets. "No. I thought it would be better to go straight to L.A. and try my luck while I was still young enough to do it. I figured college would always be there if I changed my mind."

"Did you change your mind?" Gabe asked, peering at her through the moonlight.

"Of course not, Dad," Carys answered for Lindy. "She's almost a famous actress. Why would she need to go to college when she's already doing so good in movies?"

Lindy smiled faintly at the confidence in Carys's young voice and she felt a pang of discomfort. She should've gone to college like Lora instead of running off to L.A. like an idiot. The reason no one took her seriously was because she was just like a million other beautiful, empty-headed bimbos whose value was found in her face and body. And Lindy hated that. She was smart—maybe not as smart as Lora, but she wasn't stupid. It was a constant uphill battle, one she'd begun to tire of fighting.

"I think I'm going to be an actress when I grow up, too," Carys said wistfully and Lindy winced. She didn't need to see Gabe's expression to know it was likely thunderous.

"Well, give it some time before you make a big decision like that," Lindy suggested. "A lot can happen between now and the time you're eighteen. Trust me."

"Okay, but I'm pretty sure I'm not going to change my mind," Carys said, turning her back on them both to watch the waves as they chugged through the water. The lights of St. John twinkled in the distance and Lindy sighed.

"Thanks for coming today," she murmured. "It was nice having you there."

Gabe smiled but didn't comment. She knew he hadn't had much fun but he'd stayed. That meant a lot to her. She couldn't remember the last time someone had done something for her that wasn't remotely advantageous for the other person. Damn, she hung out with crappy people.

LATER THAT NIGHT, after Carys had been put to bed and the door to her room closed, Gabe invited Lindy to share a glass of wine with him.

She hesitated but ultimately agreed. "You know, it's funny, for the first time in a long time, I saw my profession through your eyes and realized how strange it all must look."

He poured the wine, shaking his head at the recollection of the day. "I've never considered how hard it must be for actors to maintain some kind of relationship with another person without having some seriously nontraditional relationship rules. I mean, Lindy, I'm not exaggerating in the least when I say that when that actor kissed you, I wanted to put my fist through his face."

She accepted the wine and grinned. "Really?"

"It's not funny," he admonished, still moderately bothered by his reaction to the whole situation. "I'm not the jealous type—or at least I didn't think I was— until I saw that and then it was like I was infected with the rage virus. It was terrible. I didn't like it."

"So I shouldn't be flattered that you wanted to go all caveman on poor Brandon's ass?" she teased, brooking a small smile on his part.

"No, you should be alarmed," he said, finally laughing. "I'm a civilized guy...most of the time."

"I know you are," she murmured with a smile that lit up her eyes with a mischievous light. "Except when you shouldn't be."

Taking a sip of his wine he paused and shook his head in warning. "Stop looking at me like that or you'll find yourself thrown over my shoulder in true caveman style."

She slowly raised her glass to her lips and her tongue darted out to taste the rim. Seductively sliding it along the edge, she said, "And that's...bad?"

"Damn, you'll be the death of me," he growled, downing the glass in one swallow and then roughly removing her glass from her fingertips so he could finally taste her lips. He latched onto her mouth like a man starving and in essence, that was an apt analogy because he felt as though if he didn't get his hands on her body, he'd expire from all the pent-up need bubbling inside him. All that frustration from being unable to stake his claim, rising to the surface, choking out rational thought, was more than he could control, and he didn't want to even try.

He slipped his hands under her rear and hoisted her into his lap. She settled nicely on his groin, all that liquid heat centered right over his burgeoning erection as their tongues tangled with one another, dueling for dominance.

"I want you so badly," he said, his voice a low, throaty whisper as his hands roamed her backside, eager to touch any exposed skin he could manage without ripping her clothes from her body. "I want to erase the images in my head where he touched you and I shouldn't care but I do, Lindy. I care that he touched you here—" he cupped her rear and squeezed a handful of perfect ass "—and here." He took her mouth again in a savage kiss. "I hate it but I can't stop thinking about it."

"Stop thinking and start doing," she murmured, pulling her top free and tossing it to the floor. Her breasts, two achingly perfect globes with dainty pink-tipped erect nipples, begged for his touch, his mouth, a pinch between thumb and forefinger. She threaded her fingers through his hair and brought his mouth to her breast, saying, "I'm all yours right now. What are you going to do about it?"

CHAPTER TWENTY-ONE

LINDY DIDN'T WANT to think about what Gabe was saying. She just wanted to become lost in sensation. There'd be plenty of time to dissect the "why" and "what for" later and it was a conversation she wasn't looking forward to.

Gabe sucked her nipple and she gasped as he laved the sensitive tip before drawing it hard back into his mouth. His mouth and tongue made sensual assaults on her breasts until he was forced to swallow her soft moans for fear of waking Carys.

He carried her to the bedroom, his arms hooked under her rear as they kissed. He shut the door with the push of his foot and then they collapsed to the bed in a fit of heated giggles that quickly changed to heavy breathing as Gabe stripped himself and she wiggled from her own clothes.

She pushed him down and playfully pinned his arms as she bent to tease his nipple with her tongue. He sucked in a tight breath when she nipped at the smooth skin, encouraging his nipple to harden with a soft blow, followed by another tease with the rasp of her teeth.

"Oh, you're killing me," he gasped, jerking his hips so that his erection strained and bobbed. "I can't take this much longer!"

"So impatient," she murmured with a throaty laugh as she traveled his stomach to the hard length that begged for her attention. She grasped his erection firmly and raked his balls with the edge of her fingernail with just enough pressure to cause him to suck in a tight breath but not enough to hurt. He groaned against the assault. She closed her mouth over him and he moaned as his length hit the back of her throat. She teased him, made him writhe, made him babble nonsensical words as he came close to orgasm, but suddenly, he panted, "Baby, I want to be inside you. I have to feel you now! Condom. First drawer. Hurry!" he urged, gesturing to the dresser.

She found the condom and shredded the wrapper with her teeth. Within seconds, she'd sheathed his member and straddled it to sink onto his erection with a shuddered groan. "Ohh, that's it," she said, nearly purring with delight at the sensations flitting across her nerve endings. She arched against him, giving him a better chance to rub that elusive spot deep inside her and he hit it unerringly. She rocked against him, eyes closed, focusing on the pleasure beginning to build and riding each thrust as she clenched her muscles around him, driving him mad until his thrusts were hard and deep, sinking into her.

"Yesss," he groaned, his hands anchoring on her hips, lifting her so he could pound into her wet and hot core. She gasped and tensed as every muscle spasmed, radiating in deliciously carnal waves that spiraled out from her insides, igniting a firestorm that sizzled and snapped along every fiber of her being.

"Gabe!" she gasped against the pleasure rocking her. "Ohhh, Gabe!"

Seconds later, Gabe stiffened against the orgasm that found him, his hands curling into her flesh as he pumped into her, his thrusts becoming spastic until he finally finished and Lindy collapsed against his chest.

She whimpered as little pulses continued to zing

through her body and reluctantly rolled from Gabe's body. He pulled the condom free and tossed it into the trash beside the bed and then grabbed her and tucked her against him, fitting her perfectly against his chest as if she'd been made to fit there.

As her heart rate slowed to a less-frantic pace, she exhaled softly and fought the urge to fall asleep. Lying there with Gabe was a special kind of torture. Casual bed partners aiming for discretion didn't cuddle. But it felt so right lying there. She swallowed and prepared herself to climb from the bed, but the words wouldn't come.

"You could stay," he murmured against her crown as if reading her mind.

She smiled. "No, I can't. What about Carys?"

He sighed. "You could leave early in the morning."

"Sneak out like some floozy after a one-night stand? No, thanks. A girl has her pride, you know."

"It wouldn't be like that," he said, affronted. "You know I would never treat you like that."

"I know, but that's how it would make me feel. Trust me, I've made that walk of shame and it doesn't do much for the self-esteem in the harsh light of the morning."

"I understand." He drew a deep breath. "It's just that I don't want to let you go. Having you here right now is the most amazing feeling in the world, and I'm being selfish. I don't want to give it up."

Sadness crept up on her like an unwelcome and un-invited visitor, and she tried to shoo it away but it remained. "There's always tomorrow," she reminded him, trying for the positive approach but it was difficult; she wanted to stay, too. But to remain in that bed would raise uncomfortable questions in the morning and would set a terrible example for Carys, and Lindy couldn't do that.

She reluctantly started to pull away but he wouldn't let her go just yet. "A few more minutes?" he pleaded.

She nodded and allowed herself to be folded into his arms again. They remained that way, curled into one another, until morning.

And that's exactly how Carys found them.

"DAD?"

Gabe's eyes flew open at the sound of his daughter's confused query and he realized with a sinking heart that they'd fallen asleep and it was now morning.

Worse? They were both plainly naked under the thin sheet.

He pulled the sheet more securely up and over Lindy and said to Carys, "Hi, honey…this probably looks a little strange…."

"Why is Lindy naked?" she asked, frowning. "Why is she naked with *you?*"

His mouth tightened against the barrage of lies that immediately sprang to mind. He wouldn't lie to her. It would only cheapen what he felt for Lindy and he wasn't willing to do that. "Honey…Lindy stayed the night here with me. Why don't you let me get dressed and we'll talk about it."

Carys reluctantly left the room and he bounded from the bed to jerk on some shorts and a T-shirt. He closed the door quietly behind him so Lindy wouldn't be bothered and then found Carys sitting at the breakfast table, staring at her bowl of cereal with a faint frown.

"Carys…does it bother you that Lindy stayed over?" he asked gently.

"Yeah, sort of," she admitted. "What does this mean? Are you dating or something?"

"Not exactly," he answered, flushing with the embarrassment of a father faced with tough questions. "We're just friends."

"Friends with benefits?" she asked, shocking him with her frank and precocious question.

"Where did you learn that term? Never mind. I can guess. Listen, it's a bit complicated but I really care for Lindy, and I don't want you to think that this is some cheap and tawdry hookup. It's not like that. I promise you." Carys nodded but looked a little lost and forlorn and it broke his heart. He cursed himself for being so selfish and falling asleep when he should've allowed Lindy to leave when she'd been ready to. "What's wrong, sweetheart?" he asked, smoothing the frown from her brow.

She shrugged. "I know it's stupid but suddenly I miss Mom a lot. I like Lindy but…she's not supposed to be in the spot where Mom was."

"She's not in your mom's spot," he promised her. "Your mom was special and amazing and no one can ever replace her."

"I know, but when it was just you and me, I could pretend that maybe Mom was going to come home. Seeing Lindy sleeping next to you…just made it feel real that Mom is never, ever coming home again." A single tear oozed out from the corner of Carys's eye and he scooped her into his arms, hugging her tightly.

"I miss her, too, sweet pea. I miss her so much sometimes I can't breathe because my chest feels as if it's caving in. But your mom was an amazing woman who wouldn't have wanted us to climb into the ground with her. She would've wanted us to live our lives. She was just that kind of woman. You remember that, right?"

Carys nodded and wiped at her nose.

"The best way to honor her memory is try and remember all the wonderful things she tried to teach you about being a good person because I'll let you in on a secret…your mom was one of the best. And I know you'll make her proud because you are so much like her already."

Carys cried softly and he rocked her, holding her close. His heart was fracturing in two from her raw pain, and he hated that he'd cracked open this fissure with his own carelessness but he supposed it'd been bound to happen sooner or later.

"I love you more than anything in this world, Carys Deanne," he said. "And nothing will change that fact. Nothing in this world."

"I love you, Daddy," Carys said between hiccups. "I love you so much."

"Ditto, moonbeam. Ditto."

LINDY STUFFED HER knuckle in her mouth to keep from crying. Gabe was such a good dad, so unlike her own father, who had bailed when the going got tough and never looked back to see how they'd all fared after his defection.

Carys was so lucky to have a father who was willing to shelve his own happiness to ensure her own. No doubt, he was beating himself up for falling asleep. She knew this because she felt it, too. This felt similar to a walk of shame, only it was ten times worse because it would be witnessed by an eleven-year-old girl. Lindy gathered her clothing and quickly dressed. After finger-combing her hair, she opened the bedroom door with a bright, false smile and acted as if everything were fine and dandy.

She faltered in the face of Carys's puffy, reddened eyes. Meeting Gabe's tortured gaze, she knew with a certainty he was dying inside for the pain that his daughter was feeling. She wanted to talk to Carys, wanted to explain, but the words dried like dust in her mouth. She didn't have the right words to explain to a child why she'd been sleeping with her father. It was too complex and complicated to pare down to a sound bite of information so she wouldn't even try. "Well, I have to go," Lindy announced, moving to the front door. "Call time is at noon and I should check in with my sister before I go…so…all right. Catch you later, guys!"

And then, like a coward, she practically ran from the bungalow.

CHAPTER TWENTY-TWO

LINDY WENT STRAIGHT to her room and luckily bypassed anyone who might question where she'd spent the night. She showered and emerged, shaky but determined, and went to the kitchen.

Lora looked up when she entered and smiled. "Look at you, up so early. What's the occasion?"

Lindy blew out a breath and grabbed the orange juice. "Well, I have a small acting job in St. Thomas and my call time is noon so I figured I ought to see if there were any chores you needed help with before I took off."

Lora grinned. "Well, color me impressed. I believe you're growing up."

"Don't get your hopes up," she said wryly and sipped at her juice. "Okay, well, maybe just a little," she amended, then switched subjects. "How's Lilah?"

At that Lora frowned. "Okay, I suppose. She's been quiet. More quiet than usual. It bothers me but I haven't had a chance to sit down with her and have a heart-to-heart. Pops tried to help Heath with some outside yard work and ended up slipping and hurting his back. So we spent most of the day in the urgent care making sure he didn't break anything."

"Pops okay?" she asked, alarmed. "Why didn't you call me?"

"He's fine. Just a little bruised. I would've called if it had turned out to be serious, but I heard you were

spending the day with Gabe Weston and didn't want
to bother you."

"Actually, his daughter, Carys, was picked up to be
an extra in the film. She was pretty excited."

"How'd that happen?"

"Well, I invited them to tag along because I thought
they'd enjoy the experience and while we were there,
Paul Hossiter, the executive producer, took a shine to
Carys and put her into the scene."

"That's pretty cool. You don't hear that happening
very often. Did you have something to do with it?"

"Inadvertently," Lindy admitted, sighing. "Paul's a
bit of a player. I think he thinks if he does me a favor,
I'll owe him a favor later. I told him he's dreaming but
he keeps trying. But in the meantime, it worked out for
Carys and I'm happy for her. She was over the moon excited." She chuckled. "She's already spending the money
she earned."

"How much?"

"Two hundred and fifty," Lindy answered with a
shrug and Lora gaped.

"That much?"

"Yeah, extras on a good shoot can make some nice
pocket change. And for a kid? That's like hitting the
mother lode."

"Yeah, but you may have just created a monster.
How's she ever going to be satisfied with babysitting
money now?" Lora said wryly. "I don't envy her dad."

Lindy smiled, her heart pinging at the mention of
Gabe. She busied herself with finishing the glass of orange juice, not trusting herself at the moment. There
was too much going on in her head, stuff she couldn't
even begin to comprehend or make sense of, to risk
opening her mouth. Besides, she knew what her older

sister would have to say about her involvement with a guest. She needed to talk to Lilah. Her twin wouldn't judge her, even if she didn't agree with Lindy's choices.

"Hey, even though Paul isn't willing to move his production, my payday for this bit of work will come in handy," she said. "It should help with the next IRS payment."

"I hate to ask because it's so personal, but how much are we talking?" Lora asked.

Lindy shrugged. "After my agent takes her cut, it should be about $35,000."

Lora stared, as if not quite sure she'd heard the amount correctly. "Did you say…?"

"Yes. Normally, this kind of job could sustain me all year. How else do you think I've been able to stay in L.A. all this time without having to get a real job? I'm probably the only starving actress who's not moonlighting as a waitress. I land a gig like this and I sock it away."

"You have some pretty good budgeting skills if you manage to make this kind of system work," Lora remarked in surprised awe. "I'm impressed, little sister."

Lindy grinned. "Yeah, well, you learn real fast not to blow those paydays because sometimes work is scarce."

"You've turned into a pretty savvy woman," Lora said, offering a rare compliment. "So, our next payment is due at the end of the month. We're about halfway there. Do you think you could kick in a few bucks to the pot?"

"Of course. I'm willing to put it all in if you need," Lindy said, surprising Lora. "Hey, I said I'd help and I meant it. I might not be good at customer service or fixing plugged toilets but I can at least do this, right?"

Lora looked away for a second but not before Lindy

saw tears in her eyes. Lindy hesitated, not sure if she should go to her or not. Lora was always the iron woman; to see her show this kind of open emotion was foreign. But no matter what, Lora was her sister and that bottom line caused Lindy to cross the room and fold Lora in a tight hug. "We'll get through this," Lindy promised. "We'll get it all figured out and then everything will get back to normal."

Lora nodded and pulled away, wiping at her eyes. "Some days it feels hopeless, like no matter what we're doing it's not going to fix things. Pops seems as if his bad days are becoming more frequent, and I'm so worried that one day he's going to be more than we can handle and then what?"

Lindy didn't have an answer and the helplessness she felt in the face of Lora's stark questions only served to make her feel small and useless. "I don't know, Lora," Lindy answered honestly. "But we'll get it figured out together. Somehow. That's all I know."

Lora released a pent-up breath on a laugh and said, "Funny how it takes a really messed-up situation to bridge the gap between us."

Lindy sighed. "Yeah, I know. I'm sorry for not trying harder."

"I wasn't innocent in that, either," Lora admitted. "I got caught up in my own stuff and forgot that I was leaving behind the ones that mattered the most. But I'm trying to fix that. I really am."

"I know you are. And you're doing a great job with everything here," Lindy said, hitching a jerky breath. If she wasn't careful, she'd end up crying, too. "Listen, if you don't have anything for me to do I could use some beach time to clear my head."

"Everything okay?"

She nodded. "Yeah. I mean, yeah…I think so. Or I should say, I'll get it figured out. Don't worry."

"Okay…I'm here for you if you need me."

Lindy smiled. "Thanks, sis."

Lora grabbed a banana from the fruit bowl and exited the room, leaving Lindy to think about everything that had transpired within the past twenty-four hours.

Instead of simplifying things, she'd made a mess of things. And now Carys was hurt. That was the worst part. She'd never wanted to hurt Carys. A sigh rattled out of Lindy and she grabbed a banana for herself.

She needed some serious beach time before she lost what little sense she had left.

LILAH FOUND POPS on the terrace eating papaya like he and Grams used to when she was young. She smiled and sat opposite him.

"Morning, Pops," she said, letting her gaze track out to the sea. It was so beautiful, so serene. When she looked at the ocean stretching out as far as she could see, she felt peaceful, which was a rarity these days. Seemed it was all she could do to keep from crying all the time. A tight breath seemed caught in her chest and she struggled to release it, which caught Pops's attention.

"What's wrong, sugar bird?" he asked, scooping a spoonful of the succulent fruit. "Why the long face?"

She forced a smile but her eyes tingled, signaling tears weren't far. "I'm just feeling a little blue this morning, I guess."

"Anything I can do to help?" he asked, and for a moment, Lilah was almost lulled into a false sense of security, that Pops was fine and everything was going to work out. But then he said, "Well, you know if you can't talk to me, there's always Grams. She's a great shoulder for young girls…and one old guy, too," he said, winking.

At that, Lilah's shoulders sagged and she ground away the tears that sprang to her eyes. "I wish I could talk to Grams," she murmured, hating how awful she felt inside. It was as if she were constructed of pitiful sadness and black days. Where'd her sunshine go? She'd had sunshine once. Hadn't she? She couldn't remember any longer. Fatigue from her insomnia had begun to take its toll. Her feet ached from all the walking she did at night and her head felt stuffed with sand. "Grams is gone, Pops," she said softly, the words drifting from her mouth as if someone else were orchestrating the conversation. She snapped her mouth shut before the rest of the words fell. *She's not coming back. And you're losing your mind. Larimar is screwed and we don't know how to fix it. Everything is a mess, Pops. How come you can't see that?*

"Sugar bird…what's wrong? And what do you mean, Grams is gone?" he asked, concerned. "You don't seem yourself. Where's my sweet, sweet Lilah girl?" He peered at her, his blue eyes soft with love. She sucked in her bottom lip and fought the tears that were always much too close to the surface.

"I don't know, Pops," she answered honestly, her voice cracking. "I really don't know."

"You need to talk to Grams," he announced. "She'll get things straightened out. She always does."

Lilah wiped at her eyes and nose and nodded, her eyesight blurring from the tears. "Yeah, Pops. I need to talk to Grams."

Pops smiled as if glad she'd come to the same conclusion and then patted her hand. "Papaya?" he offered and she smiled.

"Not today, Pops. I think I'll go find Grams."

He nodded with approval. "Sounds good. When you see her, let her know Celly is making her special Caribbean-blend coconut pie. She'll love it."

Lilah felt disconnected from her body, floating away with the slightest breeze. She didn't even realize when she'd left Pops on the terrace. The next thing she knew, she was standing on the beach. Then, she was in the water.

Her eyes fluttered shut and she slipped under the surface.

I'm coming, Grams...I'm coming.

CHAPTER TWENTY-THREE

LINDY WAS ON the beach, soaking up some sun and solace, when for no particular reason, her eyes snapped open and she was overcome with a sense of panic. Her heartbeat fluttered like a bee caught in a Venus flytrap and she sucked in big, gasping breaths trying to get a deep lungful of air. Her gaze went out across the water and she thought she saw Lilah but then she was gone in a sun flash.

She scrambled to her feet, spraying fine sand all over her blanket, and she ran to the water's edge. "Lilah!" she screamed, unable to quell the rising terror in her chest. She didn't know why but something felt terribly wrong. "Lilah? Where are you?"

She closed her eyes and pictured where she'd seen Lilah a second ago and then struck out in that direction. She swam in long, clean strokes to the area where she'd seen her and then dived under the water. The water, crystal clear and hiding nothing, revealed a flash of white sinking slowly to the bottom. This area was only about ten feet deep, but there were chasms that opened up farther out and the bottom dropped significantly. She kicked hard and started swimming as if her life depended on it. She grasped at Lilah's trailing blond hair and used a chunk to pull her sister's limp body to her. They broke the surface and Lindy rolled to her back with Lilah in front of her and swam for the beach. "Lilah, what did you do?" she gasped, crying as she stumbled to shore, dragging Lilah with her. "What did you do? You promised me you wouldn't ever do this! You promised!"

Lindy screamed until her voice turned hoarse, "Help! Lora! Pops! Heath! Help!" Then she dropped to her knees to give her twin mouth-to-mouth. She tilted her sister's face and positioned her mouth over hers. With a prayer that her decade-old lifeguard training was still in her memory she began trying to blow life back into her sister.

Lora ran out of the private area of the resort and skidded to a stop when she saw Lindy working on Lilah, her hand going to her mouth. "Oh, God…" she breathed.

"Call an ambulance!" Lindy cried, stopping mouth-to-mouth to pump on Lilah's chest. "Hurry!"

Heath's face blanched when he saw Lilah but he moved into action. "Lora, call 911 and keep Pops away. I'll take over for Lindy. We need a steady rhythm for her heart. Go."

Lora stumbled in her haste to run and get the phone, but she recovered quickly and she was gone. Heath hustled over to Lindy and she reluctantly turned Lilah over to him. "I don't know how long she was under the water," she said, sobbing. "I just saw her and then she was gone and I don't even know why I looked up at that moment. I almost didn't catch her. I pulled her hair.… I think I ripped out a few strands but I couldn't reach her bathing suit strap," Lindy said, almost babbling as Heath ignored her to work on Lilah.

"C'mon, kid," he urged. "Breathe! C'mon, you can do it. Don't you dare check out like this! Lilah Bell, don't you dare!"

"Why'd she do this?" Lindy asked, going into bewildered shock. "Why?"

Heath ignored her and continued to work on Lilah but his actions were becoming desperate. Too much time had passed and Lilah remained still as the grave. "Don't give up, Heath," she begged, grabbing Lilah's hand and squeezing tightly. "Please don't stop. Please. *Please.*"

"There's no response, Lindy," he said, gritting his teeth against his own tears.

"I don't care! Don't stop. Keep trying. She's in there somewhere. I can feel it!"

Paramedics rushed in and Heath moved out of the way so they could do their jobs.

Seconds later they were shocking her heart and Lindy flinched each time Lilah's body spasmed from the electric shock. Tears streamed down Heath's face as he watched. The third time the paddles went to her chest, the paramedics exclaimed, "We've got a pulse! It's weak but it's there. Let's get her loaded up and to the hospital. Now!"

"I'll go with her," she said, scrambling after the paramedics but Lora stopped her.

"I should go. I have all the insurance information and I know her Social Security number," Lora said, her face deathly pale from the fear they were all feeling. Lindy sobbed into her hands, unable to fathom what had just happened. Lora didn't wait for Lindy's agreement and simply followed the paramedics.

Heath watched them go, slightly unsteady on his feet. "What happened?" he asked in a grief-stricken voice.

"I don't know," she answered. "I...I know she's been depressed but I didn't think it was this bad. I mean, if I'd known..."

"Don't go there," he admonished in a sharp tone, probably sharper than he intended for he immediately gentled his voice as he added, "You couldn't have known she was feeling this way so don't beat yourself up over this. Can you drive? I want to be there for Lora, too."

Lindy jerked a short nod and they trudged back to the resort to grab shoes and keys to the Jeep but not before Gabe intercepted them.

GABE WALKED OUTSIDE the bungalow to see paramedics carrying a wet figure on a gurney to the awaiting ambulance.

He saw Heath talking with a plainly distraught Lindy and he quickly crossed to see if there was anything he could do. The moment she saw him, he could tell she was struggling to remain rooted to the spot but he could read in her eyes the fear and pain. "What's wrong? What happened?"

Heath's mouth tightened, looking to Lindy for permission to share and at her imperceptible nod, he said, "Lilah had an...accident. We don't have any details, just that Lindy managed to pull her from the water and give her mouth-to-mouth and CPR before medical aid could get here. They're airlifting Lilah to St. Thomas right now. We were just about to get to the car ferry and meet them there." Heath turned to Lindy and said, "Can you be ready in five minutes?"

She nodded and Heath headed back to the resort, leaving Lindy behind. She looked at Gabe with a trembling lip and eyes that were red from crying and he simply gathered her into his arms to hold her tightly. "What really happened?" he asked in a low voice.

"I think she tried to...tried to...kill herself," Lindy sobbed against his chest, clutching at his magnolia rayon shirt and crushing it between her fingers. "I should've known. I should've seen it! I knew she'd been acting strangely, like, out of it, but Lilah's always been a bit different, and I didn't give it much thought. But I'm her twin, I should've *sensed* that she was hurting inside and done something about it!"

He rocked her and remained silent. Lindy was hurting; nothing he could say would soothe the wild beast raging inside her. "Do you want me to go with you?" he asked.

"What about Carys?" She pulled away to stare at him with red-rimmed eyes and a runny nose. "She's too young to stay by herself."

"She could stay with Celly. The two seem to have hit it off lately," he answered, checking his watch. "We'd better get moving if we're going to catch the ferry."

Lindy nodded and appeared relieved that he'd taken control of the situation. She seemed lost and frantic, unsure of how to deal with simple tasks, and he couldn't blame her; he'd felt the same way when Charlotte had died. It'd been so bad that he'd momentarily forgotten how to fill out a check to pay a bill. He'd simply stared at the checkbook, his mind as blank as the paper, wondering how to properly fill it out to pay the water bill. The memory returned in an embarrassing flash but for a full minute, he'd been lost. His mind had simply shut down, unable to fathom his reality. That's what was happening to Lindy. He could see it.

"Thank you, Gabe," she whispered, moving to cling to him again. Her fingers dug into his skin as if she were trying to meld into him and he simply bore the pain for her. Her shoulders had begun to shake and silent tears followed. "I'm afraid she's gone. That we'll get there and she'll be gone."

"I'm here for you, Lindy," he murmured, kissing her crown, wishing he could take away the pain. "You have to keep hope alive. And until we get there, we don't know anything. Okay?" He lifted her chin and gazed into her eyes, hoping to give her strength when she had so little of her own. She slowly nodded and he bent down to brush a kiss across her lips. "Let's go. Heath's probably waiting."

He kissed her hand and then slowly let go so there wouldn't be questions they weren't ready to answer, but he wanted to hold her close and damn the questions. He needed to be there for her. He sensed she was near her breaking point. And he wasn't about to let her fall.

Not now, not ever.

CHAPTER TWENTY-FOUR

LINDY, HEATH AND GABE arrived at the St. Thomas Hospital emergency room an agonizing forty-five minutes later. They saw Lora in the waiting room, her eyes bone-dry but devoid of any color in her cheeks. Lindy's knees threatened to buckle as fear weighed on her shoulders. "What's the word?" She was almost too afraid to ask. "Is she…?"

"The doctor hasn't come out yet. I'm still waiting. Her heart wouldn't stay beating. They had to shock her a few more times in the helicopter. When we got here, they told me to wait in here and they'd let me know."

"Oh God, I have to know what's going on," Lindy said, turning to Gabe. "They can't just expect us to sit in here twiddling our thumbs. What are we supposed to do? I'll go insane if I don't find something out right now!"

Her voice had taken on a hysterical note and Gabe placed both hands on her arms to calm her down. "I'll find out something," he assured her. "Try to relax."

She jerked a nod and went to sit by Lora. Lindy felt ready to jump out of her skin.

Gabe went to the lobby receptionist and made a few inquiries. The woman shook her head in answer and he walked back to them. "No information yet, but it shouldn't be much longer. The emergency room doctor treating her is known for always keeping the families in the loop. Lilah's in good hands."

"I hate that saying," Lindy said, grabbing a tissue to wipe her eyes. "I don't know that she's in good hands. I don't know this doctor from anyone." Lora put a hand on Lindy's knee and gave it a subtle squeeze and tears sprang to Lindy's eyes for her snappish tone with Gabe when he'd only been trying to help. "I'm sorry," she apologized. "I'm a mess and my mouth is getting away from me."

"No worries," he said, sitting beside her.

Lindy grabbed a magazine, not because she thought she'd find anything to distract her, but because she couldn't sit still and flipping through the pages of a stupid magazine was at least doing something.

Thankfully, they didn't have to wait long. A dark-haired doctor entered the waiting room and spotting Lora, went straight to their group. "I'm Dr. Bajaran. I assume you're all family of Ms. Bell's?"

"Yes," Lora answered, and they all stood anxiously. "How is she?"

"She's in recovery," he answered but his expression was grim. "She's lucky to be alive. I'm not going to sugarcoat this—she was without oxygen for too long. She might've sustained permanent brain damage."

Lindy stuffed her knuckle in her mouth to keep from crying out, her eyes brimming with tears. "Brain damage? How soon will you know?"

"We're going to run some tests but she's already exhibiting some signs of damage."

"Such as?" Heath asked.

"She's having difficulty coordinating the movements on her right side. We didn't see any point of trauma so we assumed she didn't hit her head on anything. Do any of you know what happened?"

Lindy swallowed and looked fearfully at Gabe. She

didn't want to admit her fears that Lilah had done this to herself but she didn't know if withholding that information could affect her treatment and recovery. "Well... I...uh...I think she may have been...confused...and..."

"Our sister tried to kill herself," Lora answered for Lindy when Lindy couldn't get the words out. "She walked into the ocean and tried to drown herself. That's all we know."

Dr. Bajaran nodded. "That confirms our suspicion." He sighed. "Well, as with all cases of attempted suicide we have to follow a specific protocol and an officer is here to take her statement. You can see your sister soon if she's up to visitors."

Lindy looked to Lora, alarmed. "What does he mean, an officer? That's the last thing Lilah needs right now. That will freak her out big-time," she protested, but Gabe pulled her aside before she could start railing at the doctor. Angry, she stared at Gabe, uncomprehending. "What the hell is this shit? My sister is lying there trying to recover from almost dying and they want to take her statement like she's some kind of criminal?"

"Lindy, be reasonable. Whether you agree or not, suicide is against the law. And when there's a suicide attempt most places have a mandatory seventy-two-hour hold on the person to make sure they're not a danger to themselves or others. It's not like Lilah is going to spend a night in jail or anything, but she needs help, Lindy. You have to realize that, right?"

Lindy stared at Gabe, hating that he was right. But it cut her to pieces to know that her sister would be put under a microscope for one misguided action that she likely regretted this very moment. "I need to talk to her," she said stiffly, ignoring the tears rolling down her cheeks. "I need to see Lilah, right now."

"Do you think that's a good idea?" Gabe asked.

"I want to see my sister," she repeated, moving past Gabe to where the doctor was still quietly speaking with Lora and Heath. He looked up when Lindy approached. "I want to see her."

"Maybe we should wait until after the officer talks to her," Lora suggested, but Lindy adamantly disagreed.

"She's not going through that alone," Lindy said hotly. "I want to be there with her when she gives her statement. You don't understand—she's very fragile right now and I want to make sure she knows she's not alone. Not anymore."

Lora seemed to know that Lindy wouldn't back down. There must've been a wildness in her eyes that warned everyone to back off because the protests died down and Dr. Bajaran nodded with a promise to return momentarily after he'd spoken with Lilah.

Five minutes later, Dr. Bajaran shocked everyone when he said, "I'm sorry but your sister…well, she doesn't want any visitors right now. Maybe you can come back tomorrow. She's probably just overwhelmed with everything that has happened. It's not uncommon for near-death experiences."

Lilah didn't want to see her? Lindy swallowed the lump of grief in her throat. "Even me?" she risked asking. "I'm her twin."

Dr. Bajaran looked uncomfortable as he answered, "She said especially you. I'm sorry."

Lindy stared at the doctor as he made a hasty exit after dropping his bomb, and her knees buckled. Gabe caught her just before she sank to the floor.

"We'll come back tomorrow," he murmured, helping her up. "She just needs a little time. It's going to be okay. She's safe here. Let's go." He looked to Lora and Heath, who seemed to agree as they gathered their stuff.

"We'll come back tomorrow," Lora promised. "Like Gabe said, she's safe and that's what matters for tonight. We'll sort everything out later."

Lindy nodded numbly, still reeling from the unbelievable pain of her sister's rejection.

What had she done?

The mystery was as painful as the reality that Lilah had tried to kill herself.

CHAPTER TWENTY-FIVE

IT WAS A silent ride home, first on the ferry and then in the car. Lindy sat quietly crying, the tears seeming unending, while Heath and Lora simply held each other's hands as they looked out their separate car windows.

Back at Larimar, Heath and Lora branched off while Gabe and Lindy went to relieve Celly from watching Carys. The minute Carys saw Lindy she asked what was wrong.

"Celly said something happened to Lilah," Carys said in a small voice. "What happened?"

"She had an accident," Gabe answered gravely. "She's in the hospital in St. Thomas. But she's going to be okay—that's what's important."

Carys looked to Lindy, who remained silent. "Then why is Lindy so sad?"

Lindy closed her eyes and said, "Because Lilah scared me…. I'm just really worried about her."

"Is this because of her art?" Carys asked, concerned. Gabe frowned with open confusion and Carys admitted, "She said that she's not good at anything, not even her art, but I told her she was wrong and that she was amazing with her paintings but she wouldn't believe me. I mean, sometimes the art was kinda scary, like when you looked at it, it made me feel all sad inside but it was still really pretty."

Lindy stared at Carys, trying to understand what art

she was talking about. She'd seen Lilah's art and she couldn't remember anything that looked like that. She wiped at her face and then came to Carys and bent down to her level. "Do you know where Lilah kept her paintings?" she asked.

"It's a secret. She only showed me because I was sad, too, and she said I would understand," Carys said.

"Please show me. I'm sad inside, also," Lindy said, grasping Carys's hand. "It would mean a lot to me if you showed me where Lilah keeps her art."

"It's in the atrium, behind the secret door."

Secret door? Lindy stared hard, trying to remember. Suddenly a memory unfolded, slowly opening like a door with rusty hinges, and her hand went to her mouth before she broke out into a run for the atrium. She didn't wait to see if anyone followed. She just had to see what was on those paintings. Whatever had caused Lilah to plunge herself into the ocean was on those paintings—she'd be willing to bet her eyeteeth.

"Lindy, wait!" Gabe called after her, but she wasn't about to stop.

She burst into the atrium, immediately assaulted by the tropical humidity in the garden room that'd been Grams's favorite place when she wasn't in the water, and went straight to a place she'd since forgotten about.

It wasn't actually a hidden room but the door was hard to see if you didn't know what you were looking for. She pulled on the wall where the seams met and a section opened up to reveal a small broom closet. But instead of brooms and cleaning supplies, there were rolls upon rolls of completed and hidden-away paintings. Lindy pulled the first one and unraveled it. Nothing but green tropical foliage, which is what she'd expect to see from Lilah. She realized she could be searching for hours. Lindy turned to see Carys and Gabe had caught up. "Carys, do you know which paintings Lilah showed you?"

"Yeah, they were on the top shelf. I remember that because she had to stand on her tiptoes to reach them."

Lindy saw the rolls and jumped to grab them. She unrolled one and secured it on the empty easel.

She gasped at what she saw.

Endless darkness against a melancholy sea, a woman walking the beach, her expression bleak and broken, giving the sense that salvation could only be found in the water. It was beautiful and evocative but sadness dripped from the canvas in a wash of blues, black and gray. The woman's blond hair trailed in an invisible wind, her face half-hidden in shadow.

"Oh, Lilah…" she said, slowly removing the painting to roll it back up. She unrolled another. It was similar. And yet another. And another. It was painting after painting of sadness and grief; heartache and pain. "How long have you been feeling this way?" she murmured to herself. She tried to recall snippets of conversations she'd shared with Lilah while Lindy had been in L.A. Lilah had seemed more reserved than usual, but Lindy had been too busy with her own life to stop for a minute and question. Now she felt sick to her stomach for missing an obvious marker of her sister's private pain.

The last painting chilled her blood.

It was the same beach, the same midnight sky. But the woman was no longer walking the beach. She was in the water, her blond hair drifting in the caress of a thousand waves, her eyes closed in surrender.

It was Lilah's suicide note.

LILAH STARED LISTLESSLY ahead, hating herself. She couldn't even kill herself properly. *Congratulations,*

Lilah. You have now successfully failed at everything you ever put your mind to.

Her right hand twitched and she glanced down at the useless appendage. The consequence of being without oxygen was brain damage, so the doctor had told her. She had months of physical therapy to look forward to and even then, she might not return to normal.

A tear squeezed from the corner of her eye, but she didn't bother to wipe it away, not even when the officer walked in, looking stern and forbidding. "Ms. Lilah Bell?" At her nod, he sat and continued, "I'm here to take your statement."

"What's to say? I walked into the ocean trying to drown myself. Simple, eloquent, but ultimately a failure. Anything else?"

The officer stopped writing and peered at her as if trying to determine her mental health with the strength of his stare. She glanced away, suddenly tired. All she wanted to do was sleep. She hadn't slept in weeks. The fact that she wanted to sleep was something. "Do you take medication for your depression?" he asked.

"I'm not depressed," she retorted with a sigh. "I just don't want to live any longer. Why does there need to be some mental illness to support that explanation?"

She heard herself and winced at the flippant tone, but she couldn't muster the energy to care. That seemed to be the problem in a nutshell for everything she was going through. If she wasn't hurting, she was apathetic. Not that great as an either-or.

"Ma'am, because only mentally ill people want to die," he stated simply. He stood and said, "For your protection, you're being placed on a seventy-two-hour hold for evaluation."

"Whatever," she mumbled. "Go away, please."

The officer left, only to be replaced with a woman who had the air of a counselor. Lilah closed her eyes and tried to purposefully shut her out but the woman didn't take the hint to leave her in peace.

"Lilah, you can pretend you're sleeping but I'm going to talk to you about your situation and it's very important that you listen. I'm Dr. Veronica. I'm a mental health counselor at Dolphin Cove, a facility for those in need of extra help before they can return home."

That caught Lilah's attention. "A facility? You mean a mental institution?"

Dr. Veronica's smile was indulgent as she corrected Lilah. "We prefer not to use that term. It has a negative connotation we'd like to avoid."

"It's negative for a reason," she muttered. "Listen, I understand how my actions may have been alarming, but I'm just really tired and need some sleep. Honest. I'm so tired I can't think straight anymore. I haven't slept in… I can't even remember the last time I got a good night's rest."

"Trouble sleeping?" Dr. Veronica asked, jotting down some notes. "How is your appetite?"

Lilah sighed. "I'm not a big eater on a normal day," she said evasively. The truth was, food didn't much interest her, either. No sleep, very little food and this constant presence in her head that dragged down her every thought. How long had she been suffering from this feeling? She'd lost count of the days, weeks…possibly months. Possibly even before Lora asked her to handle what was happening at Larimar. But it would come and go, not like this pervasive blanket of doom that had been draped around her shoulders that she couldn't quite shrug off.

"Is this the first time you've had thoughts of harming yourself?" Dr. Veronica asked quietly. Lilah blinked and looked away, which was answer enough. "There's no shame in admitting you're depressed. Clinical depression is a real and treatable mood disorder if you seek help. If your sister hadn't dragged you out of the ocean, you would've become a statistic. The best part is, there is help out there. Do your sisters—specifically your twin—know how depressed you've been?"

Lilah shook her head. "I didn't want her to know."

"Why not?"

Lilah made a sound of self-derision. "My sisters are superstars. My oldest sister, Lora, is a barracuda in the boardroom and is so smart, she had her choice of Harvard or Yale graduate school. My other sister, my twin, is a beautiful actress who makes people forget their name when she walks into the room. I couldn't tell either of them that I was *sad* inside. To even say it out loud sounds embarrassingly pathetic."

"It's not pathetic. It's how you feel and your feelings are valid. But it can change. I promise you that," Dr. Veronica told her. "But you're going to need treatment that will include medication and counseling. Most people with clinical depression have hormonal disruptions that make it impossible to recover without outside help. You can't will away depression…. You can't wish it way. You have to have help."

Lilah groaned and wanted to bury her head in the pillow. What would her sisters think of her now? Poor fragile Lilah who couldn't handle anything and now needed medication so she didn't go off the deep end again. *Hide all the sharp utensils…Lilah's here!* "I wish she would've let me drown," she cried softly, hating herself, hating her life. "Everyone would've been better off."

"I don't think your family would agree. They love you very much and just want you to be well. So, let's work on that. Everything else will fall into place when your outlook has changed."

Lila cast the counselor a dark look, hating that self-assured tone she was using, despising that she was so weak that she couldn't handle her own problems. "I'm fine," she said. "I made a stupid mistake. It won't happen again."

"Clinically depressed patients who don't seek treatment are statistically favored to try suicide again. And the second time they're usually more successful. No one wants to see that happen to someone they love. And you are loved, Lilah. Your family is very supportive of your healing. They're all behind you, believing in you. All you need is to believe in yourself, and that's where I can help you."

Lilah wanted to cover her face with her hands but her right hand only jerked in uncoordinated movements that shamed her. She turned her head away from the woman, unable to face her or anyone. "Please just go away," she whispered.

Lilah thought of Pops and closed her eyes. Lora was a rock; she could handle anything. She couldn't think of Lindy. A fresh stab of pain rocked her body and she whimpered without realizing it.

"It's Lindy, isn't it?" Dr. Veronica surmised. "Twins have an unusual bond. Some say it even borders on psychic. Somehow your sister knew you were in trouble and found you in the water. Think about that for a second. She risked her own life to save yours. You mean the world to her. Without you, her life would change dramatically."

Lilah stared, hating the valid points Dr. Veronica

was making. Lindy would never forgive her.... She'd hate her for being so cowardly, for leaving her behind. The tears started fresh and her shoulders shook from the force of her weeping. "I don't want to hurt her. I just wanted this pain to end. I'm so tired...so tired of it all!" Lilah didn't have the strength to argue any longer. Her will felt sapped and she simply wanted to disappear. At least if she were ensconced in a facility, she wouldn't have to face her sisters right away. Maybe that was for the best. She nodded. "Fine. What do I have to do?"

Dr. Veronica smiled in understanding and handed her the paperwork. "I just need your signature here—" she pointed to a line at the bottom of the paper "—and your initials here. And we'll take care of the rest."

Lilah didn't hesitate and simply scrawled her name where directed. "Can I sleep now?" she asked, weary to her bones.

"Absolutely, dear. I will return tomorrow morning to arrange your transfer."

Lilah shut out everything and buried herself under the scratchy hospital blanket, desperately hoping the floor would open and swallow her up.

But she knew that wouldn't happen.

That wish had never come true—no matter how many times she'd asked for it.

CHAPTER TWENTY-SIX

LORA LAY WITH her head on Heath's chest, caught between two different emotions.

"Is this my fault?" She whispered her secret fear to the man who knew her best. "I should've seen this coming. I was too harsh on her. I should've known not to put that kind of pressure on her with Larimar."

Heath tightened his hold around her. "This is not your fault," he said gravely. "Lilah is suffering from a mental illness. She's going to get the help she needs and everything will go back to normal."

Lora sat up, frowning. "That's the problem, Heath. What is normal? What is normal for us? I can't go back to Chicago. My life is here now, but what happens once we get Larimar back on track? Where does that leave me? You have your glass fusion art but I'm useless here. There's nothing that I can do to put my skill set to work."

Heath paused, as if reluctant to broach this subject, but he threw it out there anyway. "We could start a family."

Lora did a double take. "A family? We're not even married yet. I think you're putting the cart before the horse."

"Okay, but saying we got married, then what? Would you be ready to start a family?"

Lora had to stop and think for a minute. A family? Kids? She'd never considered herself mother material.

She'd never pictured herself being the soccer mom and PTA president. But as she gazed at the man she loved more than life itself, she saw that being a father was something he'd always wanted. She could see the desire in his eyes, though he would never pressure her to do anything she didn't want to do. She was torn between wanting to make him happy and staying true to herself. "I'm not ready right now," she started, proceeding with caution so as not to seem as if she was shutting and locking the door forever. "But I might be ready someday soon. I just need to get some things figured out first."

He smiled with love in his eyes and sealed the deal with a soft kiss on her lips. "When the time comes and it's right for both of us, you'll be a great mother."

She blinked back tears at the easy confidence in his voice and she wondered aloud, "How do you know?"

"Because I know you" was his simple answer and Lora felt completely unworthy of his love and support. She closed her eyes and cuddled up to him.

"I love you, Heath Cannon," she murmured and closed her eyes. Tomorrow was likely to be hell and she was so thankful she would face it with Heath by her side.

LINDY HAD CRIED herself to sleep in her own bed, but she'd sorely wished she'd had Gabe holding her instead. So when she woke the following morning, she looked as if she'd been dragged behind a bus. She went straight to the kitchen and poured herself a liberal cup of coffee and as she wrapped her fingers around the hot mug, she grimaced when Pops walked in. She didn't have the strength or stamina to deal with him right now, but she knew she didn't have the option of just telling him to stop being afflicted with dementia so they could deal with one crisis at a time.

"Morning, Pops," Lindy said wearily, sipping at her coffee, willing it to power her sluggish thought process into something more efficient. "What's on your agenda today?"

"Going to putter around as usual. Maybe go into town to get some parts for the new mailbox I'm making for your grams for Christmas. Don't tell her. For one, it's a secret and two, if I don't get it finished on time she'll be none the wiser that I was making one!" He snickered and Lindy offered a wan smile. He didn't seem to notice it was lacking in the enthusiasm department and she was grateful.

"Make sure you let someone know if you're leaving the resort, Pops," she reminded him. "Maybe Celly can drive you later."

"Oh, that's a good idea. Or maybe Lilah. I think she needs to get out more, see some different scenery than these walls, you know? Lilah is a bird that needs to fly now and then, but I think she's been cooped up with us too long."

"What makes you say that?" she asked.

"You know she's an amazing artist, and I'm not talking about that glass fusion art she's been doing for Heath while he's laid up. She's the real deal—like your grams says—she creates from her gut. I was real sad for her when that fancy art school turned her down in Florida. It was their loss, I'm sure."

"What school?" she asked, disturbed that she'd been unaware of this aspect of Lilah's life. "She never mentioned it."

"No, she wouldn't. She's too damn modest. But she's something else. Mark my words, someday her work will be worth something."

Pops ambled on, completely clueless about the turmoil in their lives, leaving Lindy to wonder over the latest piece of Lilah's puzzle. There'd been a time when they'd been joined at the hip. When one sneezed, the other said, "God bless you," but when Lindy had moved away, the distance had taken its toll. Lindy rubbed at her face, feeling every hour of lost sleep, and wondered if anything might've been different if she'd stayed in St. John, too.

Maybe they would've gone to Florida for college like they'd planned or maybe Lilah would've gone to study art somewhere while Lindy pursued a degree in…*something*.

It was painful to speculate given the circumstances, but Lindy couldn't help but wonder.

How could she not feel the burden of guilt? Her twin sister had tried to take her own life and Lindy had been completely oblivious to the fact that she was in trouble.

Because she'd become too damn wrapped up in the Hollywood crap. God, she was so sick of all the bullshit, which was probably why she'd been on a short fuse with Brandon two days ago. It wasn't as if she acted like a diva on a regular basis; in fact, in most instances, she was pretty laid-back. But something about that guy just rubbed her the wrong way and then she'd snapped.

Oh, damn. Maybe she had the same mental disorder as Lilah? She immediately discarded the idea with a deep breath. She was exhausted. And confused. And wishing she had the right to go to Gabe and simply be with him like a normal couple.

She closed her eyes. A normal couple? What's that? She didn't have any experience with that. Her therapist had essentially labeled her a serial dater with an extreme ADD streak. At the time, Lindy had taken offense, but now that she was forced to take a hard look at herself she was sad to admit the expensive crackpot may have been right.

She needed to see Gabe. Dumping the rest of her coffee down the sink drain, she replaced her rinsed mug and headed for Gabe's bungalow.

GABE TRIED TO focus on work, having neglected it for the past few days. His voice mail was clogged and his emails were backed up.

"How's Lindy doing today?" Carys asked, coming to the counter and sliding onto a barstool. "Have you heard anything about Lilah?"

Distracted, he shook his head. When he'd decided to take a month-long vacation he'd left the company in good hands, but there were certain decisions that could only be made by the boss. And those were the ones all clamoring for his attention, each request more important than the last.

"Dad?" Carys said, exasperated. "What's the point of going on *vacation* if you're still *working?* You said you would delegate more," she reminded him with a dark scowl.

"I know, honey, but if I don't stay on top of these calls and emails I'll be buried in them when we return and you won't see me again until your high school graduation." Gabe frowned when he saw that his joke had sailed right over his daughter's head. Either that or she hadn't found it funny.

"Aren't you worried about Lindy? She seemed real sad last night."

At that he looked up and he exhaled softly. Yeah, he was worried, but they were in a weird place. Not quite sure where they fit into one another's lives, and neither had the time to figure it out. He wanted to be there for

her but then, he also didn't want to crowd her. So, he figured work was a safe bet for his time today. "Well, I'm
just trying to give her some space. She's going through
a tough time and I don't want to get in the way," he explained.

"That's crap, Dad," she said, startling him with her
language and her frank assessment.

"Excuse me?"

"Well, it's like when you thought that not talking
about Mom because it was upsetting and sad was the
best way to handle our grief. That didn't make it better,
only worse. You know? So maybe Lindy doesn't need
space…she needs her friends. Aren't you friends?"

Gabe stared, shocked that such insightful advice was
coming from an eleven-year-old. A precocious eleven-
year-old but a tween nonetheless. "I suppose you're
right," he allowed. "But it gets a little more complicated than that when you're an adult."

"Why?"

"I don't know. It just does."

"I don't believe you. I think Lindy needs us, and
you're avoiding her because you don't want to get your
hands dirty emotionally. That's what Dr. Phil says,"
Carys said primly as if she were a thirty-five-year-old
therapist from New York and not some kid who often
forgot to brush her teeth on weekends. She hopped from
the stool and traipsed to her bedroom, leaving Gabe to
wonder when his daughter had started watching Dr. Phil
and why the hell he wasn't following her advice.

Because he was scared.

Plain and simple.

He wanted to be there for Lindy but they'd started
on this crazy journey, free-falling into a kooky hands-
off—unless they were in the bedroom—relationship,

and he didn't know the rules to this game. Should he go to Lindy and just step into the role of supportive boyfriend and let the chips fall where they may? Or should he give her a respectful space like an acquaintance should?

C'mon, Gabe, you're more than an acquaintance, a voice reasoned. He'd touched and kissed every inch of her body. He'd held her tightly as she'd sobbed. To hell with that acquaintance crap, and he hated the term *friends with benefits* so he ought to just man up and figure out where the hell he stood.

"I'll be right back," he hollered to Carys, then opened the front door to find Lindy. As luck would have it, she was just about to knock on his door. "Never mind," he told Carys as he stepped aside to let Lindy in.

"Hi," Lindy said, almost shyly. "I know I shouldn't just barge in like this but I really needed to talk to you."

Carys popped her head from her door and seeing Lindy bounded into the room to wrap her arms around her. "How's Lilah?" she asked when she'd let go. "Is she going to be okay?"

"Well, she has to do some physical therapy and some other stuff but I think she's going to be all right," Lindy said, smiling. "Thanks for asking, kiddo."

"I was real worried about her. Celly was, too. She has a soft spot for Lilah."

"Yeah, we all do. Lilah is a special person. I can't imagine my life without her. Hey, Carys," she said, smoothing a lock of Carys's hair behind her ear. "Would you mind if I talked with your dad about something in private?"

"No problem," Carys said. "I'll just go to my room and listen to my iPod with my earbuds so you can talk about whatever you like." She smiled at Lindy and then winked at Gabe before going into her room, which made him roll his eyes and Lindy chuckle quizzically.

"Do I want to know what that was all about?" Lindy asked.

"Apparently, unbeknownst to me, my daughter has become an avid Dr. Phil watcher."

"Kids nowadays. You gotta watch them. You never know what kind of influence they're getting from the television," Lindy joked as she took a seat on the sofa.

"Yeah, tell me about it," he quipped, sitting beside her. "Listen, I'm glad you came by. I wanted to talk to you, too."

"Yeah?"

"Yeah… First off, how's Lilah really doing?"

Lindy sighed. "Good, I think. She's checked herself into Dolphin Cove, where she'll stay for her mandatory seventy-two-hour hold for evaluation and then she's going to stay for another two weeks to seek treatment for her depression."

"You still haven't been able to talk to her, have you?" he surmised by the sadness in her eyes. Lindy shook her head and his heart contracted painfully for her. "She'll come around when she's ready and you'll be there for her when she does."

"I'm just hurt that she's shutting me out like this, but I'm trying to keep it in perspective, too. I mean, maybe I'd want some privacy and to be left alone, too, if I'd tried to kill myself. There's gotta be some kind of emotional roller coaster deal going on for her." She shook her head and twisted her fingers. "I just want her to get well. I never want to go through that again."

"Understandable," he said and risked taking her hand in his. She glanced at him, uncertain, but she squeezed his hand. "Lindy…I want you to know that I wish you'd been able to stay here with me last night. I felt terrible about you leaving. But when you said you had to go...I just let you because...well, I don't know what we're doing here. I mean, it was all well and good when it was all superficial, but I gotta tell you, this doesn't feel superficial to me."

"I know," she acknowledged softly. "I feel the same. I was conflicted. I didn't know what was the right thing, but I know I didn't want to leave. I didn't sleep at all last night."

"I'm sorry. If it makes you feel any better, I didn't fare much better."

She chuckled, admitting, "A little."

He laughed and leaned over to kiss her. It felt as natural as breathing to be there with her, sharing this moment. His lips brushed across hers, and she leaned into him, as if needing his support. He deepened the kiss, his hand going around the back of her neck to pull her in, while his tongue gently sought hers.

After a moment, Lindy pulled away with a frustrated groan and he didn't know in what context the groan was intended. He didn't have to wait long to find out. "I'm a terrible girlfriend," she blurted out, seeming distressed by her own admission. "I used to think the problem was with everyone else, but I've since realized that the common denominator was me. I mean, I've cheated on great guys—I've pushed away men who were awesome because of some perceived flaw so I could move on to the next bigger, better deal.... I'm a total commitment-phobe and quite possibly a wretched person!"

That was a lot of information to take in. Gabe pulled away, digesting her admission. He was a smart man, one who knew better than to get involved with a woman who was clearly and succinctly laying on the table the reasons why he ought to run the other way.

"Why are you telling me this?" he asked.

"Because I care about you. And I care about Carys, way more than I want to, trust me. And I don't want either of you to get hurt. Aside from Lilah, I've never had to really consider the feelings of anyone else. Given the circumstances, I've just been doing a lot of introspection, and I'm scared that I will hurt you. It's what I do! Maybe not even on purpose, but it will happen and I don't know how to stop it. I'm an actress, for crying out loud. I can kiss another guy without blinking an eye. And that bothers you because it should! I think something is broken inside me that I've only just realized needs to be fixed so that puts me in a bad place with you and Carys. You get what I'm saying?"

"Sort of," he said, shifting against the growing ball of dread in his gut. "You're saying we should end this… whatever *this* is."

"Oh, damn. Yes, probably. That's the responsible thing but I've never done the responsible thing so I don't have a lot of experience."

"Yeah…usually the responsible thing is certainly the one that doesn't feel as good," Gabe said wryly as he squeezed the bridge of his nose. She made valid points. He'd be stupid to ignore them. "I appreciate your honesty."

"Sure," she said, suddenly glum. "This sucks."

In spite of the situation, he chuckled because he agreed. "Being an adult isn't always what it's cracked up to be, right?"

"You're telling me. But then, I don't feel like a grown-up most days. Not surprising, given my line of work." A self-deprecating grin found her mouth and he longed to kiss it away. It took everything in him to keep his impulse in check. Her smile faded and was replaced by a somber expression that seemed completely foreign to the fun-loving Lindy he'd come to know. "I want you to know that this isn't easy for me. I really care for you, probably more than I've ever cared for anyone in my life. To be frank, it scares me. You're the first person to make me realize that I needed to be a better person in order to be worthy of someone good."

"Lindy, you're being too hard on yourself. You are a good person," he disagreed softly. "You don't give yourself enough credit."

"Gabe, I love you for your willingness to see nothing but the good in me but you don't know my track record. It's not stellar. I'd rather walk away from you and Carys now than ruin all those wonderful feelings you have about me later. You know?"

"You're assuming that you would," he protested, frustrated with her fatalistic opinion. "Recognizing your flaws is the first step to changing them."

"Nice try, Buddha, but whatever's broken inside me takes more than just good intentions to fix. I'd never ask you and Carys to come on that ride with me when I don't even know if my cart is capable of staying on the tracks."

He sighed, struggling with a deep sense of loss, hating that her argument was solid. But damn it all, he wanted to shout, *I think I'm falling in love with you,* and then demand that they figure it out together. But he held back. She'd made her case, and if it was just him, he'd say, *screw it, let's go for it,* but his little girl had been through enough. She didn't need more piled on her plate.

"For what it's worth…when you get it all figured out, you're going to make someone an amazing partner."

Lindy's eyes watered and she jerked a short nod. "I

should go," she said, rising. "I appreciate you listening. My life is a mess right now.… I don't know what the hell I'm going to do but I want to thank you for everything. From not letting me scare you off that first day, to being there when I needed you the most. I'll never forget that."

"Does this have to be goodbye right now?" he said, plainly wanting to squeeze every last moment with her.

"Shouldn't it be?" she asked, a tear dribbling down her cheek. "Wouldn't it be cruel to continue our current arrangement given the circumstances?"

"I have two more weeks before we leave," Gabe said. "Let's spend it together as friends." She arched her brow and he clarified, "Just as friends. I promise."

She laughed at his earnest assurance and he frowned. "What's so funny?"

Lindy cupped his cheek gently with an impish smile. "I think it's adorable that you think I'm worried about *you* trying to taking advantage. Sweetheart, if anyone's in danger of being thrown down on the nearest bed, it's you."

He sucked in a wild breath and laughed shakily. "Okay, I get your point. We're both attracted to each other and we'll have to fight it."

"I don't know," Lindy said. "Seems safer to just agree to keep our distance from each other."

"It won't be for Carys," he said. "Frankly, I'm worried about how she's going to take it when we leave for home. She's wiggled her way into your family with surprising speed."

Lindy grinned. "The girl knows a good thing when she sees it."

"No arguments here, but it will pose a problem when we can't pack everyone up into our suitcases."

"All right, for Carys's sake, I say we go forward as friends and act accordingly. Sound good?"

"It sounds…doable but not optimal," he said, wondering how he was going to train his thoughts to behave when all he could think of was how beautiful she was on any given day.

Her expression said she agreed. At least he wasn't alone in this. "One last kiss?" he asked.

"Just one," she murmured and leaned in eagerly. "And then, it's strictly friendship…."

"Right." He grinned. "Then we'd better make it count."

CHAPTER TWENTY-SEVEN

TWO WEEKS FLEW by and each day, Lindy waited for Lilah to reach out to her but it'd been radio silence. The lack of communication killed her inside but she covered her pain by spending lots of time with Carys and Gabe.

She'd talked Billy into taking them on a boat ride around the island, and Carys was so excited she could barely sit still.

"Do you think we'll see dolphins?" Carys asked.

"It's possible," Lindy answered, smiling. "We'll just have to wait and see."

"This is the coolest thing ever!" Carys exclaimed as they climbed onto Billy's boat.

"Welcome aboard de *Jumbie Moon,*" Billy said in greeting, as they moved past him to take a seat at the starboard bow. "Today we's gonna go on a true island excursion around St. John. Hands and feet stay in de boat, cuz I ain't gonna swim after yah if yah fall in," he said, winking at Lindy then Carys. "Well, I might go aftah the pretty ones." He gestured to Gabe, saying, "Yah outta luck. Yah fall in, yah swim on yah own."

"Good to know," Gabe said good-naturedly, and Lindy chuckled at Billy.

"All right, who's ready to see amazing tings that only St. John can provide?"

"Me!" Carys exclaimed, jumping in her seat. "Can we find dolphins, Mr. Janks?"

"First, call me Billy…my no-good father is Mr. Janks, yah hear?" he said with a smile on his dark face and Carys giggled. "And second, we will do our best to find de dolphins for yah."

"This was a great idea," Gabe said, smiling. "Although I'm not quite sure I should've left my phone at the bungalow."

"If you'd brought your phone you would've been fiddling with it instead of spending quality time with really cool people," Lindy said, not feeling the least bit sorry she'd bullied him into leaving his phone behind. Of course, Carys had readily agreed with her and had offered to toss the offending bit of technology down the toilet. Lindy had to remind her that the septic system wasn't up for another of her disposal antics and opted to just leave the phone on the counter as she pushed Gabe out the door.

"You're right," he agreed, his gaze roaming Lindy's face in a way that made her blush. "I can't imagine anything I'd rather be doing right now."

"Excellent, then we're agreed. I was right. I like the sound of that, by the way," Lindy teased.

Billy entertained them with stories—all likely completely made up—about the island and its folklore. By the end of the evening, they'd seen dolphins and turtles and stingrays and all manner of fish, so that by the time they returned to Larimar, Carys was plain tuckered out.

Gabe returned from Carys's room and closed the door softly behind him, approaching Lindy with a smile. "Out like a light. Would you like a glass of wine?" he asked.

"Tempting, but I remember what happened the last time we shared a glass of wine," Lindy said, smiling. "And I'm having a hard time remembering why we said we wouldn't do that anymore."

"Ah…right," he said, pulling a frown. "How's Lilah? Heard any news?"

"Just bits and pieces. She's doing well in physical therapy. Miraculous actually. The doctor said she might sustain long-term damage to her right side, but she's nearly gotten all her mobility back, which is amazing. But I still haven't been able to talk to her."

"She can't have visitors?"

"No, she can…she just chooses not to. I'm trying to give her the space she needs to heal but it's hard. What I want to do is charge in there and demand to see her."

"You're a good sister," he said.

"Yeah, well, sometimes I worry it's not just for her but for me. I have some unresolved guilt about the situations that led up to her accident."

"It wasn't your fault," he reminded her, and she nodded.

"I know, but it's hard. She's my baby sister by one minute and I feel like I let her down."

"You're going to need to let that go before it eats you up inside."

"I'm trying. I really am. It's just…well, hard."

"You'll get it figured out."

Lindy tried not to lean in but it seemed a natural thing to do, so when she felt herself getting closer to him, she didn't stop. And he didn't, either.

It didn't surprise either of them that they ended up in bed.

Again.

"This could become a habit," Gabe murmured, placing a kiss on the soft skin of her neck.

"Mmm," Lindy said, tilting her neck to give him better access. "What time is it? I should go."

Instead of answering, he said, "What do you think of San Francisco?"

"I like it," Lindy said, yawning. "Great sourdough bread if I remember correctly. It's been a while."

"What if I suggested that you relocate?" he said, almost holding his breath. She twisted in his arms to stare at him with a quizzical frown.

"Come again?" she asked.

"I'm saying…let's make this official. You know this isn't ending like this. I know for a fact that I can't go home and just forget about you and I think you feel the same about me. Am I wrong?"

"No," she answered reluctantly. "But I told you…"

"That you're a bad girlfriend. Perhaps. But you've never been a wife…. Maybe you're a phenomenal wife."

She stared, and he realized he might've just scared her off. True, he'd made a leap, but the minute he'd said it, he knew it was the right thing to say because it was how he felt.

"Are you asking me to…marry you?" she asked incredulously. "Seriously? We've known each other, like, a month. That's crazy talk and way too early in the morning for a practical joke."

"I'm not joking and I'm not crazy. I love you, Lindy. I've known it for a while but kept it to myself. I knew with Charlotte and I know with you."

"Gabe…I can't marry you," Lindy protested, pulling the sheet up to cover her bare breasts. "What about my career?"

"Last I checked, there are actors in San Francisco. Robin Williams comes to mind."

"He's an A-lister who's already made his name. He can live on the moon if he wants. The action is in L.A. I have to be there."

"What kind of career are we talking, Lindy? Correct me if I'm wrong but to date your career has consisted of bit parts and 'B' movies. What's next? Porn?"

She blinked, stung. "Low blow, Weston."

"I call it as I see it."

"No, you're being a petulant child who's lashing out because I don't want to run off and be your corporate wife. I told you in the beginning, I wasn't cut out for that crap. Hell, I told you I wasn't cut out for being a girlfriend, much less a wife and now you're cutting me down for being honest?"

"No, I just think you need to start being realistic about your expectations. You're a beautiful woman. How many parts have you been offered that didn't rely on your looks? How many parts did you get based solely on your acting ability? Sometimes the truth hurts but the reality is, beauty fades. And then what are you going to do?"

"I'm a good actress," she said in a tight voice. "Someday I'm going to get the role of a lifetime that will prove it."

"Yeah, you and ten thousand other beautiful wannabes. You can continue chasing after a dream that's ended in heartache for so many before you or you can start fresh someplace new and maybe start doing some quality theater where you actually might be discovered by someone interested in more than your ass!"

Lindy stared in open shock at his blunt statement, but a storm quickly gathered behind her eyes and he knew it wasn't going to be a gentle wind. "How dare you judge me," she said, throwing the sheet from her body and bounding from the bed. She jerked on her discarded clothes and tied her sarong around her hips with enough force to strain the fabric. "I've tried to be open and honest with you. I can't help that you don't like what I'm saying. I don't want to be your wife, or anyone's wife for that matter. I want fame and fast cars and bad boys, not stuffy dinner parties where people stand around and quietly judge one another and simper behind false smiles while doing meaningless things to fill my day."

"Really? Because that doesn't sound much different from your Hollywood lifestyle where everyone is sleeping with everyone else but pretending otherwise. It's all the same, Lindy. If you're drawn to that lifestyle, you'll find it wherever you go."

"Well, I guess I'm drawn to it then because not only am I a terrible actress but a raging slut, as well." She seethed with anger so hot he thought the floor might melt where she was standing.

"I didn't say that," he said, trying to correct her wild leap from one point to the next. "I'm just saying—"

"I don't give a shit what you're saying," she interrupted in a harsh whisper. "You don't know a thing about my career or my life, so I'd stick to what you do know, and leave me out of it. It's been fun, buddy. Thanks for taking care of the part where I miss you when you go because I sure as hell won't! Screw you, Gabe!"

"Lindy!"

But she was gone.

"Damn it," he cursed, punching the mattress before rolling to his back to stare at the ceiling.

He'd royally screwed the pooch.

So much for hoping she'd be swept off her feet by his declaration.

Ah, hell.

He should've kept his mouth shut.

LINDY WANTED TO wreak havoc on everything around her. How dare Gabe throw a marriage proposal on the table as if that were the answer. As if she'd drop everything that was important in her life to traipse off with him to play house and corporate Stepford wife. Hell no. She missed L.A. She missed her friends. She missed parties and clubs and spoiled celebrities who bought into their own press and made ridiculous demands on the set to be fulfilled by some hapless production assistant.

She stomped to her room and closed the door, still fuming. If it were possible, steam would be curling out of her ears.

Theater in San Francisco? It was cold in the Bay Area. And it was always foggy.

She thought of her dinky apartment in Sherman Oaks and sat on the edge of her bed with her fingernail tapping the bed with an agitated staccato beat. "Who the hell does he think he is asking me to marry him? Was he nuts? Who does that?"

How did you go from friends to "hey, marry me!" in the space of two weeks?

But even as she raged, a very small part of her was ridiculously thrilled by the sappy gesture.

Unlike the cavalier offers that'd been cast her way over the years, this one felt wholly genuine even if it was just as implausible.

If she didn't know how to be a good girlfriend—which was simply a training ground for marriage—how could he possibly make the assumption that she'd be a good wife? She was a terrible housekeeper, couldn't really cook to save her life and had the attention span of a goldfish, which was why acting suited her.

Lindy dropped into her large cushioned wicker chair

and stared at nothing, too irritated and angry to do much more than fume and sulk.

Damn you, Gabe Weston, for getting under my skin.
And into her heart.

CHAPTER TWENTY-EIGHT

LINDY DIDN'T HANG around Larimar when Carys and Gabe checked out; it was surprisingly painful just knowing they were leaving.

But because she didn't want Carys to think she'd abandoned her, she left her a gift with a heartfelt note. For Gabe she left nothing.

It wasn't that she hadn't wanted to leave him a short note, too, but each time she tried to write it, tears had blurred her vision and she gave up.

Lora found her staring morosely out at the sea shortly after the Westons had checked out.

"You didn't say goodbye," she noted, coming to sit beside her on the terrace.

Lindy shrugged. "Should I?"

"C'mon, are we going to play that game? I knew you were more than friends. I wasn't stupid or blind."

Lindy cut Lora a short look and said, "Well, I should've listened to your advice and kept my distance. It didn't end well."

"Oh? What happened?"

Lindy's sigh was punctuated with a scowl. "The damn man asked me to marry him! Can you imagine that? Me? A wife? If he knew me better, he'd know that his offer was nuts."

Lora was silent for a moment then asked, "Why?"

"Because I'd make a terrible wife," she answered bluntly.

"Hmmm…it's interesting, because the other night Heath asked if I'd like to start a family soon," she mused, and Lindy turned to regard her sister with curiosity.

"What did you tell him?"

"I told him I didn't think I was ready for that yet… but I might be ready soon. I need to work some things out before I take that step."

"What do you need to work out?"

Lora exhaled a short breath. "Well, since returning to Larimar, I've lost my identity. I'm a workaholic by nature and having no job to speak of is really messing with my head."

"Isn't Larimar and handling Pops a full-time job?"

"Not really. I mean, yeah, it's work but not like I'm accustomed to. But here's the thing—I don't want to go back to what I was doing. My life is here with Heath. It's a change and I'm struggling to find my bearings, but it's all worth it in the end, because he makes my life so much better than it was."

"So if you know that you don't want to go back to Chicago when this is all fixed, where's your struggle with starting a family?"

"Probably the same reasons you don't want to marry the man you're in love with."

"I'm not in love with him," Lindy insisted, though the words fell strangely flat. "That's ridiculous. I've only known him a month."

"Pops and Grams enjoyed a whirlwind courtship, if you remember all the stories. It worked out for them."

"A different time, a different set of people. I'm nothing like Grams was," Lindy retorted.

Lora shrugged. "I don't know about that. None of

us know who Grams was before she was a wife and a mother. I'm just saying, there's probably a lot about Grams we'll never know. Maybe we're all just like her in some ways. My point is, the reason you're so worked up is the same reason I fought my feelings for Heath. You're scared. If you admit to loving Gabe it puts you in a vulnerable place, one that will require change to make it work."

"I'd have to move to the Bay Area," she said, grimacing. "It's cold there. All the time."

"It's beautiful and has some of the best wineries," Lora countered with a smile.

"He says I should do some theater instead of the crap roles I've been taking based on my looks."

"I think it's a valid point. You're a good actress…but the roles you've been taking…they're nothing more than tits-and-ass parts that could be filled by anyone with a great body and a pretty face. You're more than that. And the fact that Gabe sees it and you don't says volumes."

"My therapist said I'm a serial dater," Lindy admitted. "And she's right. I don't want to hurt Carys or Gabe because I can't make a commitment."

"There it is…the fear. Lindy, we all have flaws, parts of ourselves we're not overly proud of, but it doesn't define who we are. Let's use Lilah as an example—she tried to hurt herself. Are we going to let that define who she is? No. Of course not. She's our sister and we love her. We know she's so much more than a clinically depressed person who in a moment of pain and desperation tried to end it all. You need to stop defining yourself by your past and move on. You can choose to be a better person. You can choose to be a better wife and mother than you ever were a girlfriend. It's all up to you."

"Mother," Lindy murmured, swallowing at the realization that she would step into that role with Carys if she accepted Gabe's proposal. Charlotte left some pretty big shoes to fill. Was she really up to the challenge? "How'd you become so wise?" she asked with a small smile.

"Lots of mistakes," she joked, and they both laughed.

"In that case, I ought to be Ghandi," quipped Lindy.

They chuckled together and fell silent, watching the waves roll in and out. After a moment Lindy looked at her sister and said, "You're going to make a great mom. Whatever you're struggling with, let it go. You're strong, amazing, smart and loving.... What more could a kid want?"

"Patience?" Lora supplied with a self-deprecating smile.

"That will come," Lindy said. "You're selling yourself short. You put up with twin sisters. You likely have the patience of Job and just never realized it."

Lora laughed softly as if she hadn't thought of that and then reached over to squeeze Lindy's hand. "Thanks, sis."

"Ditto."

The conversation meandered to less heavy topics until they finally went their separate ways to start their day. But Lora's advice rang in Lindy's head.

Lora was right—she was afraid. Not only of ruining everything but of hurting the two people she'd come to love—yes, love—in a short period of time.

She wanted to know how Carys's school day was and take her on shopping sprees. She wanted to cuddle up with Gabe after a long day and simply watch television together. Or share a bowl of popcorn at the movies.

Normal stuff.

Stuff she'd previously put no value upon.

After really evaluating things, she realized it'd been a long time since she'd enjoyed going out to the clubs until the wee hours of the morning, helping drunken starlets into a cab, being seen with the right people. At first it'd all been a grand adventure and she'd been high on the adrenaline of the lifestyle. But now she was simply irritated by all the ridiculous shenanigans that had nothing to do with creating good films and everything to do with spoiled celebrity life. Most of her friends were simply people she partied with because when she wasn't drunk, they were too vapid and shallow for her to handle in the harsh light of the day. And she really, really hated her apartment.

So…why did she want to return to L.A.?

At the moment, she couldn't think of a single reason.

GABE TRIED TO forget how things had ended with Lindy, but he couldn't quite push from his mind the ugly things they'd said to one another.

He shouldn't have said what he did about her career. It was rude and insensitive and she had every right to be hurt.

But when she'd outright rejected his proposal, even the very *idea* of marrying him, he'd lashed out and used the easiest ammunition to create the most damage.

What a prick.

"When are we going to see Lindy again?" Carys asked, admiring the Larimar pendant Lindy had given her. "I want her to come visit us soon. I miss her."

"I don't know, sweetheart," Gabe said, dancing around the issue. Should he tell Carys the truth about their parting? Or should he just be deliberately evasive whenever Lindy's name was brought up? In the end, he took the evasive route. "She's real busy with the resort and stuff…. We'll see."

Carys looked at him and announced, "I think Mom would've really liked Lindy. She's funny and Mom loved to laugh. Do you think they would've liked each other?"

"I think so," Gabe answered, smiling. "Your mom was always a great judge of character."

"I think so, too," Carys said, happy Gabe agreed. "Can we call Lindy and invite her to stay with us soon? Maybe Lilah, too? She'd love it here, I think. I mean, there's so many artists here in the Bay Area that she'd fit right in. Can we call and check on Lilah? I'm worried about her."

"Lilah is in good hands. She's busy getting well," Gabe said. But he added, "We'll give Larimar a call in a week or two and see if there are any updates, but I should warn you, they might not want to share that personal information with us because we're not family."

"We're *like* family," Carys said, not missing a beat. "I can't wait to go back to Larimar. It's like home away from home. Lindy is going to take me diving when I'm old enough."

Gabe did a double take, shocked at how at ease Carys had become with the Bell family.

"Honey…" He started to explain how it was likely they wouldn't return to Larimar, but something held his tongue. He couldn't quite say the words. Instead, he simply nodded and let it be.

But later that night, when he tossed and turned in his bed, his thoughts continued to circle around Lindy. He missed her smile, her laugh, her quirky sense of self. He'd never met anyone like her, and he never would again.

Of that he was certain.

And the knowledge that she'd never be his hurt like a son of a bitch.

He grabbed his cell phone and stared at it in the darkness, the glow from the LCD screen illuminating his face. He ought to call and at least apologize for his cutting remarks.

But if he heard her voice, he might crack and beg her to change her mind.

A man had his pride.

Still, his fingers hovered over the buttons, ready to call in spite of the knowledge that he ought to leave it be.

Muttering a curse to himself for being a sappy fool he shut off his phone and tossed it to his nightstand before deliberately turning his back on the phone with the intention of forcing himself into sleep.

Yeah…great plan.

Surprisingly, he fell asleep quickly.

Only his dreams were filled with Lindy and when morning came, he felt worse.

He didn't know how he was going to get over Lindy Bell.

He wasn't even sure he knew where to start.

CHAPTER TWENTY-NINE

LILAH WAS COMING home today and Lindy was a nervous wreck.

"Will you stop?" Lora admonished in irritation when Lindy had zoomed past her for the third time to check the driveway for Lilah's cab. "You're making me want medication, too."

Heath chuckled at Lora's wry comment, but Lindy didn't find the humor at all.

"We shouldn't joke about medication or anything related to her disorder or disease, or whatever the hell is wrong with Lilah. Oh damn, I need to get the lingo right or that could be upsetting to her," Lindy fretted, looking to Lora for help.

Lora rolled her eyes and said, "Calm down and act normal. The worst that we could do is act like we have to treat her with kid gloves. She's not an egg and she's not going to break."

"You don't know that," Lindy countered sharply, then gasped when she heard a car come up the gravel driveway. "She's here!"

"I'll alert the media," Lora said drily.

"Shhh," Lindy said, scowling fiercely. "We need to be as supportive as possible. Okay?"

"I will but—"

Before Lora could finish, Lilah appeared at the door, carrying a small rolling travel bag. Lindy was hesitant at first but when she saw Lilah's sweet, if tremulous, smile, she ran to her and clasped her to her chest.

"I've missed you so much," Lindy said, tears springing to her eyes. "Please don't ever do that again. I'd die without you."

"I'm sorry," Lilah whispered, clutching her tightly. "I'm so sorry."

"Can we get in on some of this action?" Heath teased, as he and Lora opened their arms for Lilah. Lindy reluctantly let go and wiped her eyes as Lilah gave her other sister and almost-brother a squeeze, too. "Good to have you back."

"Where's Pops?" Lilah asked when all the hugging had ended.

"We thought it would be best if he were off doing something else when you came home, so Celly took him to town for some supplies he thinks he needs. This way, when he sees you around, he'll forget that you were gone for almost three weeks. His memory is getting worse," Lora admitted sadly but then brightened. "But that's neither here nor there. You're home and that's what we're celebrating."

Heath grabbed Lilah's bag and they headed for the terrace for fresh papaya and pineapple with omelets and thick-cut bacon. Lindy had wanted to make sure that all of Lilah's favorites were on the table so there was really an obscene amount of food for just four people, but Lindy didn't care.

Lilah sat down with a smile, relishing all the food she saw and she didn't wait to dig in.

"Glad to see you're hungry because we're going to be eating leftovers for a while," Lora joked.

"I'm starved. When I was sick, I never wanted to

eat but now that I'm feeling better, I feel as if I need to make up for lost time. I've already gained five pounds!"

"You look wonderful," Lindy said immediately, at which Lilah chuckled.

"You don't have to do that. I'm okay. Really."

Lindy peered at her sister and something broke inside her, washing over her in giant waves of equal parts grief and relief, and she couldn't stop the tears from flowing. "I'm sorry, I'm trying to hold it together—I really am! But not being able to talk to you all this time has really messed with my head. I was so worried about you."

Lilah fell silent as if she were contemplating how to handle Lindy's outburst, then she addressed them all. "What I did was an action borne out of extreme desperation and a hormonal imbalance. I am not the same person I was three weeks ago. I now understand that it's okay to seek help when I hit the low spots. I don't have to suffer alone. Dr. Veronica has been a godsend and I know I'm going to be okay. It's not going to be easy all the time. Some days will be hard but I can get through it. I'm so sorry for putting you all through this. Especially you, Lindy. I promised you I wouldn't hurt myself. I didn't know how to tell you that I'd been thinking of it for a long time. I'm so, so sorry." To Lora, she said, "I should've told you that I was struggling with something really big. Maybe if I had, none of this with Larimar would've happened but I was ashamed at being so weak when my sisters were so strong."

"You're not weak," Lora said fiercely. "It takes guts to go through what you did and come out the other side. I'm so proud of you."

Lilah blinked back tears and suddenly the entire table

was crying until they realized how ridiculous they all looked and the tears turned to laughter.

Lindy wiped at her tears with her napkin and then exhaled a long breath before saying, "Enough of all this stuff—let's eat!"

And so they did.

Everything felt right and normal, even though there was so much that still needed work.

Which left one last dilemma that needed solving.

And Lindy knew exactly what to do.

GABE OPENED THE door and nearly fell over when he saw Lindy standing there, shivering on his stoop in a fuzzy wool scarf and a long coat wrapped tightly around her luscious body, muttering about the damn Bay Area fog. He didn't have time to usher her inside or question what she was doing in the Bay when she launched herself into his arms, taking his mouth in a possessive kiss filled with pent-up longing and yearning that he immediately responded to because he felt the same.

"I've missed you so much," she murmured against his mouth, as she quickly divested herself of her coat and it dropped at her feet. "It feels like forever since I've seen you even though I know it's only been a few weeks."

His arms wound around her and he held her tightly against him, almost afraid to let go. "What are you doing here?" he asked in a pained, tortured voice. It seemed both a dream and a nightmare to have Lindy here in his arms.

"Isn't it obvious?" she asked, pausing to shut the door and unwind her scarf from her neck.

He was speechless; afraid to ask. She smiled and kicked off her shoes.

"Lindy…" he started, but she wasn't interested in

a deep, soul-searching conversation. Her mouth covered his again, hungry and needy, and her body pressed against his as if trying to blend them together. She groaned and pulled away. "Clothes off," she demanded as she stripped.

It was the middle of the day and Carys was at school. The house was empty except for him and a rapidly disrobing Lindy Bell.

It was a dangerous combination.

"Lindy…" he said, swallowing, finding it hard to believe that he was actually going to refuse her body. "I can't do this…."

She unclasped her bra and let her breasts come into view. His Adam's apple bobbed painfully as the scrap of lace hit the floor, followed by her panties.

She stalked him as he tried to keep his hands off her, until his knees hit the back of the sofa and he sat with an abrupt *oompf.* She didn't waste time and straddled him. "You, my handsome executive, are wearing too many clothes for what I had in mind," she teased, popping his shirt buttons.

"What are you doing?" he asked in a tight voice. His erection had sprung and it was desperate to be inside her body again but he wasn't about to embark on some pointless affair with the woman he wanted in his life every day, every hour and not just when it suited her schedule. He wasn't a booty call, damn it! He groaned as her palms spread out across his chest, seeking and finding the flat nipples to pinch and tease. He caught her hands and held them. "I can't do this!"

She ignored her captured hands and bent down to nuzzle his neck, nipping at the skin. "I have a very high sex drive, Mr. Weston, and I have to know if I'm going to be *Mrs.* Gabe Weston that you can keep up with my needs."

He stilled, his heart nearly stopping at her words. She pulled away, all teasing gone from her expression. She swallowed and met his stare with one filled with uncertainty and vulnerability. He cupped her precious face with trembling hands. "Are you saying…?"

"Yes," she answered softly. "I will be your wife, but if I turn out to be the worst wife in the history of wives, you can't say I didn't warn you."

"Oh, my God," he cried, kissing her again and again, unable to get enough of her. "I will make you the happiest woman on this planet. I will make it my life's work to ensure you want for nothing. I—"

She laughed and cut him off with her mouth, murmuring, "I just want you and Carys. Everything else is gravy."

"I love you, Lindy Bell, soon-to-be Lindy Weston!"

"And I love you," Lindy said, but she placed a hand against his chest with a somber expression. "First, I need to tell you right now, I'm a demanding person. I'm not going to be the trophy wife you prop up in the corner and forget about until it suits you. If I'm giving you the best of me, you sure as hell better be willing to give me the best of you."

He smiled. "I've already started delegating more at the office. Since returning from St. John, I've been implementing changes to my schedule. I'm a more hands-on dad. I'm ready to be a hands-on husband, too." With that, he emphasized his point by sliding his hands under her rear and squeezing a handful of her flesh. "Starting with this right here," he growled, and her pupils dilated with fresh arousal.

"I like the sound of that," she murmured, her expression morphing into pure sexual hunger as she plucked at his shirt with a sidelong glance. "Now that that's out of the way…as I said earlier…someone is wearing way too much clothing for what I had in mind…."

And with that, his restraint fled.

She squealed as he ripped his shirt from his body, hardly noticing the sound of buttons flying and skidding across the mahogany hardwood, because he had Lindy and Carys and that's all that mattered in this world.

Everything else was just gravy.

EPILOGUE

"WHEN ARE WE going to get there?" Carys complained, as she glanced out the plane window. "I hate the long plane ride. It's *sooo* boring."

Lindy smiled indulgently at her soon-to-be step-daughter and said, "I know but before you know it we'll be at Larimar eating boiled bananas and playing in the surf. Just keep that in mind and the time will go by faster."

"No, it won't. It makes it worse," Carys grumped, reaching into her backpack to grab her earbuds and iPod so she could at least listen to music while she watched the clouds go by.

The sparkle from Lindy's engagement ring caught her eye and she smiled on the inside, lighting up from the joy that continually cascaded through her at the knowledge that she was going to become Gabe's wife and Carys's stepmother.

She couldn't imagine loving Carys more than if she'd given birth to her. The kid was amazing and she was proud to be in her life.

Lindy had relocated to the Bay Area but she still made frequent trips to Larimar to help her sisters. Gabe never winced at the expense and encouraged her to go whenever she felt the need. He said someone ought to be able to cash in on the frequent-flier miles he banked from business trips, and she was happy to take him up on his offer.

Carys had insisted they all go to Larimar on this trip, saying she had to have her island fix if she was going to make it through the chilly Bay Area winters. And the kid was an island girl at heart. So much so that she scared the life out of Gabe but made Lindy laugh at her antics because they reminded her so much of herself.

It was interesting; once she left L.A. and moved to the Bay Area with Gabe and Carys, she'd discovered an awesome theater group who recognized her talent and not just her pretty face. She'd landed a small role in their last production and she'd learned that she had a passion for theater. Now she wasn't chasing the nightlife in the hopes of gaining a career; instead she was studying acting techniques and becoming versed in the debate over Method acting and classical acting. It was a change she realized should've happened a long time ago if she'd ever hoped to be taken seriously in the acting world.

Lilah was doing well in her healing and Lindy was so grateful for the change. Lilah continued to see Dr. Veronica but the combination of art therapy and medication had lessened her need to see the doctor so frequently. For the first time in a long while, Lilah was in a great place and it warmed Lindy's heart to know her twin was doing so well, though in a private place that she didn't talk about she still worried that Lilah could relapse. Even thinking about the possibility gave Lindy the chills so she tried to banish the thought whenever it arose, but seeing Lilah's sunny smile always helped allay her fears, too, which was another reason for the frequent trips home.

With the help of her paycheck from Paul Hossiter they were able to make the quarterly installment payment to the IRS but there was one final large payment looming over their heads, which was why they were all traveling to St. John on this trip.

It was time to put into place some sustainable practices to save Larimar.

The only problem? Pops was getting worse by the day.

Lora, Heath and Celly had their hands full with the day-to-day running of Larimar, not to mention the babysitting of Pops so he didn't hurt himself.

Heath had proposed to Lora and had fashioned symbolic rings out of fused glass. Some rich guest at Larimar had seen it and commissioned his own. Now, Heath was creating fused glass rings for a decent sum of cash, which was nice for the resort and for Heath because he'd begun to worry that he'd made a wager on his talent and come up short.

But even as serious as everything was around her, Lindy couldn't help the smile that constantly found her lips.

She was happy.

Blissfully, ridiculously happy.

And she knew that whatever came their way, they'd handle it as a family.

All of them.

Just the way it should be.

* * * * *

Be sure to look for Kimberly Van Meter's last book in her FAMILY PARADISE *trilogy,* SOMETHING TO BELIEVE IN, *available in January 2013.*

COMING NEXT MONTH
from Harlequin® SuperRomance®
AVAILABLE OCTOBER 2, 2012

#1806 IN THIS TOWN
The Truth about the Sullivans
Beth Andrews

Getting out of Mystic Point has long been Tori Sullivan Mott's dream. And when special investigator Walker Bertrand shows up, she may have her chance. Until he looks into possible police misconduct in her mother's murder case—focusing on Tori's sister!

#1807 NO MATTER WHAT
Janice Kay Johnson

As a vice-principal, Molly Callahan has seen it all. But none of her experience matters when she discovers her teenage daughter is pregnant. The situation becomes more tangled when a powerful attraction develops between Molly and Richard Ward, whose son is involved.

#1808 TO BE A FAMILY
Joan Kilby

John Forster isn't ready to be a single dad. So he reaches out to someone who can help his six-year-old girl. Given his past with Katie Henning, John needs to be clear he's not using this situation as a chance for reconciliation...even if the thought crosses his mind.

#1809 THE NEW HOPE CAFÉ
Dawn Atkins

Having her car break down miles from her destination is not what Cara Price needs. She only wants to get her daughter to safety and a new life. Although she wasn't looking, Cara might find exactly what she needs here in this desert town...and in Jonah Gold.

#1810 ONE FINAL STEP
Stephanie Doyle

Madeleine Kane works her PR magic from the sidelines. Yes, there was a time when she shared the spotlight with her clients, but no more. Then Michael Langdon hires her. His dynamic energy draws her in, makes her risk publicity...until her scandalous past reappears!

#1811 A DAUGHTER'S STORY
It Happened in Comfort Cove
Tara Taylor Quinn

After the unsolved abduction of her sister twenty-five years ago, Emma Sanderson learned to live a safe life. Then all her careful plans fall apart and she risks the unthinkable—a single night with the mysterious Chris Talbot. Before the night is over, they both know once isn't enough.

You can find more information on upcoming Harlequin® titles, free excerpts and more at www.Harlequin.com.

HSRCNM0912

*What happens when a Texas nanny learns she is
the biological daughter of a prince? Her rancher boss
steps in to help protect her from the paparazzi, but who
can protect her from her attraction to him?*

*Read on for an excerpt of
A HOME FOR NOBODY'S PRINCESS
by USA TODAY bestselling author Leanne Banks.*

Available October 2012

"This is out of control." Benjamin sighed. "Well, damn.
I guess I'm gonna have to be your fiancé."

Coco's jaw dropped. "What?"

"It won't be real," he said quickly, as much for himself
as for her. After the debacle of his relationship with Brooke,
the idea of an engagement nearly gave him hives. "It's just
for the sake of appearances until the insanity dies down.
This way it won't look like you're all alone and ready to have
someone take advantage of you. If someone approaches
you, then they'll have to deal with me, too."

She frowned. "I'm stronger than I seem," she said.

"I know you're strong. After what you went through for
your mom and helping Emma to settle down, I know you're
strong. But it's gotta be damn tiring to feel like you've
always got to be on guard."

Coco sighed and her shoulders slumped. "You're right
about that." She met his gaze with a wince. "Are you sure
you don't mind doing this?"

"It's just for a little while," he said. "You mentioned that
a fiancé would fix things a few minutes ago. I had to run it
through my brain. It seems like the right thing to do."

She gave a slow nod and bit her lip. "Hmm. But it would cut into your dating time."

Benjamin laughed. "That's not a big focus at the moment."

"It would be a huge relief for me," she admitted. "If you're sure you don't mind. And we'll break it off the second you feel inconvenienced."

"No problem," he said. "I'll spread the word. Should be all over the county by lunchtime. No one can know the truth. That's the only way this will work."

Coco took a deep breath and closed her eyes as if preparing to take a jump into deep water. "Okay" she said, and opened her eyes. "Let's do it."

Will Coco be able to carry out the charade?

Find out in Leanne Banks's new novel—
A HOME FOR NOBODY'S PRINCESS.

Available October 2012 from Harlequin® Special Edition®

SPECIAL EDITION

Life, Love and Family

Sometimes love strikes in the most unexpected circumstances...

Soon-to-be single mom Antonia Wright isn't looking
for romance, especially from a cowboy. But when
rancher and single father Clayton Traub rents a room
at Antonia's boardinghouse, Wright's Way, she isn't
prepared for the attraction that instantly sizzles between
them or the pain she sees in his big brown eyes.
Can Clay and Antonia trust their hearts and build the
family they've always dreamed of?

Don't miss

THE MAVERICK'S
READY-MADE FAMILY

by Brenda Harlen

Available this October from Harlequin® Special Edition®

www.Harlequin.com

HSE65697

celebrating 15 YEARS

Love Inspired

Another heartwarming installment of

← TEXAS TWINS →

Two sets of twins, torn apart by family secrets,
find their way home

When big-city cop Grayson Wallace visits an elementary
school for career day, he finds his heartstrings
unexpectedly tugged by a six-year-old fatherless boy and
his widowed mother, Elise Lopez. Now he can't get the
struggling Lopezes off his mind. All he can think about
is what family means—especially after discovering
the identical twin brother he hadn't known he had
in Grasslands. Maybe a trip to ranch country is just
what he, Elise and little Cory need.

Look-Alike Lawman
by Glynna Kaye

*Available October 2012
wherever books are sold.*

www.LoveInspiredBooks.com

LI87770